"BUTCHERTOWN IS NO PLACE TO WALK ALONE."

"As I read this darkly fascinating novel, I kept having two strong associations. The first was with Jim Thompson. This is the novel he would have written if he'd ever set a story in the Bay Area. The second was Anthony Mann's noir classic *Raw Deal*. I half-expected to see Raymond Burr as Rick Coyle stepping out of the fog to set someone on fire. He doesn't, but that's no problem. *Butchertown* is incendiary enough."

—David Corbett, award-winning author of *The Mercy of the Night*

"Thomas Burchfield is an awesomely twisted talent. As ringmaster of a murder circus in the stink-smog of Butchertown, he will make you choke for air as the human trash piles up. If you want to see how civic virtue does in such a place, watch as the hero, naïve, soft-hearted Paul Bacon, gives it a try. You won't be able to turn the pages fast enough to see what happens."

—John-Ivan Palmer, author of *Motels of Burning Madness*

"Burchfield rounds up a great cast of gangsters and gunsels to bat around his around his wide-eyed hero. For the movie, you'd have to bring back Lee Van Cleef from the dead to do justice to the villainy."

--Don Herron, author of *The Literary World of San Francisco* and *The Dashiell Hammett Tour*

ALSO BY THOMAS BURCHFIELD

PUBLISHED BY AMBLER HOUSE

Novel:
Dragon's Ark

Screenplays:
Whackers (e-book)
The Uglies (e-book)
Now Speaks the Devil (e-book)
Dracula: Endless Night (e-book)

BUTCHERTOWN

Thomas Burchfield

AMBLER HOUSE PUBLISHING

Oakland, CA

DISCLAIMER: Though *Butchertown* echoes with some history, all characters and events are figments of the author's imagination. Any resemblance to actual persons living or dead, save for a few historical figures, is purely coincidental.

PCIP: Publisher's Cataloging-In-Publication Data
(Prepared by The Donohue Group, Inc.)
Names: Burchfield, Thomas, 1954-
Butchertown: a novel / Thomas Burchfield.
Description: Oakland, CA: Ambler House Publishing, [2017] |
Identifiers: ISBN 978-0-9847755-4-5 | ISBN 978-0-9847755-5-2 (e-book)
Subjects: LCSH: City attorneys—California—History—20th century—Fiction. | Gangsters—California—History—20th century—Fiction. | Racketeering—California—History—20th century—Fiction. | Prohibitionists—California—History—20th century—Fiction. | Nineteen twenties—Fiction. | LCGFT: Thrillers (Fiction)
Classification: LCC PS3602.U73 B88 2017 (print) | LCC PS3602.U73 (e-book) | DDC 813/.6—dc23

Published by Ambler House Publishing, 584 Vernon Street, #1, Oakland, CA 94610

First Edition

Cover design by Cathi Stevenson/Book Cover Express
Images by Adobe Images
Interior design with templates from The Book Designer.

For Elizabeth, as always!

Contents

The land shall be utterly emptied and utterly spoiled . . ."
                                        —*Isaiah, 24:3*

"If I don't get away soon, I'll be going blood-simple like the natives."
                                        —Dashiell Hammett, *Red Harvest*

BUTCHERTOWN

Chapter 1

Promised Sunshine

"It ain't called Butchertown for nothin', chum," the ferry barman said, grinning and winking like an imp through the blue smoke of his black cigar at me, the sporty young fool leaning on his bar.

Until that moment I knew only that I was on the ferry boat *Nicosia*, on a late Friday afternoon. I was bound for Evansville, across San Francisco Bay, where a sunny romantic weekend awaited me. At last I would find the California I was looking for when I stepped off the same ferry two months before, looked around and asked, where are all the palm trees? Where are all the oranges?

And what the hell is it with all this fog? When will it go away?

"So you think this is bad, do ya, Bacon?" my boss, San Francisco District Attorney Brady, sneered on my first day at the office. "You Eastern boys, you think it's all sunshine out here. This is nothing! I've seen fog so thick you couldn't see your goddamn toes." Even so, some of the old-timers I knew disagreed, saying no, that summer's fog was the worst ever since before the '06 quake and fire, all the way back to Gold Rush days.

The worst or not, the fog looked bad enough to me. For two months straight, day after day it rolled in like a silent white tidal wave around noon, whipped by strong Pacific Ocean winds. The difference between night and day became shades of gray, except for a meager respite in the morning, when the fog lurked offshore, under the surf. The streetlights remained lit all day long. Foghorns and ships howled and whistled around the clock, hooted, tooted and boomed from all points of the compass. San Francisco was more like a Hades, damp and dismal, than the Heaven splashed with sun I had been led to expect.

True, it looked rather romantic to me at first. I liked how the fog piled up on the hills in the morning, like the early-winter snow on the hills back east. I enjoyed watching it from a restaurant window as its veils swept down Haight Street. My fancy conjured it into ghosts hurrying to work at some haunted house or the wedding trains of angels marching to an altar.

But San Francisco fog was different from fog elsewhere. For me, foggy nights had always been still, quiet, mysterious like a Sherlock Holmes story. San Francisco fog blew and stung like a January blizzard tearing through Westchester. Its droplets sank into my pores, down to my marrow, turned my blood to slush.

The mist condensed in my lungs, infused with fuel exhaust and sewer smells. I lost two good hats that summer, blown off my head, crushed under the wheels of streetcars. My best suits became spongy and moldy. As my soul rusted away, I became stooped over with melancholy.

Then, just when I thought I had tripped up badly in moving all the way out here and leaving behind everything I knew, something happened—that "something" called "woman."

One night three weeks before my fateful August weekend, I was seated at a long table in a back corner of the Poodle Dog restaurant on Bush with some of my senior colleagues in the DA's office, passing the flask, toasting somebody's birthday. I was also celebrating the news that I would be handed my first real case—in a few weeks I would stand up in a real courtroom before a real judge.

But instead of making me merry, the whiskey I was sipping from my ten-dollar silver flask loosened my tongue, always a little bit fast, and sent it whipping into a tirade.

"When's all this fog gonna stop?" I finished, pounding my fist on the table. "When are we getting some sun? My brain feels like my grandmother's flannel nightie."

And then someone said, "If you don't like the weather here, mister, why don't you do something about it?"

The voice came from outside our circle, a couple tables away, sultry and throaty like smoky burgundy. A striking high-boned female face peered at me from around a candle on the table, as though it were a bedroom door. She wore a fetching smile, her lovely cheek on her closed jeweled fist.

"Instead of talking," she added.

"Like what?"

"Like come on over to my side of the bay. You'll find plenty of sun there. Especially in the morning." She winked. You know. That kind of wink, like bedroom blinds closing. "My name is Molly. What's your name, handsome?"

"Bacon," I answered. "Paul Bacon."

The more I looked at Molly, the more her cocoa-brown eyes locked into mine, the more she had of me, until by evening's end she had all of me. My cold marrow melted, my blood ran like a spring brook, my sap rose up the tree. She could have carried me out in her purse. I got so dumb and dizzy, I sat there like a dope when she rose, said good night and walked her voluptuous figure to the door. She stopped and stared, turned to show breathtaking curves under a clinging blue silk dress. I tripped out after her, caught up with her in the street, found her standing on the sidewalk in the fog, inside a circle of light cast by a streetlamp overhead.

"Yes?" Her jet-black eyebrows arched like a rising harbor bridge.

I sailed on in. "I'd like to do something about the weather. Instead of just talking."

"Think you're man enough for it?"

I laughed. It was almost like sparring in the ring.

"I know pennies about the East Bay, except that it's dry as dust over there." I drew out my flask, waved it at her. "I hear everyone's thirsty all the time."

She took the flask and took a drink. "You ever hear of Evansville?" My face must have broken into puzzle pieces. "That's my hometown. I'm the mayor's daughter, in fact. It may not sound like much, but one thing my town isn't is dry, and we never go thirsty, just like here." She looked around at the towering buildings. "It might look pretty dull to a big-city sport like you—"

I broke in with a fib. "I wouldn't mind taking the ferry over. See for myself."

Molly drew a cigarette from her purple velvet, gold-chained purse. I brought out my lighter. As our faces drew close together, she said, "I've never found much reason to come over here myself with all that sunshine." She winked again at me through the smoke. "But maybe now I have."

For our first two dates she ferried over to my side. Being the mayor's daughter kept her busy in Evansville, and she was glad for the chance to escape to the big city, the Jewel of the Pacific Coast, even for a few measly hours. "Besides," she added, "wherever you live there's always a better party elsewhere, don't you think?"

Molly had a point I thought. From where we stood, Alameda County, where Evansville was located, had a reputation as the driest county in Northern California. The fed, state and most of the local cops read the Volstead Act like the Lord's Gospel. But not, it seemed, the cops in Evansville.

"They're always trying to get us to clean up. But we're not the kind who give in."

"Might be my kind of town," I replied. "Are there are a lot beaches there?"

"We're right on the water."

Already I could see us walking hand in hand, digging our toes in sunbaked sand as seagulls swept by on salt-scented wind, the fog far across the bay, where it belonged.

But for our first two dates, Molly Carver and I did San Francisco on a Friday night. The first date she met me outside City Hall, the next in the St. Francis lobby, whose high-ceilinged opulence made her gasp; then followed dates at Il Trovatore restaurant on Broadway; *Orphans of the Storm* at the Castro Theatre; a Seals baseball game at Seals Stadium; the Singer Midgets at the Golden Gate Theatre. She seemed awestruck, enchanted and delighted by it all. And every step of the way we bantered, sparked and teased like we did the night we met.

Molly may have been a small-town Californian, but like me she was up on all the new fashions coming in from back east. She dressed as though she had read all the catalogs cover to cover, outfitted to stun me and every jumping young Joe for twenty miles around. The first date she wore a pink cloche hat over her black bobbed hair and another clingy silk number, robin's-egg blue with high heels to match. The next date she wore red from top to hem, and both times she had carefully wrapped a matching silk scarf around her neck. She was a package begging to have its ribbon untied, the wrapping torn away.

At evening's end we took the train down Market, standing close together, joined hip to shoulder. I guided her across the footbridge over the train tracks that ran through the busy dockyards. I was her protector in that gamy seafront world, no place for a lady. She stood at the ferry stern and we waved at each other until the red lights vanished. Then I turned around, looked at the looming city and realized I had not noticed the fog all evening. And my heart sank again. I could not wait to get across the bay.

The second Friday, as we approached the dock, the ferry whistle calling to separate us, I drawled with New York café insouciance, my hands in my pockets, "The Seals are playing the Oaks in a doubleheader next Friday afternoon at Oaks Stadium. In Evansville," I added, shooting up my eyebrows. I would be a little late for the second game, I explained, but I could be at the dock by, say, six o'clock?

She happily agreed. Then she kissed me, a full one this night. We mapped the insides of both our mouths. Hers tasted like fresh cherry as she pushed her full body against mine, her arms going around me, squeezing. She walked her mouth step-by-step up to my ear and made herself a meal.

Then with a naughty giggle she whispered, "Don't forget your toothbrush."

It was on that momentous Friday afternoon that DA Brady chose to keep me after work. I was already dressed for the evening when he pinned me to the chair in front of his desk and lectured me on my first trial, scheduled for next week, telling me what to expect and what he expected. I was barely listening. There was a name, Dago Loosner. It sounded like an off-key ukulele chord. A bootlegger. Or something. Instead of seeing DA Brady behind his desk, I was seeing Molly Carver (now there was a name!) as I unwrapped the red ribbon from around her throat while her fingers drifted down to her breasts. I would worry about the Loosner file come Monday morning.

"You'd better not be dressed up like a dance hall fruit when trial starts," Brady snarled as I flew out the door.

I hopped on board seconds before they raised the plank. Right after the *Nicosia* left the dock at five thirty it plowed into heavy chop and slowed to half speed, rocking side to side, stem to stern, on steep, sharp, frothy waves. It was my first time back on the water since the ferry in. Remember my little fib, when I said I was happy to take the ferry? My stomach started to roll against the waves, and vague, nauseating memories of my navy service smoked the back of my throat.

Nevertheless, I proudly stood on the *Nicosia's* foredeck, clutching a spray of flowers, wearing my two-tone, full-brogue wingtip oxfords, each heel carved with the image of a chess knight, and matching wool socks. My new blue "jazz suit," ordered on credit from back east and retailored, consisted of stovepipe pants creased like a razor, the cuffs high up the ankles, while the jacket was short in the sleeves and cut slim and straight from shoulder to waist. A white handkerchief blossomed from the pocket, complementing a thin red tie and matching a brand-new crisp white shirt and silk detachable collar, the collar my one concession to tradition. For the topper I wore a bright white boater, its crown circled with a red and blue band. With pomade in my dishwater hair, and a splash of Sushi Imperiale Bois cologne at five dollars a bottle, no woman could resist. Together, Molly and I would light a bonfire seen from all over the bay.

As I stood with my hat tucked under my arm to keep it from blowing away, my slicked hair impervious to the wind, I envisioned Molly waiting for me at the end of the Key pier. Would she wear red on this night? Or green (for "go")? I imagined her lit like a harbor light as we sailed in, while I stood heroically at the bow like Neptune, our eyes meeting through the murk, guiding us into each other's arms.

"Gonna be a long crossing tonight," a passenger said. I glanced behind me as he headed inside. My heart sank as worry suffused my seasickness. Molly would be kept waiting and we would be late for the game. The engines strained as the rocking increased. Salt water sprayed over the bow. If I stayed out here, I would soon be soaked, my suit ruined, and the night too.

I made for the ferry house, clapping my boater on my head as I pushed through the door. The interior was packed and sunk in thick blue smoke, thicker than the fog outside. The other passengers were packed shoulder to shoulder. The pitch was not as bad near the center of the ship and so my stomach calmed. From a far corner a colored woman was singing "Vampin' Liza Jane," accompanied by a small group of other colored musicians. They played well enough to make me think they should be playing somewhere else.

Most of the other passengers were older, a chunky stew of Mexicans, Chinese and a scattering of Negroes, with only a few whites. They looked to be poorer than I, than most of the folks I had met in the city since I landed; more like the types I saw standing around the jail or before the judge. Like the people I would be prosecuting. They wore frayed brown and gray suits, cinched high at the waist but cut of tweed or wool, with vests. Most wore bill caps or greasy homburgs and derbies, fashion from the 1910s, before the Great War, shed long ago by the crowd I ran with, especially the café crowd back east. Even their girls looked heavy and slow, in musty finery from the 1890s, cut from their grandparents' brown-and-green-flocked curtains, then draped over their petticoats. I had not felt so overdressed since my navy discharge.

I stuck out here, not just because of my new white man's suit, either. I was the tallest man in the room. As I slid politely through, I caught a few hostile glances. "Peacock," a voice muttered, but when I turned to face the insult, everyone was looking askance.

The air was choked with blue smoke from cigars fat and big enough to plug a leak in a destroyer. Pipes fumed like factory chimneys and cigarette tips glowed like distant buoy lights. I was a smoker myself, but I found it a bit much, nearly choking in fact.

My eyes watering, I found the bar and ordered a whoosh of sugared soda and ice from the square-jawed, sandy-haired bartender, whose stogie poked impudently from the center of his pursed mouth. Volstead had been in force—so to speak—for over two years, so I poured my own Haig & Haig (as the label alleged) from the flask given to me by my Uncle Lloyd, who taught me most everything I knew about good times.

As I paid up, I asked the barkeep why everyone was smoking like a coal steamer convoy. Winking, he nudged a box full of fecal-looking black stogies at me with the back of his hand. "Nickel each." I smelled those stinkers around city hall every day, especially around the jail, and disdainfully waved my pack of Chesterfields.

The barkeep laughed. "Where you headed?" he asked.

"Evansville. Ball game at Oaks Park. If we get there on time."

He nodded. "Yeah, on a night like this you'll need somethin' stronger than Chesterfields where you're goin'. New here, right? I haven't seen you on this boat before. You ever been to Evansville? East Bay? No? Step out on deck, take a whiff. The wind's from the north tonight *again*. We'll be passing Buena Vista Island soon."

I hung by the bar, nursing my drink, pretending indifference to this white-coated wise guy. No boy likes being treated as one. What did he know anyway? I would be petting with the mayor's daughter, while *he* would be stuck behind this bar all night and forever.

Finally, my nerves softened and my belly found its keel. I held my boater down tight, flowers tucked under my arm, and stepped back out on the port outer deck. I expected to find some sign of clear evening sky. Instead I found the same soggy northwest wind and fog, the fog now low enough to touch. I sensed a black lump sliding by to the south. Sunset was still a couple hours away but we were in full gray sunless twilight.

The ferry was still chugging at half speed, but now the water seemed to have turned to a thick soup that slopped against the hull. I looked down over the rail. A rainbow-colored surface scum stretched away into grayness. A school of pale white flotsam floated by. I inhaled and was nearly felled by the stench of dead rotting fish, hundreds of them making a gray-and-white carpet. Beneath it all I recognized another foul odor from the troop transport ships I had served on, from bilge and backed-up pipes.

I pulled out my handkerchief in time to catch a big sneeze. Up ahead the fog became an oily, ochre crepe. A black smokestack rose and vanished ominously in the fog above like a castle tower. Above that, from within the fog a fuzzy orange tongue of fire pulsated in the brown sky.

What port, I suddenly wondered, was I really bound for? Molly got me talking more about myself than she talked about herself or the town she lived in. Nobody said anything, not even at the office. *Oh,* they smiled and shook their heads in wonder. *Evansville? Who wants to go to Evansville, even for baseball?* I thought Molly had said Evansville was right on the bay. Or somewhere inland? Far inland, I hoped. I saw us dancing under the stars, not under a belching smokestack.

At that point, San Francisco was all the California I knew. Even Oakland, the largest city in the East Bay, was a distant village "over there somewhere," populated by preachers and dry old maids.

Oh well, I assured myself, Molly would know where to go. How could I turn back now? I was more than halfway across. Sparkling Molly Carver, the mayor's daughter, could not possibly live in a slum. Evansville had to have some pleasant neighborhoods. There had to be one if she lived there.

I retreated inside, back to the bar. The barkeep's eyes glinted. I must have looked greener than newly printed money.

"Three for a nickel for you, mate." He nudged the box at me again. "Think it's bad now? Wait till you step off the train downtown. My advice is to have a good time and keep smokin' so you won't notice the stink." Then he leaned over the bar, pointed his stogie right at me. "And whatever you do, stick with the beer and wine. *Don't* drink the hard stuff. Not a drop."

Then he winked again, gave that warning. "Butchertown," he added. "That's what it is."

Then the ferry whistle blew. The engines slowed, the props churning up a stinking froth. We nudged the end of a pier that jutted a half mile into the bay. No breakthrough into dusky sunshine; only more heavy fog and the fuzzy tangerine glow of streetlamps. I shuffled along with the herd, cigars and cigarettes lighting the way. My belly started to yaw again, but once I set foot on the dock my nausea eased.

I had spent two years sailing back and forth across the Atlantic during the Great War, but now I seemed to have disembarked at a truly foreign port. I turned and took a step back, but there were only red lights fading as the ferry horn blasted a sad farewell.

I wondered if Molly had grown impatient, decided I had stood her up. But then I turned back and saw her waiting, like she promised, leaning against a wrought-iron lamppost in a pool of light, a cigarette dangling from her left hand. The lumpy, swarthy men around me had their plain girls, but I had Molly, a girl only I would know. I forgot all about the dim, malodorous world around me.

Tonight she wore another cloche hat, this one cherry red, with her bobbed auburn hair wound gracefully behind her left ear. Thick blue eyeliner circled her warm eyes under fine black eyebrows; rouge highlighted her high cheekbones; her wide, lipsticked mouth was already open for a kiss. Once again a wide scarf—bright crimson—circled her throat. Her slinky red silk dress flirted with her knees while she filled up the top. Warm and saucy, that was Molly. As the space between us closed, I saw how artfully she applied her makeup to catch the light from every angle.

She beamed at the flowers, then pulled me in and kissed me deeper than before, in full view of everyone. Her lips tasted like iced cherry; the flavor spread all through my mouth. The scent of jasmine further washed away the bad air.

"I could see you all the way from out in the bay," I whispered in her ear.

"I could see you too, sailor."

We boarded a packed Key train at the end of the pier. She leaned hard against me as I lit a Chesterfield for her with my new sliver-plated lighter and then lit mine off hers, the glowing tips of our cigarettes hissing as they pressed together.

The train carried us down the pier. It reached land, then chugged up a steep incline. As we climbed, Molly let her full body press down on mine, until she was almost lying on top of me.

"Good. You brought your toothbrush."

I laughed, looking away in pleasurable shock, and glimpsed steel bridge railing and trains passing below, side by side, north and south, over silver streams of tracks, their thin gleam visible even through the fog and soot-crusted windows. I felt too dizzy to wonder about it.

As the train descended the far side, our weight shifted so I was leaning on her. She felt as soft as a new bed. Everyone was watching, but we did not care. I slipped my hand around low on her back to support her. Her eyes half-closed, she opened her mouth. "Oh my God! I forgot my girdle at home!" Then she added, "And my slip!"

Oh, she forgot all right. There was nothing under my hand but smooth thin silk and her warm flesh. I nearly died right there as she tilted her head back, her red mouth open. I had never known such promise, not even in the gamiest French ports.

And then the train leveled and stopped. The doors slapped open. I stepped down into a cloud, the tarmac soft under my feet. The perfume bubble around me burst. My eyes watered, my sinuses swelled and I sneezed violently into the sleeve of my new jacket. I pawed for my handkerchief, squinting into brown air, looking around for Molly.

"Where am I?" I asked, and waited for an answer.

Chapter 2

Man Without a Face

"Sorry about the weather, Paul!" Molly's voice had turned raspy. "The wind's bad tonight. It's not like this all the time, believe me." She smiled a comforting smile, then leaned over and kissed me on the cheek, a long smack, a balm for my initial disappointment.

"It's all right. I bet it'll be sunny tomorrow." I winked. What was a little bad air after all? It would bother us none.

The train slid away like a stage flat to reveal downtown Evansville. A bent street sign said we were on San Pablo Avenue, a broad boulevard. I was expecting a West Coast Podunk, maybe with some small-town charm, but it was as loud and jam-packed as Market and Powell when the navy blew into San Francisco. But San Francisco was an international city, where all the colors of the wider world mixed and swirled together. Here, the crowd was made up of mostly working men and very few women, only some of them the respectable kind, all dressed in brown and gray. They jostled shoulder to shoulder, full of hustle and howl, many deep in their cups or well on their way. San Francisco may have had the skyscrapers, but Evansville, in this patch at least, churned with just as much energy, though it certainly lacked the color.

Blocks of one-story brick buildings stretched up and down the street, quickly disappearing into fog. Few of them sported signs, their front doors blank and sullen. But behind each of them, I knew, waited a cornucopia of sins: speakeasies; gambling halls and card rooms offering pai gow, dice, poker, roulette, blackjack, every game in town; and porticos to more profound forms of wickedness—opium dens, whorehouses. On the roofs of a couple of buildings, floozies stood waving and calling like half-naked circus Sirens, making the structures into candlelit party cakes. Even at my young age I had seen my share of vice, but never had I seen so much crammed into such a small area.

Make no mistake. San Francisco had more dazzle by far, spread out over miles. And I had read the colorful tales about the Barbary Coast days of long ago. But seeing Evansville for the first time, I wondered if the Barbary Coast had really gone away after all. Maybe it had just packed up its gaudy trunk and dragged it over here, where no one would pay attention and everyone would be left alone to do as they willed.

Along with the people there were cars everywhere bumper to bumper, spewing blue exhaust, honking like cattle. A half block away to the north, a Ford and an Olds had locked fenders, sending the drivers onto the street for a shoving match. Meanwhile a hugely overweight traffic cop, ignored and alone, waved hopelessly for attention in an intersection as everyone tried to drive around him. The sidewalks were a carpet of paper, cigar and cigarette butts, candy wrappers and scraps of metal, tin and other waste.

The wind blew here the same as it did out on the bay: hard and cold. Dense brown fog blew close overhead. The low, dirty sky turned red towards the west, towards that smokestack I had seen from the boat. I fumbled for a cigarette, wishing I had bought some of those black cigars and praying the wind would change soon.

Then from underneath the brass toot of car horns rose a noise like actual music, hung on frames of rhythm and melody. It came from down San Pablo, from Oakland way, marching and strident. I looked at Molly to see her bedroom smile capsizing like a ship. Her brown eyes smoldered, not with sex but with a surprising deep anger, boiling to rage. It was the first time I had seen her mad.

I followed her stare. Down the middle of San Pablo a row of tubas floated towards us, their bells waving like shiny gold flowers, flanked by a police escort. A parade! Another party coming to join the one underway, though God knew where everyone would fit, or if there would be enough booze for one and all.

But as the parade drew closer, grew clearer through the growing mist, my dazed smile sank like Molly's. I recognized the strains of "Onward, Christian Soldiers," saw the white signs waving over the marchers, barking in large black letters:

TEMPERANCE NOW AND FOREVER!
EVANSVILLE MEANS E-VILLE!
CLOSE DOWN BUTCHERTOWN!

A trio of marchers led the tuba line: a short, blondish young chap on the left, hefting a black Bible like a brick; in the middle a tall, young, hard-looking brunette female dressed in pure black, bravely lugging a man-sized sledgehammer in both hands. The third marcher was a big fellow whose appearance gave me the willies—it was, of all people, Earl Warren, the Alameda County deputy DA. My boss would not like Warren catching me in his jurisdiction. DA Brady may have been a wet, but this kind of trouble our office did not need.

I turned to Molly saying, "Let's get away from these killjoys." But she already had me by my arm. (She thought fast, stayed on her toes—another thing I like in a woman. I swooned for her all the more.) She firmly guided me down a side street of brick buildings, past more bustling dens of sin. "Ballpark's right here." Oak Stadium's brick and steel suddenly loomed overhead, its roof nearly lost in the dusky fog.

As we drew near the gate, I heard the familiar crack of ball and bat, and another kind of cheer, a happy one, rose from inside the giant bowl. Baseball. This time I pulled ahead of Molly before realizing I had no idea where to go. But then came the thrill at the sight of that sward of green, barren though it was in spots. Unlike Seals Stadium, it looked to be barely maintained, but I was happy to be there nonetheless.

We were late, as I feared, but it did not cost me a dime. After all, I had the daughter of Evansville's mayor on my arm. And thanks to her high falutin' status, the Carver clan got the best seats, first row along the third base line, close enough to see wrinkles on the uniforms, beads of sweat dripping from the pitcher's nose and globs of tobacco juice raising dust as they plopped in the dirt.

The stadium was packed and it was the middle of the sixth, with the light rapidly fading. My attention immediately dived into the game. The score was, incredibly, Seals 15, Oaks 13. I jumped when Molly sharply tugged my sleeve.

"Paul, say hello."

A big pork-white hand slid towards me, a boxer's hand, swollen around the knuckles, the fingers bent from years of bare-knuckled bouts. A fat diamond ring glinted on the third finger. An expensive cigar, gold wrapped, stuck like a thick stump from yellowed dentures, bared in a friendly grin set in a square, fat, veiny red face. His steel-gray hair was greased back on his head. The smile looked distant, the small porcine eyes unfocused, oddly blank. My hand was big too, but nevertheless his swallowed mine whole as my stomach dropped. I felt under pressure.

Gee, I forgot to bring the engagement ring, I almost joked, but Molly spoke first.

"Daddy, I want you to meet Paul Bacon. Paul, my father, Mayor Cobb Carver."

He slowly released my hand, looking at it carefully. Then he winked at me with a scraggle-browed eye, brown like Molly's. "You a boxer, son?"

"I used to be. In the navy during the war. Amateur bouts, pickup fights on the troopships going back and forth, that kind of thing. Nothing professional."

"Me too," he murmured. "I fought Sullivan." His eyes went even blanker, as though he were reliving a memory of standing toe-to-toe with the greatest. I was going to add that I moonlighted as a referee in the city, but Molly was talking to him and I saw his grin turn to a grimace.

"He is?" Cobb Carver's face turned red as a vein pulsated in his forehead.

Uh-oh. What happened? What did she tell him? Panic seared me. Two seconds in and I had flunked Daddy's test. My dreams of Molly burned up like cheap paper. This might be our last date. I plunged into a mood like the fog, seeing myself seasick on the lonely ride back across the bay.

But then Cobb Carver turned to his right to someone seated next to him, as though relaying a message. Maybe they were not talking about me after all. I leaned out to look down the row to where two pairs of long legs stuck out, the first pair in cream-colored pleated pants and two-tone wingtips like mine, the second in razor-creased black slacks over sleek, shiny black shoes. This last one also held a fancy polished bent pipe with a silver band and a glowing red eye.

The tip was missing from the middle finger. I glimpsed a hawkish tawny eye under a sleek black eyebrow. He seemed to be looking at me. Except for Molly, none of them wore hats, though the fellow in cream-colored slacks held a straw boater like mine.

I hurriedly returned to the game. At some point Molly's arm curled through mine. I leaned against her. Maybe she still liked me, even if Pops did not. Soon the hot dog boy came by and served me one for free as Molly's guest. I was so hungry I almost missed the odd smoky flavor as the dog's juices burst and filled my mouth. I recalled the ferry bartender's warning about the booze. Did that apply to the food? I took a grateful sip from my flask and passed it to Molly, who accepted it with a graceful smile.

The game was a joke. With everyone in the stadium smoking (including the kids, I swear) and the smoke rising to meet the brown fog overhead, and the sun nowhere in sight, visibility was about zero. Fly ball after fly ball was swallowed by the fug, leaving the fielders below baffled as the balls landed everywhere but in their gloves. The base hits kept coming. In the eighth inning, both teams batted through their lineup. At any other park they would have called the game, but the crowd was tense and rowdy, and the umpires did not dare risk starting a riot.

At the bottom of the ninth, it was 26 to 19 Seals, not looking good for the Oaks. I detected movement to my right. Cream Slacks was on his feet. I glanced over carefully because I did not want be Mr. Nosy, especially when I heard hoarse voices rising. "No! I said don't go!" Cobb Carver called. "C'mon Danny, stay here! Wait!" Molly said.

But Danny, in his cream pants, rose and went sideways away, his back to us, slapping on his bright straw boater. It sat on him like a crown. He wore a blue blazer, and besides being the only Carver wearing a hat, he was blonder than I, his hair razor-cut in a straight line over his white collar. I never saw his face.

Then came one more crack of the bat. Line drive out. Game over. Coarse boos blew through the stadium. As Molly gave me a resigned shrug and a loyal fan's weary smile and I gave a thumbs-up (the Seals were *my* team after all) I saw Mr. Carver leaning over, talking to the man with the bent pipe and the eagle eyes.

As Eagle Eyes stood up, Molly rose too, calling, "Chess!" *What a strange name.* As they talked in murmurs, Chess looked over her shoulder, this time right at me. I prickled all over. He had a large, handsome hawk nose too, with a perfect black mustache slashed over thin lips. He really did look like a devil with its talons out. I brushed my fingers over my throat as I jerked to my feet.

"You okay?" Molly looked more distracted than concerned as she turned to me.

"Yeah, I'm fine." I felt anxious to escape. As we went up the steps, I realized Molly had forgotten the flowers, but we seemed in a hurry and the petals were already wilted at the edges.

Molly, the mayor and I left the stadium together. As we emerged, people were running past us, looking upset and scared. There was a great hoo-ha rising from San Pablo a long block away: shouting, yelling, breaking glass and cawing sirens. Some kind of riot going on. A huge cop waddled hurriedly up to us, breathing heavily. I recognized him as the one haplessly directing traffic, but now he carried an enormous heavy-gauge shotgun across his huge chest, an elephant gun by my guess. Mayor Carver stepped away to talk to him. The cop puffed urgently at him, jabbing his thumb over his shoulder.

Then Carver turned. He looked at me like he did not recognize me, holding out his gnarled paw. "Nice meeting you, Joe."

"Paul," I said, but I doubt he heard me.

"A little get-together at our place, if you're interested, after you're through dancin'. Around nine, ten?" His hand swallowed mine once more. Then he bounced a funny nod at Molly and followed the fat cop towards San Pablo.

I was coming down with an attack of nerves like a flu. My date with Molly was not following my dream. Evansville was the strangest place I had ever been in. I had only seen towns like it from train windows. It was like standing near a drain with the world's dirt swirling around my shoes. I had walked in on some secret family argument, a drama taking place behind closed doors. And I felt too dependent on Molly Carver, an unwanted feeling, maybe because I was a man, and a man is always supposed to be steering the ship. Instead I was the one feeling steered.

Molly watched her father walk away, her face drawn and tired. Her artfully applied makeup failed to conceal her worry.

And then I understood. I knew why I was here: to rescue her from this place; to be an Orpheus to her Eurydice, leading her out of Hades, as it was told in Bulfinch. It explained her initial reluctance to have me come over here first. It also explained why she was so evasive about what Evansville was like. She wanted me to get to know *her* first. Molly needed desperately to be saved from this dungeon the rest of the world called Butchertown. She needed somewhere to light out for (as Huck Finn said) and the right man to show her the way.

And I would be the one! The hero who would rescue her from her miserable life in this miserable place. Then and there I determined to ask her for her hand that very night. I carried no engagement ring, but that was a mere detail. Urgency was all! *Carpe diem!*

I took out my Chesterfields, tapped one up from the bottom of the pack and offered it to her. Molly took it with a wan grateful smile. I lit it for her, then lit mine off hers, like before. This was becoming an intimate ritual. She took a puff, exhaled and shook her bad mood away with a toss of her head.

"So, babe, where's this dancing?"

She nodded with her chin past the ballpark towards the industrial area.

"Thataway, sport. We'll have to take the long way, down Hollis here. San Pablo's a little wild for strolling."

I gulped and crossed my eyes like Ben Turpin. "Good golly, Molly! You're taking me dancing at the stockyards?"

"Don't be such a goof!" she said laughing. "Believe it or not there's a park that way, with a dancing pavilion. Open till midnight."

"What's it doing over there?"

"It keeps the factory workers happy and spending their wages in town. They don't come over this way, except for the games. I'm sorry that my hometown's a little rough tonight. The wind makes people a little crazy sometimes. My father can fix a lot of things around here, but he can't turn the wind in the right direction."

We reached the corner of a street called Hollis. To the left stood Evansville City Hall, a small building, looking abandoned with the windows boarded over. Molly steered me right, behind the stadium. Across the street stood more redbrick warehouses and small factories. Not far away, towards the bay, the trains rattled slowly by, blowing their whistles. It occurred to me that they never stopped moving. Evansville had grown and branched out of its rail yards. There was not a sandy beach in sight.

I started my engagement proposal in roundabout fashion, telling Molly more about San Francisco: that there was so much more to it than what she had experienced on our previous two dates; how much I enjoyed living there, despite the fog, an aspect I downplayed. I slipped in phrases such as "next time you come over" and "if you lived there." She smiled at my clever hints: *Yes, next time I come over. Yes, if I lived there.*

My confidence grew as we walked arm in arm through the yellow pools of light cast by the widely spaced streetlamps. I enjoyed the sight of our shadows moving as one, magically flowing from under our feet and stretching out ahead to fade into darkness. "See that?" I pointed. "There we go, you and me forever."

I started creeping closer to the moment I would bend my knee and take her hand in mine. Maybe on the dance floor. But then I got a little too confident, because I suddenly put my foot in another shadow, one concealing my mouth:

"Before long you'll be singing 'So Long, Butchertown.'"

Her step slowed. I looked up just as our blended shadows disappeared in the darkness.

"Where did you hear that?"

"Butcher—?"

"Yes."

"On the ferry over. What—?"

"*We* don't call it that. Ever." She lifted her lovely chin with offended civic pride, as prim as my Temperance-minded aunties. "It's Evansville. My grandfather—my mother's father—founded this town."

I winced, bee stung from tip to toe. I clumsily apologized. Swamped with confusion, blushing with embarrassment, I swiftly changed the subject.

"Speaking of family, where's your mother tonight anyway? When do I—?"

BOOM!

"—when do I get to meet her?"

The boom came from the fog up ahead, too explosive for an auto exhaust pipe. Molly stopped short. I slid from her grasp, wandered a few steps ahead. As I turned, she hunched her shoulders as though she had suddenly grown cold.

BOOM!

"Oh no! Goddamnit . . ."

Molly ran past me, plunged into the fog. I followed the sound of her heels clacking on the cement. Then the footsteps stopped, followed by a shrill scream. I tripped over cracked asphalt and staggered. When I came up, I found another brick factory looming in front of me, its loading dock opening onto a street corner. I smelled the sting of cordite.

Molly was kneeling over a pair of shoe soles, off to the right, past the loading dock. The shoe tips pointed up at an angle from each other. I slowly approached with short steps, as though creeping to the edge of a cliff.

Two-tone wingtips, cream-colored slacks and a blue blazer. Both his arms were stretched straight out from his shoulders, as thought he had been crucified to the concrete. A straw boater lay on its crown a few feet away.

"Danny!" Molly screamed the name over and over, pounding on his chest.

I should have jumped right in and pulled her away, but I was paralyzed with horror. Danny's face, the one I missed at the ballpark a short time ago, was gone. All of it. Nothing left but a soup bowl made of bone, brimming with a pulpy stew of blood and gore.

I turned away, shaking and heaving. My knees broke. My hot dog came up as I fell on all fours. I heard Molly's raging cries through my queasy fog.

"Bastards! Sons of bitches! Why didn't you listen? Goddamn you, Danny!"

I wiped bile from my mouth, struggled to my feet, needing to do something, anything. I went to her, knelt and gently grabbed her shoulders, trying to avert my eyes. "No, don't, Molly. Come on. We'll go get—"

Suddenly a pair of talons sank into my left shoulder, yanked me up and shoved me away. I scraped my hands and knees on the tar road. My hat flew away as white lights flashed in my head. I rolled on my back, then onto my side and scrambled around to look up into a pair of eyes I was hoping to never see again.

Chess stared coldly down from a hell far above, a sawed-off double-barreled shotgun cradled in his arm. Half-lit by the streetlight, he looked like a vulture, like a rat, like a snake, like all three bred perfectly together. I was a field mouse who had wandered out of his burrow. I was sure I would die. And he would be the one making me dead. My eyes squeezed shut.

But seconds passed and I remained alive. "Buckram!" Chess called. I opened my lids as he tossed the shotgun to another stranger in the shadows. This one toted what looked like a large club of some sort. Buckram caught the shotgun easily. Then Chess firmly lifted Molly by her quivering shoulders and led her a few steps away.

"Stand back." His growl carried more weight than my lover's croon. He shot me a bullet-eyed look that said, *Stay put, you.* Then he knelt and swiftly lifted Danny into his arms. As he turned, the faceless head swept past inches away, dangling upside down, gore flying everywhere.

I swayed to my feet as he strode off towards the shadows, his back straight, the corpse dangling in his arms. His partner walked beside him, carrying both the shotgun and big stick.

Molly followed them, her shoulders bowed. I ran after her, calling her name. Just as I caught up, she turned on me, staring at me as though I were an intrusive stranger. Her makeup streaked down, as though her own face were cracking apart. She cut me off as I mumbled something about calling the cops, about not moving the body.

"Go home, Paul. Get out of here. Take the next ferry back to the city."

"Molly, a man's been killed! We have to call—"

"It's got nothing to do with you, see?" She shook her fist, her voice dead and flat. She was no longer the woman I had known, no longer the one whose hand I would have begged for. "You can't be involved. Get out of here. Forget this happened. Don't ever come here again."

She spun away and hurried off.

"Chess! Chess! Wait up!" It sounded more like a command than a plea. She caught up with them under a pool of light cast by a streetlamp.

They disappeared into the darkness. I stood alone, a stranger in this very strange and very dirty town, surrounded by fog and wind as the trains rumbled by and lonely foghorns called from far out in the bay.

Chapter 3

Step Back Into Darkness

I stood hunched, shivering, my arms wrapped around me. I felt I had been flung to Mars like John Carter. I thought about the Tarzan books on my bedside table, about how heroes such as he, Carter and Zorro would spring into action at moments like this: ready, willing and able, moments they lived for. How did they always know what to do? Standing alone in the windy gloom, I started to hate them with every fiber of my being.

I fought the urge to cry. Tears would have finished me. Had I not seen worse? What about the wounded soldiers I had helped bring back home with their faces destroyed? But those wounds had been bandaged over. I had also seen troop and hospital ships torpedoed and sunk. But those incidents mostly happened far away, near the horizon.

I had no map, no compass, no sextant and only a nebulous idea of where I was. I fumbled my watch from my pocket, tried to read it by my lighter, but my hand shook and the wind flattened the flame down to a nub. The flame went out and I cursed the darkness. I had stopped praying some years back and would have felt ashamed to start again.

I felt terrible shame as it was. I had been absolutely wrong about every damn thing from the second I laid eyes on Molly Carver. One misread signal after another. But she had read *me* all right, as easy a McGuffey primer: always follows a fine full figure, a saucy voice like the Siren's call and—

Suddenly the streetlights in the surrounding blocks flickered and went out. The wind picked up. Darkness clung like a second skin.

I tried to suppress thoughts about the dead man and the hole where his face had been, but they stuck in my head like a Victrola needle in a record. The shotgun must have been held—he must have seen both barrels, a pair of cold black eyes—and that other pair of eyes, belonging to his killer—

"That'll do, Ensign Bacon," I hissed. I forced myself to attention, my shoulders back, responding to the call "All hands on deck."

With my head wet, cold and bare, I decided my first action would be to look for my boater. I stepped carefully around in the darkness until my foot found one. I put it on, but it almost sat on my ears. *Oh God, the dead man's hat!* "Danny!" I heard Molly's scream again and threw the hat aside.

A few steps later I came upon my boater further out in the street. Its snug fit made me feel better, a first brick laid towards rebuilding myself.

I struggled to focus, to do something besides chug in circles. Despite the bad air, I felt like having a cigarette and fumbled one from my pack. I lit it with my back to the wind. As I straightened up, I saw a glow through the fog, the lights washing in from surrounding neighborhoods. I could make out the looming curve of the stadium. I remembered Molly and I had walked by Butchertown's city hall from that direction. The police station should be right nearby. I would go there and bring them back, though I was not sure what I could show them in the dark with the body now carried off, along with the likely murder weapon. Whatever remaining clues (say the bloody scatter from the victim's terrible injury) would only reappear at daybreak.

I walked with slow steps. The sting of cordite and the tang of blood still hung about me. Wanting to avoid stepping in anything gruesome, I made my way across the street in the direction I had come from.

Only a moment had passed when my shadow suddenly materialized on the ground before me as a car engine growled from behind. I turned around into the blinding glare cast by a pair of yellow bug lights bouncing along. A large '21 Model T touring car formed itself around the lights. I waved, but it was already pulling up a few feet away, as though it expected to find me. I stepped out of its glare as two guys got out and walked towards me, hands in their pockets.

Both were shorter than I and wore newsboy caps; one looked Mexican, the other Oriental.

"Hey, sports, can you lend me a hand?" I tried to sound both calm and friendly. "I have to find the police. There's been some trouble." I drew out my cigarette pack and held it out.

As the Mexican stepped towards me, the Oriental shook his head, said something, maybe in Chinese or Japanese, with a lot of vowel sounds. The Mexican stopped and looked at him, said something that sounded not quite Spanish. Then the Oriental said something like "Nah Tim!" The Mexican shook his head, uncomprehending. He pointed at his cap, then at my hat.

I kept trying to explain that I needed to get to the police station, when I should have been keeping my boxer's eye on the Mexican as he stepped up to me, drawing his hand from his pocket, the hand that carried a sap.

A thud sounded inside my head. A big ball of light and pain exploded. Then the light went out.

I came to feeling jiggled about as though in a drinks shaker. I had been stuffed into the backseat of a moving vehicle. Metal plates clanked and rumbled beneath as a choking haze of oil and gas overpowered me. Two men coughed; one swore in that funny not-Spanish. As we passed out of the cloud, I sneezed and knocked myself out again.

I next awoke sitting on a hard chair, my aching head lying on a hard wooden surface. I looked up, blinking. The right side of my noggin throbbed as warm liquid dripped from my earlobe. I looked down to see I was wearing two pairs of cuffs, hands and feet.

I was in some kind of office, dark except for harsh light from the hallway. When I stepped off the train earlier, I had caught the strong scent of the stockyards. Now it surrounded me, as heavy as the fog: tallow, blood, cow shit, moist and smoky. From somewhere nearby livestock mooed and bellowed in a chorale sung by frightened animals.

The desk was made of oak and scarred by cigarettes and penknives. The office was about ten by ten feet, its gray walls blank, except for a 1922 calendar with a color illustration of happy cows in a sunny field. The only other furniture was a metal chair in front and the wooden wheeled chair I was sitting in. Bound hand and foot, I envisioned me escaping, hopping along as though competing in a sack race. Escape would have to wait.

Voices chattered from out in the hall. An Oriental entered, pushing a button in the wall. Yellow light burst from the ceiling. He looked to be one of the punks who had conked me. His tan face was like polished stone. His Mexican partner rolled in right behind him, a feline smirk under a scrap mustache.

The Mexican addressed me, saying something like "Alo."

I said hello, asked where I was, putting on a brave but polite mug. He shrugged, spread his arms: *Don't ask me, I only work here.* The Oriental spoke and the Mexican frowned at him, replying in his off-Spanish, uncomprehending. The Oriental shook his head, exasperated at both of us. *Oh, peachy,* as my Nana would say. I did not know their lingo, they did not know mine, nor did they know each other's. A long night lay ahead.

The pair turned and left, arguing past each other. The Mexican gave the Oriental a shove down the hall out of sight.

Idiots, I thought. I started searching the desk. The drawers opened easily. Of the two on the right, the top one was empty, while the bottom contained folders. I tried to pull the folders out, and dropped them on the floor. They contained manifests with a pen-and-ink drawing of bull horns on the letterhead. In the center drawer a jumble of ink pens and pencils with half-used erasers, a compass whose needle end made it suitable for stabbing, a ruler, and an unopened inkwell.

More of nothing in the top left-hand drawer, except for a blurry family photo portrait: mother, father, an older boy, a young girl, an even younger boy. I slammed the drawer shut with a miserable sigh. What was the matter with people? No one thought to leave either a handcuff key or a gun handy.

Right then another man rounded the corner, strode into the tiny office. Right away I knew he was the Boss. His face was dark like the Mexican's but he was much taller, round, big and broad, well dressed with a rugged elegance, like a wealthy farmer going to town. A bright-red boutonniere blazed like a gunshot wound on his coat. In one hand he gripped a brand-new pine baseball bat, in the other a fat smoking cigar. An elegant Van Dyke beard circled his mouth as his round face swelled with furious disbelief.

"*Madre dio!*" That I recognized as Italian. "*Fottuto idioti!*" He backed out as quick and neat as a roadster out of a parking space and drove off down the hall, shaking the ball bat, barking in Italian. His barks faded away, leaving behind the distant lowing of the cattle. I buried my head in my arms, turning from trying to think my way out to not thinking at all, looking for a patch of relief for my sore head.

Not long after, a popping noise came from outside. I jerked my head up. Then came a bang, this one closer. Then the pops, cracks and bangs swelled and sputtered like a string of firecrackers. Then an unnervingly familiar boom, from a shotgun. Gunfire drew closer. Shouts and screams echoed down the hall, human cries mixing with the bellowing of cattle.

Then came footsteps, and a shadow spread across the wall outside.

The Oriental staggered into the office, one hand holding his bleeding belly, blood sheeting over his splayed fingers, the other holding a pistol. Shock and fear twisted his face, but he was in too much pain to cry out. His knees buckled and thumped down hard on the cement floor. Then with a whimper he crumpled on his side against the wall.

The gunfire drew closer, louder. I hopped out from behind the desk and promptly fell down next to the Oriental. His face was a foot away. His eyes and mouth were open, his mouth saying "Awww" with every breath. I could use the pistol in his hand, but I had another idea. He might have the cuff keys on him.

I moved fast as the gunfire drew closer, like thundering footsteps. I started with his jacket pockets. No soap. I probed his shirt pocket. No dice. I twisted around like a contortionist to get my hands inside his pants pockets. His blood was running out on the floor, forming a red pool, soaking the edges of my suit. He cried out in pain as I tried to turn him on his back to get a better reach. I mumbled apologies he could not understand.

I found the cuff key all right—right pocket, made for both cuffs. It took one of the longest moments of my life to free myself, as the shooting drew closer, louder, like a hungry giant going "Fee-fi-fo-fum!," determined to turn my bones into bread.

The Oriental's eyes were still and empty when I took the pistol from his hand. It was a Luger, the kind doughboys brought back from France as souvenirs. I had never fired one myself, hardly knew anything about guns beyond my old .22 hunting rifle and basic training. I grabbed the desk to get to my feet and slipped in the Oriental's blood. Both my heels were sticky and squelching on the floor as I tore out the door and turned left.

I ran down the hallway, the narrow gray kind you see in bad dreams. Two other darkened offices opened on the left. I turned right at the corner. Up ahead a block of light, a rail running across, darkness beyond, the lowing of cattle, gunshots. I had nowhere to go but straight on.

Straight on into the middle of a full-blown shoot-out.

I ran out onto a second-floor walkway surrounding a giant cattle pen. The roar was deafening. The air reeked of cow shit and gunpowder. Bullets flew everywhere, whining and spanging. On the far side a man flipped over the railing and fell screaming, spinning as he landed among the dozens of panic-stricken steers milling below. The bulls jumped and slashed at each with their horns, as though fighting over his corpse.

I saw another one to my right, sagging face-first, clinging to the railing, maybe the Mexican. Like the Oriental, he had been shot through the middle.

I crouched low and ran the other way. *If I think myself invisible, then I will be invisible.* Bullets zipped by inches away, striking the far wall, steel beams and glass. Any ricochet might find me; my next step might be my last. I made it to a door at the far end. As I shoved through, I felt relief. Now I would be free, clear and safe.

But I was wrong. I met a man at the top of the stairs. He had a long face, small slitted eyes, wavy hair and pencil-thin mustache. He wore a long blue wool coat, no hat, carried a gun. Big surprise for us both. This time I wasted no time. I passed on the Luger for the one weapon I did know how to use: my hardest left jab, quick, hard, a shocker to the point of his chin. I felt his whiskers scrape my knuckles. The blow rang all the way up my shoulder.

I still remember how his jaw cracked, his head snapped back, like his neck was on a hinge, and how his teeth splintered from his mouth; and how he rolled, somersaulted backward down the steel steps, doll limp in his heavy coat; how he sprawled on his back across the landing, his head slamming into the wall by the corner, his hair flying free. And then the final snap as his neck broke.

That was the first man I ever killed.

I knew right away he was dead. But this was not a thinking situation. I was lizard-scared, wanted to live too badly to think. But before I could even take the first step down I heard more commotion from below, two mean, rough voices echoing off the walls. Gunfire behind me drew closer. The only way out was up the next flight of stairs, two at a time, to the third and last floor, my heels still sticky with blood.

I dashed out onto another walkway ringing the cattle pen, like the one below. I staggered down the walkway on heavy legs, along a row of windows made of thickly frosted rectangles, the kind that open on hinges set in the middle.

I found one that was open. I must have looked like an idiot trying to squeeze through it, my ass and feet dangling, all the harder because of the Luger I stupidly clutched in my hand as though it were a life buoy.

I strained a shoulder muscle as I landed and rolled down a wide, sloping tar paper roof. The sky was black except for a fuzzy orange glow. Behind me the shooting was tapering off as the cattle kept bawling.

I crouched in the shadow, outside the blocks made by the lights from inside. Two silhouettes floated along behind the frosted windows. They had found the dead man on the stairs, then followed the bloody footprints. One of the shadows cast a profile like a hawk's. I knew that profile. Now he was after me. I would be his next victim. He let me live last time. This time he would not.

His face filled the open window. His vampire eyes over his sharp cheekbones sought me out, bore into me, seeing me in the dark, a helpless mouse miles away. Panic lifted me up. I backed away, down the roof, gripping the Luger, though it would do no good.

As he stuck his head out the window, I stepped back and down into darkness.

Chapter 4

Saved for the Moment

As always happens when I sleep in a strange place, I dreamt strange dreams.

I was lying in the backyard of my grandparents' house near Peekskill on a humid August afternoon under a blue jay sky. Uncle Lloyd, my father's brother from New York City, was dancing solo on the badminton court, performing pirouettes, gavottes, handsprings, backflips and cartwheels, cavorting without music. Uncle Frank, my father's other brother, from Illinois, wearing his tightest, most uncomfortable mud-brown suit, his derby squashed over his ears, was firing a single-barreled shotgun at Uncle Lloyd, growling incomprehensibly, every shot missing its target. He never had to reload. Uncle Lloyd did not seem to care and kept spinning like a top until he became a blur.

And then my father was standing over me, his priest's collar blinding white, the cross swinging from his neck winking with sunlight. He held his butterfly net over his shoulder, while a butterfly on his finger waved its blue wings at me.

I reached for it, my body rising through damp soil, the loam sliding over my skin as though I were being pulled from a grave. The sky turned gray. The grass under me shrank beneath the ground.

I peeled open my gluey eyes, my nerves buzzing, my cold, wet skin tingling. I was lying at the bottom of a V-trench under a gray sky. On one side a wall of cement blocks stretched away in a plain, on the other a dirt slope rose to a plain gray heaven. I inhaled the aromas of livestock and petrol. My shoulder and head throbbed. My ears rang.

I sat up slowly, then crawled up the dirt slope until I was vertical on the incline. I felt my body all over and found a collection of lumps, bruises and strained muscles, as though I had been beaten with a small hammer. No broken bones, though.

At first, I could only remember fragments. Assembling them was like cutting together a picture show, as I understood the process, with images jerking and jumping past: sailing through wind and fog; a woman's blurry face framed by shiny silk; a body sprawled in the street. Then that part in the movie came where the mustachioed bone-faced villain stared through a window, his evil eyes fixed on me, his prey. Then that other face returned, or rather the man without a face, because it had been destroyed by a shotgun blast.

I became furious with myself. I should have *known* or at least suspected. I remembered Aunt Agnes's voice like a wrinkled carpet, declaring with fundamental Protestant certainty that I would wind up in a gutter if "I didn't mend my sinful ways." Well, here I was: in the gutter, her prophecy come true. "Just as I thought!" her cry rang with triumph in my mind.

I looked behind me up the slope. I had fallen from the roof opposite as I backed away from the villain's stare. He had not seen me like I thought, or concluded I had broken my neck and left me here. Indeed, a straight fall might have killed me. Instead I had landed on the mound at precisely the right angle, then rolled and slid down here, twenty feet or so, judging by the track I left behind.

I patted myself down, doing an inventory. I had been picked clean: billfold, cigarettes, keys, silver lighter, silver flask, my toothbrush, all gone. The bastards even took my shiny red tie. Both front buttons had been ripped from my collar, leaving it stuck out from my neck like a flimsy pair of soiled wings. Feeling ridiculous, I tore it off and flung it away.

Worst of all, they had taken my gold-plated Elgin watch, my father's last gift to me just before I left for the navy and the war. Those dirty thieving bastards.

All I had left were my muddy two-tone oxfords, my new pants ripped and soiled at the knees, my suit coat and cotton shirt. My head felt cold. My boater was in the street where I had been sapped by that Mexican and his Oriental partner, the one grabbing his belly, holding the Luger as he stumbled through the office door before dying with his face inches from mine.

The Luger lay close by. I remembered more of last night: fleeing down a walkway, my heels sticking, bullets flying by. Another dead man rolling head over heels down steel stairs, his neck snapping. I looked at the scraped sore knuckles of my left hand, the one that delivered the blow. I had killed someone. I turned each foot up to look at my shoes. The carved knights on the soles were caked with blood, further evidence.

I had to get out of there. On one side the trough stopped at another gray wall, intersecting a one-story building with a barred window. On the other it emptied into soupy fog, where stood a lonely, thin tree.

The Luger held seven rounds and needed cleaning, not possible now. I slid the gun into my pants pocket, thinking I would clean it later. Maybe I would not have to fire it, just wave it around and yell. I had a big enough voice. A big man with a big voice waving a gun could go far around here, far enough to get out of Butchertown.

I walked unsteadily out of the trench, leaning my hand on the wall. My knees quivered. I stopped to relieve myself. The reek of my waste whirled with the noxious fog. I itched all over and would have given my life for a bath.

The trench opened up into flat, empty dirt. Off behind me a deep hole yawned under the pile on which I had fallen. Construction equipment, including cranes and mechanical diggers, sat near the rim. Not a laborer was in sight. Maybe they had been scared away. No police, no curious citizens. Someone must have heard the shooting. Yet, except for the trains, the foghorns from the bay and that empty wind, there was only hollow silence. A crumpled tarmac road stretched before me. Across the street a long row of one-story brick-and-concrete buildings, silent and empty, ran alongside it.

The tree turned out to be an old lamppost, the bulb inside the burnt glass housing long dimmed. I leaned on the post, but its painted surface had no traction, nor did my legs have much strength. I slid to the ground at the base, leaned my head against its cold metal. I needed more sleep. I wanted to return to that dream of home, where I would stay forever.

Then something popped from deep within the fog. Then another pop. *Oh no, shit, here they go again, crazy bastards.* I could try to run. Or hide. I decided to curl up like a possum, hoping they would mistake me for a pile of rags, or maybe another corpse.

Then under the popping rose the growl of a car engine gasping and sputtering and the smell of car exhaust. I prayed they would drive past without seeing me. No rides for me, not anywhere. I would walk out on my own feet.

Then came a woman's voice came from above, hoarse but tender.

"Are you all right, mister?"

A pair of fierce blue eyes, tight with concern, stared down from under a flat, lacy black hat, the kind my mother's Methodist mother wore. This woman wore a similar black dress. Its high ruffled collar was ringed by a gold chain with a plain tarnished gold cross. The black sleeves were puffy though torn, the voluminous skirt smudged. She had no gun, no sap and looked both sincerely worried and very perplexed. And she was not scared at all, though she had good reason to be. A young woman needed to beware of strange men lying in ditches on foggy mornings, especially around here.

Behind her at the curb a black prewar Model T idled, shaking as though cold, smoke puffing from its tail. In the front passenger seat sat a youngish man who stared at me with wide pale blue-white eyes. He wore a coarse, plain black suit, except for a white collar circling his neck. His soft sparrow-brown hair, parted on the left, swept over his head, framing a forehead like the blank wall of a large building, the kind of frontage built to house a large brain.

The woman gripped my elbow as I pulled myself up the light pole. "We have room in the jump seat. Do you need a hospital? The closest one's in Oakland. That's not too far away."

Her voice sounded strangely familiar. With her hand on my elbow, I walked stiffly beside her to the car, squeezed my big frame into the jump seat, groaning through my teeth. She looked at me carefully as she got in behind the wheel. I had the same I-know-you feeling.

The exhaust pipe backfired as she adjusted the gas mixture. My head bobbled as the vehicle jerked forward and we lurched down the street.

"Where you headed, pilgrim?" The preacher glanced over his shoulder with a pained smile. Seeing him close up, I guessed him to be around my age, but his skin looked pale and weathered, his face like a rock beaten into human shape with hammers. He was older than his years.

"I need to get to a police station. Evansville City Hall. At least I think that's where it is." I looked down at my muddy clothes. "Sorry. I'm dirtying up your car."

I trailed off. The car may have been comical, but there was a somber quality about these two that made me cautious. I realized that they may well be Prohis, drys, like my mother's people, sniffing everyone's breath. Aunt Agnes would love it; all my aunties' hearts would sing hosannas to the church rafters! *Grabbed from the gutter by Jesus!* I had more reasons to be careful now.

"Where are you comin' from?"

Instead of answering, I asked the time. Six thirty, he said, pulling a silver-plated watch from his pocket.

"Morning or evening?"

He laughed coarsely, like an old navy salt, ex-pug, cop or a newspaper guy, a jasper's cackle. He laughed like a man from the wrong side of the tracks. My prim, snooty aunts might not have liked him after all. And he would have scoffed at their prim certainties.

"Morning. What else?" He sneered at me like I was a mug.

"I lost my watch. There's no sun around here."

"Yeah, there's something timeless about Butchertown. Not like in fairy tales, though. You need a torch to find your way in daylight. You know the story of how the world fell dark when our Lord died on the cross? It stayed dark in Butchertown." He paused. "Looks like the town painted *you* red instead of the other way around."

I figured I would keep mum about what happened, not only because of my shame. I felt protective towards them, especially the woman. They had no need to know. However strange, they were straight and square, and telling them too much would be like putting them in the line of fire. I needed to talk to experts, to professionals. Though what I would tell *them* I had no idea.

I glanced at my sore knuckles and changed the subject.

"Is this your missus?"

He gently placed a hand on her shoulder. "My betrothed. We'll be married soon, with the Lord's blessing. I'm Taggart by the way." He stiffly offered me his hand. His handshake was strong, though the flesh was soft. "And this is Louise."

Now that the voice and the eyes had a name, the picture puzzle finished itself: a blue-eyed girl, her mouth open, leaning back against a tree on a long-ago spring afternoon in a blue and windy world. My heart burst like yolk. Indeed, this was a miracle. An insane one.

Louise was nodding, her eyes on the road, steering carefully and confidently, shifting gears gracefully, especially for a woman—better than some men—her grip firm without being rigid. She neatly threaded the potholes pocking the road.

"And you?"

"Paul Bacon," I said slow and deliberate. "From New York."

Louise's foot slipped off the gas as her square shoulders covered her ears. The car slowed down and swerved. The preacher frowned with loving concern.

"You all right, Lou?"

"Fine." Her foot found the gas again. The car lurched forward, then steadied.

"Bacon." Taggart chuckled. "You kinda look like you just jumped out of a hot skillet."

"I tipped a few," I said, though I hardly had any. A drink would have been good about then. A good stiff scotch, the kind Scots in kilts drank. I coughed, spat over the side and excused myself. A slight smile on his face, Taggart kept asking questions.

"We drove by here last night, where we found you. We heard shooting. Did you?"

"Me? Yeah, I did. I was too busy getting waylaid and robbed to be honest. They took everything I had."

"Your flask too? That could be a sign, pal." He pointed his finger skyward.

"The only sign I'm looking for is the one that says 'Police.'"

"You're a stranger here."

"From the city. I was on a date and we got separated."

"Is your girl safe?"

"Oh, she's safe I think."

The car slowed as we approached a metal bridge over a creek. Handwritten signs were posted all over, on the bridge and on utility poles:

NO SMOKING! PROBITTO FUMAR!

We plunged into a stinging petrol mist. My whole face ran as I coughed and gagged. Taggart covered his nose with a handkerchief. Louise shook her head violently and groaned as her hat nearly came unpinned from her hair. As metal plates rumbled under the tires, I wondered if this was the road I had ridden last night on my way to the stockyards. To our right a huge oil refinery towered like a rusting castle, stretching towards the bay, smoke pouring out its minarets into the ashen sky.

Taggart grinned, wiping his face, blinking the fumes from his watering eyes. "That's just one of our major oil refineries. The creek used to be called Grizzly Creek. They say bears lived around here a long time ago. Indian and Mexican children used to play it in it, catch fish for their supper." He shook his head. "But that's just a fairy story. It's Gasoline Creek now. Even the maps say so. It actually catches fire from time—"

Suddenly a large pop came from up ahead. *Pop . . . pop pop . . . popopop.* Then a percussive BOOM like a kettle drum. I nearly jumped out the back.

"We'll be fine. Keep driving." Taggart patted Louise on the shoulder. Then he turned to me again with a clever smile.

"So you were havin' fun last night. And then the fun stopped. Like it always does. And what were you left with?"

"Things happened."

"You came all the way here from San Francisco to go courting?" Louise called over her shoulder.

And no chaperone either, I thought. Instead I said, "She was the mayor's daughter."

The car slowed again as Taggart sat up straight, looking away, murmuring. Louise glanced at him, taking her eyes off the road, barely missing a giant pothole. The car jerked as she swerved and regained control.

"I know just where to take you," Taggart said with an insinuating drawl.

Suddenly Louise took her foot off the gas again. By the side of the road a man lay facedown in a ditch, unmistakably dead, gore and brain protruding out the back of his skull, spattered over his leather jacket. In my mind I again heard that *boom* from last night.

Taggart raised his hand. Louise steered to the curb, stopped a few feet from the dead man. "Be careful." She looked away, her voice shaking. I was afraid for her. She should not have been seeing things like this.

Taggart slowly got out and stood over the corpse. He bent carefully to one knee, his back to us. He lifted the body up and felt for a heartbeat, a fruitless gesture. He then gently laid the dead man down, as though he were an infant. He bowed his head, continuing to move his hands over the body.

Louise murmured a prayer. He joined in, their voices singing a familiar duet. I knew the prayer but remained silent. Finally Taggart crossed himself and rose with effort. He hitched his trousers, buttoned up his black coat to the top, then turned and eased himself back in the car. I wondered if he had been in the trenches. I felt a little embarrassed, as I sometimes did around frontline veterans.

As Louise drove on, Taggart bared his yellow teeth at me in a mirthless grin.

"Butchertown's a high old time, eh?"

We now rode through a semi-residential neighborhood of grimy clapboard and shingle houses, some of them sagging, and false-fronted stores and apartment buildings. The smell of cow shit and burning oil faded, to be replaced by burning rubber, paint fumes and paper mills. The fog was more like smoke from a great fire. I imagined a fairy-tale giant lounging on his back, a huge stogie jutting out of his mouth, its tip glowing like that smokestack, lazy and happy in his filth.

There was not a touch of green about, not even a weed. A few oak trees hid between the houses, with black, bony branches. I wondered when springtime would arrive, then realized my sense of time had been capsized. This was August. Those trees were not awaiting spring. They were dead and would never bloom again.

"Stop here." Taggart pointed off right. "This is it," he said to me.

"Are you sure?" Louise's voice quavered. He brusquely nodded. She may have held the wheel, but this Taggart fellow did the driving.

She pulled the flivver over to the curb and made a perfect stop.

Chapter 5

First Time by Daylight

Wherever we had landed, it looked like no police station I had ever seen.

Three large houses set on barren ground, enclosed by a low, ornate brick wall, spread before us. A mossy green three-story Victorian towered on the right at the end; the one in the middle was a hunky two-story clapboard house, broad across the front, painted a grimy off-white with blue trim; the third house, the one we had stopped in front of, was a lime-shingled box and looked to be the most neglected of the three. Across the street stood a broad redbrick building with a sign that read, "CHAS. CLARK PAINT COMPANY, Founded 1899": the place from where the paint fumes emanated.

Louise shut the engine off. The violent barking of angry dogs rushed to fill the sudden silence.

"Are you sure you—?"

"I know this town." Taggart cut me off. "Every lane and alley. Every gutter."

I started to follow him out of the car, but he abruptly raised his hand. "Wait here. I want to make sure there's someone on duty. Don't want you walking into trouble."

"Like a desk officer. Well, I can—"

"Lou, don't let him go pokin' about."

"Look, pal, this is—"

"I'm in with the law, chum," he said, bouncing his chin for emphasis. "Let me open the door for ya first, make introductions, okeydokey?" He winked and jabbed a determined finger. "I'll be John. You be Jesus bringin' the Word, all right?" He spoke to Louise. "That's Scripture, right, dear?"

"Be careful, Tag!"

Taggart walked slowly along a crescent driveway in front of the second house. The tears in my stinging eyes made him look like he was moving underwater. By the time I shook the fumes out of my head and wiped my eyes, he had gone. He certainly knew more about this place than I did. My life lay wiggling nervously in his hands.

"Here." Louise offered me a snow-white handkerchief, taken from a plum-colored cloth bag stuffed with them. As I blew my nose, she said, "I almost didn't recognize you."

I squinted over my handkerchief, trying to color in the empty patches of my memory of that day: how she leaned against a birch tree by a brook in the woods with her mouth open and eyes half-closed. It was after school on a humid May afternoon. A blue something glimmered nearby, forming a halo around us as I leaned in to kiss her.

"Louise Wheeler."

"Hello, Paul."

"Goddamn. The world's sure been getting smaller."

"Still taking the Lord's name in vain I see. A priest's son should know better. I didn't like it much then. I don't approve at all now."

She turned away, stared ahead as though she were alone. She had become clipped and hard since I last saw her, her manner chiseled and hammered.

"Gotta admit, this is some kind of miracle."

"Finding Paul Bacon in a gutter hardly constitutes a miracle. Your fate was ordained."

"Putnam Valley School. Those were the days, huh?" No answer. It felt rude not to keep the conversation going, even if it sounded forced. How could we two meet again after all these years and have so little to say?

"So, what brought you out here?"

She lifted her chin as though I had cut into an especially noble chain of thought. "A train." Through all that dull black cloth, a little of the Lou I had too briefly known glinted. "And you?"

I waved my hands like a bird. "Oh, I just flapped my arms, ran as fast as I could and flew all the way here. It was foggy when I landed. It's been foggy every day since."

She sniffed. She used to close her eyes with amused exasperation at my silly jokes.

"You're as glib and silly as you ever were."

"We were both fairly amusing I recall."

"You've taken the road everyone said you would. You lost everything last night gambling, am I right? Tch!"

"Whoa. Wait—"

"You took the mayor's daughter to a dice game, like you took me. Don't you dare deny it. Only Paul Bacon would escort a girl to a gambling den. And then get into a fight. Did you bet money on that too?" She heaved a sigh. "And now you're on the streets alone."

Oh you bet I was mad. I almost told the truth but restrained myself. She would be safer not knowing what really happened, not only last night but in the years since then. Let her rant all she wanted. I was used to it. Besides, I had bigger problems to worry about.

"Maybe if you'd let me—"

"Whatever happened was a long time ago. We shouldn't speak of it."

"Hey! You're the one who brought the past up."

"But you're the one in the gutter. Still shiftless and irresponsible. I can tell. I've learned to tell." She stared at me like a fork, growling between her teeth. "The hard way. As you will."

I glanced behind us, but Taggart had not returned. The dogs had stopped barking. I grew nervous, just the two of us sitting alone in the fetid air. I wanted Taggart to hurry back and take her out of here, like he was supposed to. Let *him* protect her. What was taking him so long?

"Look, I hope you two aren't planning to stick around," I babbled. "Things got rough with me last night. It's dangerous—"

"What do you know of real trouble? You're the kind that makes it, that's all." She pounded the words in like a hammer on a nail. "God will see us through our travails, but He sees right through you period. I'd offer you a chance to join us, but your faith is thin and weak, like your father's. Go back to your drinking, gambling and whoring in your glittering Babylon. You'll be safer. Leave the saving to us."

By now I was steaming. The slander against my father and his faith (no matter the lack of mine) was more than I would tolerate. I climbed angrily out of the car as Taggart came around the corner and waved to me from the main driveway between the clapboard and the Victorian.

I glanced at Lou, but her eyes were all for her Taggart. I was just a fly buzzing past. She would not hear my thanks or my good-bye, so I gave none, just walked away. "God keep you," she called, but if she was going to act superior, I would too.

Taggart waited with a wide smile, his hand making a jingling sound inside his pants pocket. "Thataway." He waved down the dirt driveway towards the rear.

The center house stretched far back. A large garage stood at the rear, its doors open. It housed two touring cars, an old horse-drawn carriage, but no horses. Chickens clucked from somewhere nearby.

To my right, at the rear corner of a yellow plaster bungalow that fronted the next street over, stood a young fair-skinned Negro, around fourteen years old by my guess. He wore grimy gray corduroys, a white undershirt and heavy scuffed work shoes. A towering Doberman-mastiff dog sat beside him, its huge head rising past my waist. The boy held him by his collar—tightly I hoped, for the dog looked hungry and mean.

Next to the side door sat another huge dog, an equally ruthless-looking German shepherd. He rose anxiously to his feet, wagging his tail, his huge jaws opening in a slobbering, tongue-swinging smile.

"Dogs." Taggart winked as he walked up and tenderly scratched the shepherd behind the ears. The dog leaned his great head against Taggart's thigh. "They never forget a pal."

Then he stepped back, waved a hand at a steel-barred door that stood half-open. A lock and chain dangled from the crossbars. "Through there. They're waitin' for you."

"What kind of—?"

Taggart backed away. "All the real gen-u-wine law there is in Butchertown is right through that door," he said gaily.

"Hey, wait a minute—"

"Hey, bub, you're a stranger, see? I may be strange and this place sure is strange, but *you're* the stranger. Be careful. The shit you give is the shit you get."

He nodded at the mulatto and headed around the corner. The boy leaned down and whispered to the mastiff. Then he released the collar and followed Taggart.

Leaving me alone. With two large angry dogs staring at me.

Do not open strange doors, the ghost stories warn. But Jonathan Harker did not have vicious dogs creeping toward him, their fangs bared and glistening, heads down, bristling from nose to tail. The shepherd was closer, but the mastiff was madder, bigger and could have swallowed my head in one gulp.

I threw open the door and dashed inside as the mastiff leapt. The door shook as I slammed it shut, shook again as the mastiff threw his whole body against it. Both dogs exploded into furious barking.

I found myself in a narrow, short hallway. To the right a door opened into a mudroom, containing tools, shovels, brooms, buckets and a washtub. A sledgehammer lay on the floor near the entrance. In a corner rifles and shotguns lay in a jumble, as though recently and hurriedly picked through. It smelled of bleach, gunpowder and grease.

The door ahead led into a large kitchen, whose only window was in the back. Immediately to my right was a porcelain sink. Catty-corner stood a large old stove, a beaten copper teakettle on its burner. The shiny copper piping indicated that gas had recently been laid in. Next to the stove was an oaken highboy icebox with shelves above. Against the far wall sat a kitchen table, painted white with red trim around the top, and three white-painted wooden chairs. The kitchen looked disused. The walls were bare of pictures.

No, this was no police station. The only law in Evansville? Maybe it was Temperance law that was in force here, but where were the posted prayers and pictures of Jesus? And what about that arsenal piled in the mudroom? And the dogs?

A swinging door was set along the wall to my left. Right by it was another chair, oak brown, spindly and low, but it had a thick green cushion on its seat. I made for it. It felt soft as a couch under my sore rear end.

"Hello!" My voice fell, as though I were in a room lined with cotton. I sat back, trying to relax, while craving a cigarette and a strong drink.

And then suddenly a floorboard creaked from somewhere behind me. There came a soft scuffing of slippers on a wood floor. I sat up as the door opened, slamming into me.

A woman entered the kitchen. As I watched in dumbfounded silence, she shuffled listlessly to the stove, her back to me. Her shoulders were bowed, her hair was short, scraggly and tied with pathetic paper twists. She wore an old pink terrycloth robe that went to the floor and was frayed at the shoulders. Even her slippers were old and worn, the leather cracked, the soles separating from the tops.

She opened the shelf over the icebox and pulled down a coffee mug and a box of matches. She put the mug down, lit the gas stove and fumbled out a cigarette from the pocket of her robe. She bent and lit it off the flame all in one move, a lifelong well-practiced ritual.

Finally, as she grabbed the kettle to put it over the flame, she became aware that she had company.

"Excuse me." I coughed politely.

She spun around. The kettle fell from her hand, clanged on the floor.

"Jesus Christ!" she cried out.

At last I was seeing Molly Carver by daylight.

Chapter 6

Cornered

I had been in similar situations before—waking up next to a pimply, pillow-mashed face that had looked enough like Mona Lisa or Florence Lawrence the night before as I swam in my cups in a dim New York saloon, London pub or French café while on shore leave. A couple had been floozies, women of the night, pleasure for pay. I left quickly and politely, left extra money—a tip—if I had it to spare. I always walked out feeling guilty, in dread of finding the more upper-crust layer of my family lining the street outside, prim and prune faced, even my epically forgiving father.

But this was Butchertown. This was different. As I looked at this woman, this supposed Love of My Life, in the dreary light, I asked the questions betrayed lovers have been asking for eons: *What was I thinking?* The answer was, of course, I had not been thinking at all.

Molly Carver had done an artful job with her mask, makeup as good as Lon Chaney's. Just as Mary Pickford fooled picture goers into believing she was a virginal fourteen, she fooled me. Her beautiful, lustrous dark-brown hair had been a wig, concealing a mousy mop. Her skin was sallow, the lines she had carefully powdered away now plain around her mouth and at the corners of her eyes. A single deep crack split the middle of her forehead, no doubt a product of the intellectual effort it took to snare me.

Her silk scarves had concealed the cables on her throat. She still had her figure, but it was stooped and weary. Her bubbly, sparkly facade must have taken strenuous effort to maintain. Once we had said good night and she had passed out of my sight, she must have shriveled up like Dorian Gray in the painting. No wonder she had been so coquettish, only letting me close when the lights were dim and the shadows strong. Now she seemed worn out and down in the way everyone in Butchertown looked.

"What the fuck . . ." Her brown eyes were dry balls of mud, full of disgust and confusion. It had been a rough night. And now a bad penny had turned up in her kitchen.

She failed to recognize me too at first. The events of last night had stripped me also. But I let her stay confused. Maybe I should have been kinder, but I felt little sympathy.

"Paul?" She cupped her hands on both sides of her stricken face, her mouth open. "Paul, what are you doin' here? How the hell did you get in?"

"I was informed this was police headquarters."

"It's not!" She glanced past me at the door leading out.

"Then I was misinformed. Another lie, like you being beautiful and in love with me."

"That door was locked and chained! Who let you in?" She was trying to change the subject. I swiftly hunched forward, hands clasped, my elbows on my knees, staring up from under my brow.

"Why did you come all the way over to the city to step out with me? You didn't *happen* to run into me at that restaurant. I was a pigeon. You put heart and soul into lighting my fire to get me to come over to this manure hole. Why?"

"It doesn't matter anymore. You better go."

I shook my head, spread my hands, shrugging. "Go where? There was a lot of shooting around here last night and this morning. More than that dead friend of yours."

"My brother." She leaned back against the stove. My feelings softened. She had lost someone, after all. Maybe I needed to ease up. This both my mother and father would insist on. Some devils do grieve and need kindness.

"My condolences. What do the police say?"

She rubbed the back of her neck, her eyes on the floor.

"You did call in the police?"

"Paul, listen up—"

"No, no more of this."

I jumped up, the dried mud on my suit crumbling off and hissing on the floor. I crossed to Molly in one step, grabbed her elbow hard.

"What's going on?" I shook her, almost tearing her arm out of its socket. "Don't flash your eyes at me. I'm not some yokel—"

She stabbed at my neck with her lit cigarette. I grabbed her wrist, twisted it hard behind her, forcing the cigarette from her hand.

"Paul, stop!"

"I'll break your goddamn arm."

The kitchen door banged open behind us.

"What's this?" a bearlike voice growled.

I turned carefully, still gripping Molly's arm. The old man I had met at the ballpark last evening now stood before us, holding the door open: Cobb Carver, Molly's father, Butchertown's mayor, or so I had been told. His face was wrinkled and fish-belly white, his eyes red rimmed and heavily bagged. His gorilla shoulders were covered by a musty yellow tartan bathrobe, loosely tied around his ample middle over gray flannel pajamas. Last night he had looked like a big shot, with his suit and cigar. This morning he was a lumpy old hippopotamus. He let the door fall shut behind as he bunched his big fists at his side.

"Daddy, this is Paul. The guy at the ball game last night, remember? He was with me when . . . we found Danny."

No sitting down to breakfast over this. I released my grip and stepped carefully to Molly's left as Cobb Carver came at me with a phony smile made of gums spaced by a few stumps of cracked brown teeth. After last night's sapping, I would not be fooled again. The Luger weighed heavy in my pants pocket, but my fists were handier and I knew how to use them.

"Uh-huh. Howdy, son." He offered his right hand as he clenched his left. I let him pull me in, then leapt forward, using momentum to slip by. His left hook grazed the back of my head, while my left smashed him above the ear, enough to make him let go of my hand and stagger away.

I spun around and we stepped apart. Shaking his head, he moved to block me from the door leading outside. I took my stance, my chin tucked into my shoulder, my left up, my right back, my head low.

"Pug." He raised his balled fists. "I boxed Jim Corbett. You're a cheap palooka."

That may have been partially true—the boxing, not the Corbett part—but he was older, fatter and slower now, and up against a decades-younger opponent, who was also taller and had greater range. All I needed was to box like Corbett did, defensively, stay out his reach, wear him down and sneak through his defenses. I did not have to knock him out, only to send enough birds tweeting around his head so I could slip out the door.

Then suddenly I saw the teakettle headed right for my face. Molly was taking her pop's part. No fighter, she only caught me with a glancing blow. I grabbed her arm and flung her right into old man Carver, like she was a square dance partner.

The impact staggered him. So we were going to fight like that, were we? As he shoved her away, I stepped into the opening, drove a one-two jab to his face—*smack, smack*—very loud in that kitchen. As his head snapped back, I tried to slip around, but he blocked me like a tree stump. I could have dodged out the other door into the house's interior, but I would have been lost and I sensed another shadow approaching the door.

I danced away from his next swing. He was tiring quickly, but raw humiliation kept him pawing and snorting and made him impatient. His face turning tomato red, he bellowed and charged. I stepped to one side, drilled my right into his solar plexus like a lead pole.

Cobb Carver said "Ooof" and staggered past me to the kitchen table, his hands over his stomach, his knees bending. Molly crawled up from the corner she had fallen in, caught him as he slumped across the table.

I rushed into the hallway leading outside, where giant hungry dogs waited, barking. I made to duck into the mudroom and grab that sledgehammer. But then my escape hatch flew open and a monster's face came through it, a face with a jagged hole, the left cheek cratered from the corner of the mouth halfway to the ear, molars and gums showing in a pink-and-yellow grin.

The scariest thing about him, though, was the sawed-off double-barreled shotgun he jabbed into my belly.

I turned and sprung for the kitchen door into the interior, gambling he would not open fire in close quarters. But that door flew open too, smacked me in the kisser. I fell back against the shotgun barrel stabbing me in the spine. My head cleared and a familiar fearsome visage swung around the door. Those tawny hawk's eyes from the ballpark; the bony-faced fiend toting that murdering shotgun who so casually scooped Danny Carver off the street; the one Molly called "Chess"; the mustachioed devil who drove me off the roof with his evil stare.

We saw each other fully now. Him predator, me prey. He held a strange-looking machine gun, its barrel pointed at the ceiling. Smiling thinly, he calmly pointed it at my belly.

One gun in front. Shotgun behind. One wrong move and I would be leaving this life cut in two.

Chapter 7

Gangster House

"Search him," Chess said, his eyes fixed like gun sights.

A pair of big hands crawled over me as the ghastly hole in my other captor's cheek gaped from inches away. My empty stomach yawed. Another deep scar ran up from his right eye, giving a dismal symmetry to his face. Even worse, he was squinting at me intensely, like he recognized me or found me amusing, or simply liked shoving his wounds at the world. He tore the Luger from my pocket and tossed it to his partner.

"That's it?"

"That's it. No billfold, nothin'." He spoke with a slurring lisp and slight whistle. He stepped back, picked up his shotgun and leaned against the kitchen sink.

"I got robbed last night."

Chess waved me onto the chair behind the door with the gun barrel. I sat like a good boy sent to the schoolmaster's office, except here discipline would be enforced at gunpoint. Chess held up the Luger, sneering.

"You got stripped? Then where did you get this gat?"

I pretended to be tired and slow thinking. "I found it on a dead man up the street a ways. I was hearing gunfire all night. I was a little scared." My mumbling probably saved me. If I had been any more coherent, that might have been the end.

Scarface laughed. "Near the bridge on Adelyne this side of Gasoline Creek, right? Yeah, I know who he means. Got him good." He wiped the back of his head with a big, soft hand. "Boom!" Sure pleased with himself, he was.

Chess nodded tersely, then glared over to where Molly was gently tending to old man Carver at the kitchen table. "What the fuck's he doin' here? I thought you dumped him."

Molly ignored him. She wet a handkerchief in the sink and dabbed the old man's face as he sat on the floor. "You all right, Daddy?" For the first time she showed something like real tenderness. But Cobb pushed her hand away and got up, panting and grunting. Blood ran down from his nose, and his left eye was swelling. I realized then I had beaten up an old man. Maybe he did not think himself old, but my eyes told me the truth, and I was raised never to hit old people.

"How did you get in here?"

I dared not tell the whole truth to this bunch, but I had to say something.

"I got let in."

"By who?"

"Some preacher guy. After I found that gun, a couple of drys, crusader types, picked me up, brought me here. He told me this was police—"

"He give his name?"

"Taggart."

It fell so quiet, you could hear dust motes hit the floor. For long seconds they all stared at the middle of the kitchen as though a ghost invisible to me had materialized right there. Then Cobb turned on Scarface. "Did you change those locks like I told ya?"

Scarface lowered his eyes in shame, his scars reddening around the edges. A guilty sigh whistled through his cheek wound. "Sorry, Mr. Carver—"

"Goddammit, what am I payin' you grubs for?" Carver stepped towards Scarface, his fists up again, but Molly stopped him.

"Daddy, calm down, please."

He lowered his fists, then glanced at Molly. I had been wondering whether she was really his mistress instead of his daughter, but no, only a father and daughter looked at each other with that tenderness. Another time, another place I might have found them touching.

"Stetson, how did it go?" Cobb spoke to Chess. "You take it to 'em? Did you get him?"

Chess Stetson shook his head. I could see how weary, unshaven and haggard both he and his partner looked. They had been up and fighting all night. He puffed out his cheeks, frowning. "It was easy, like we caught him nappin'. Got a few of his boys. Bastard ran like a rabbit. We found that distillery he built and blew it up."

"We lose anyone?"

Stetson swallowed. "Johnny Pyle. Ran up ahead of us, took a hard poke on the chin, broke his neck fallin' down some stairs."

Biting my lip, I discreetly covered my scraped knuckle with my left hand. I snuck a glance at Stetson, but his eyes were on his boss, not me. He had looked out that window, but he had failed to see me out there in the dark. I sighed as though simply tired, which I was.

"There were footprints. Whoever killed him had blood on his shoes. We followed them a ways, but they faded out."

"I liked Johnny Pyle," Scarface said, air whistling out the hole in his cheek. "He was right by me. I'll kill that bastard when I find him." He looked very sad. They all looked even more miserable now, even Molly. I was the most miserable one of all. I had killed one of theirs. A friend.

"We'll kill him," Chess Stetson said. "Slow."

"Why didn't you go home like I told you?" Molly scolded me out of my invisibility. She seemed to expect an apology.

"You left me in the middle of nowhere. All this fog, how the hell was I supposed to know where to go? I got lost. I just walked around until some thugs sapped me." I pointed at the lump on the side of my head. "Woke up and found myself in a ditch a mile or so up the street." I prayed the lack of specific detail didn't bring more questions.

"By the stockyards?" Chess tipped his head.

"Guess so."

"That's how you heard the gunfire."

"Yeah, I heard some shooting."

"Guess he's not much use to us now," said Scarface.

"Shut up, Buckram." Cobb Carver bared his teeth at me, crazy eager to beat his pound of flesh out of me. Molly was also staring, making a chasm with that crack in her forehead. She spoke in a worried tone that was about as real as last night's powder and rouge.

"God, Paul, I'm really sorry." She shook her head with tender regret. "I'm the one who should apologize. But you saw what happened. My brother lying there like that. I was upset and scared. I didn't want you mixed up in any trouble." She put a hand on the old man's shoulder. "Now that he's here, the least we can do is let him get cleaned up. Daddy?"

She bit her lip as Cobb Carver scowled. Then he brightened. "Yeah, yeah, that's the least we can do. It ain't his fault he's here I guess."

"There's clothes in that bedroom. They'll fit him well enough." She made a smile. "There's a bed where you can rest. We have business to take care of and then we'll get you home."

This tonal shift set my head spinning. This did not sound like a swell idea, even if I did get clean clothes and maybe a bath out of it. "Listen, I don't think you need a houseguest. I'm thinking you need some *real* cops right—"

"We got that covered." Cobb looked down at me from under his eyelids. "They're working the case now. They don't need to talk to you." Molly nodded vigorously.

Chess Stetson, however, was not agreeable. His stoic facade vanished.

"You're crazy! We haven't the goddamn time for this. Bat Falcone will be back, if he's not comin' already."

Bat Falcone . . .

A large black spider scuttled down my spine. I remembered the big Italian storming into the stockyard office, carrying that ball bat; how he looked at me and blew out like an ocean storm.

"You mean *the* Bat Falcone?" I asked.

"Nobody asked you, punk." Cobb Carver glanced at Molly, then said to Stetson, "Falcone's lickin' his wounds. He won't be back till tonight. Did you alert the boys?"

"Listen!" I should have stayed closed mouthed, but that spider nibbling my spine got me babbling. "If that's who you're talking about—Bat Falcone—you *really* need help. A whole brigade's worth. Get me to a phone and I'll call my boss, Brady, the San Francisco DA. He'll contact the state police and they'll come in and clean this up . . . what?"

The room went ghost quiet again as they all glared. I could almost hear Chess Stetson's tail rattle as he slowly turned his cruel eyes upon me. My sore knuckle itched.

"Yeah, he needs a nap all right." Stetson's voice drawled like gravel in a barrel. "A long one." He spoke to his boss over his shoulder. "I got men around the property, a couple dozen patrolling the distilleries and all the breweries around Park Street." He sneered, shaking his head. "Him, I don't know if we can spare—"

"We've still got other business, Stetson," Molly said. "We can do more than one thing at a time. It's too dangerous for you to go anywhere now, Paul. You're safer here with us."

"Danny wouldn't—" Stetson turned on her.

"Danny's *dead*." Not much love lost between these two. Working his jaw like he was already gnawing my bones, Stetson looked to Cobb for support, but Molly had her hand on her father's shoulder, her face turned as though talking into his ear.

"Danny would want us to fight on," she said, her voice flat. "This will be over soon and our next step will be in place."

Cobb may have wanted me bleeding dead on the floor of his kitchen (already soaked, I wagered, with the blood of others, two legged and not), but he nodded in agreement. The air grew turbid. That a woman pulled weight in this man's world clearly put Chess Stetson in a temper. I was a little shook myself.

"Buckram," Cobb spoke. The bullet-scarred gunman snapped to like an eager seaman. "Lock him in the kid's room. We'll deal with him later. Be careful. He thinks he's a boxer."

"Yessir." Buckram waved me to my feet with his shotgun. My hands went up again and more dried mud crumbled off my suit onto the floor. Stetson pulled the kitchen door open and watched me carefully as I stepped around and walked through.

Buckram prodded me into a short narrow hallway. As the door fell shut behind us, I heard matches being struck and disputatious voices rising. We passed between walls of tobacco-cured plaster, broken by pale square patches where pictures had once hung.

Buckram sharply ordered me left. He had a straight-shouldered brusqueness about him. Army, I guessed. Doughboy. That was how he got that scar.

We passed through a large living room full of moth-eaten furniture, settees and chairs from thirty years ago, covered in faded, frayed chintz, springs poking from the cushions. The woman's touch had faded long ago. Feathery piles of dust scurried away from our feet.

We made a reverse left, up a narrow creaky staircase. Buckram allowed me to get a little ahead in case I turned and jumped him. I cooperated. I did not want to give him the pleasure of bragging and laughing at how he had done me in.

And besides, I was just too damn tired for yet another fight. They would not kill or hurt me now, so it might be safe to rest for a bit. Stetson was right. I needed a nap. "Sleep on it," my father used to say. Just a catnap. And then when I woke up, well, this cat would be alert and ready to get out of here. My way. Not theirs.

At the top of the stairs Buckram steered me right, down another dim hallway, past a bedroom, a bathroom and water closet. Red-and-yellow-striped wallpaper covered the walls here, rose vines weaving between the stripes. These walls were also sticky with tobacco tar and had the same blank squares from where pictures had been taken down, an unfinished redecoration project.

We came to two doors, leading into corner rooms. Buckram ordered me to stand back. He glanced behind him. Stetson had caught up, machine gun in hand.

"Trouble?"

"Not so far."

"Here's the key." I ducked as a small black piece of metal shot past my head. Buckram snatched it one-handed out of the air, gracefully unlocked the door to the left, keeping his eyes on me, grinning on his good side.

I entered a medium-sized bedroom at the left rear corner of the house. It looked like an older boy's room, furnished in heavy mahogany. Paintings of hunting dogs and sailing ships in faraway seas hung from the walls. A tallboy wardrobe loomed to the right. On the left a dresser stood with a window on one side; a washstand, with a bowl and a cracked porcelain pitcher on the other, and books across the top. It was a cozy place for dreaming, especially since among the books were a few of my favorites, including Mr. Doyle's *The White Company.*

"There's clothes in the tallboy and the dresser," Stetson said. "We got guards all over and you've met the dogs. We keep 'em crazy hungry." He smiled as though ready for dinner with his bib, holding a knife and fork. "Rest up."

He stepped aside as Buckram entered with a pitcher of steaming water. As he placed it on the washstand, he briefly looked me over with his half smile. "Yeah, it's you all right."

And then they left me there alone.

Chapter 8

The Badger Game

I listened carefully after they locked the door, and when I was sure they had gone I promptly sought escape. The two corner windows looked out over hard-packed dirt fifteen feet below. Out the left window was the second-floor window of the third house, a narrow alleyway in between. The rear window looked out on the carriage house, a long ramshackle chicken coop to its left. Beyond were bungalows. On the roof of the one closest, a man in a large overcoat and hat stood guard, cradling a rifle, shivering against the wind. Two other gents passed below in hats and overcoats, carrying rifles, led by that German shepherd on a chain leash.

With immediate escape out of the question, I sat on the bed to rest and think. The mattress was made of feathers and looked like a soft cloud, a narcotic that drew a yawn. I roused myself and undressed quickly, eager to get out of my dirty clothes. I washed myself with the water from the pitcher, wincing as I touched the lump over my ear. I needed a long, hot soak.

I opened the top dresser drawer and found underwear, neatly folded, and black socks. My shorts and undershirt were grimy, but I did not fancy wearing another man's foundations, so I skipped those but did take a pair of black socks, which were a little small. I found a pile of white handkerchiefs, the sight of which made me sneeze as Butchertown's stink seeped in around the windows. As I grabbed some, I saw they had been clumsily hand-stitched with the initials JC.

The second drawer down contained two stacks of well-knit, neatly pressed and folded dress shirts in whites, blues and greens. I chose a sharply cut, dark navy-blue cotton shirt with button cuffs. Holding it up against me, I studied my reflection in a long mirror behind the door. I hardly knew myself at first, but finally the familiar Paul Bacon appeared under the scrapes, bruises and stubble. I would be that man again soon.

The wearer looked to have been a size or so smaller than I, according to the mirror. I laid the shirt carefully across the foot frame of the bed and turned to the tallboy, where I found a row of suit jackets and pants in various styles and cloth hanging from clip hangers. A row of ties hung like bright flags across the back wall, all very sporty and cheering. I selected a grayish-white tie and a pair of blue wool slacks, laying them across the bed with the same care I would my own.

I had found a basic wardrobe but explored some more. I returned to the dresser, where, in the third drawer down, I found more pants, dungarees and corduroys. A picture frame peeked out from the bottom. I pulled it out.

It was a photo portrait, eight by ten, maybe one of the pictures that had disappeared from the walls. It was an artfully posed studio portrait of a little boy seated on his mother's lap. The pair subtly resembled each other. The boy, six or seven years of age, wore a Buster Brown outfit: cutaway jacket, fluffy shirt, bow tie; a tasseled sailor's cap topped his large moppy head. His mother was leaning over his shoulder. Her face was handsome, her dark hair waved and coiled high above her tall forehead, her face strong and warm. She wore a lacy high-collared light blouse and a large bow tie. Mother and son were gazing off at a faraway land, with gentle smiles and wide, wondrous eyes to where the man in the moon and angels in the air lived, just beyond the frame. The photo was so at odds with the world around me. It had been stowed away like a bad secret.

Danny Carver and his mother? I wondered. Good Lord, the horror that had been done to that innocent face. I imagined his mother nearby, sunk in her grief, while the rest of the family seemed to go on . . .

I put the brake on my maundering and set the picture back under the clothes. I turned around, looked at the wardrobe I had chosen for myself, lying across the foot of the bed, and shuddered. I was about to put on a dead man's clothes.

I yawned again. My eyelids grew heavy, my body drained of its last reserves of energy. "Nap," they had said. The word worked like a hypnotist's command. Rest would be good for me. I was gone before I even started to lie down, like falling through empty sky.

A presence awoke me. At first I thought it was one of those dreams where you are paralyzed and unable to move. A woman was lying next to me, dressed in a blue see-through silk gown. She was blond, soft-faced and heavily made up, her clownish face expressionless. I tried to sit up, my mind forming questions, but I was being held down by a strong force.

"What?" Then I looked up into the pitiless face of Chess Stetson floating above. He was pressing me down on the bed by my shoulder. Another strange woman—truly whorish, her makeup a caking mask—sat on the bed next to him, holding my arm. A sharp pain jabbed through it.

"What're you doing?" I struggled, but someone else also had me by the legs. I saw Buckram's deformed face leering over the foot of the bed.

The woman next to Stetson sat up, a hypo needle in her hand.

"That should do it. He'll be quiet for sure."

I fought desperately to rise, but now all four of them were on me as I struggled and the drug streamed through my veins. I grew heavy with lassitude.

"What're you doing?"

"You gotta rest up, that's all," Buckram said in his horrible voice.

I felt like an animal being put to sleep. The room started swimming about. Stetson, Buckram and the woman with the needle released me, but I barely noticed it. The girl in the blue gown stayed next to me, her hand slipping under my shorts.

"He's so cute! Can't we keep him awake? Can I take him for real later?"

Dumbfounded, I looked at whom she was talking to. There were three of them lined up by the bed now. There was a blinding white flash, a big *poof*, a hissing, frying sound, acrid white smoke billowing across the ceiling. The flash cooked a frosty halo into my retina. In the middle of it the silhouette of Chess Stetson held a large wooden box. A goddamn camera. Buckram, next to him, held a flash device like a crucifix. The stink of magnesium powder filled the air, but I was now too numb to sneeze.

And Molly stood by the door, dressed now with some formality, arms folded, face cold.

The floozie flew off the bed like a fairy, her powder-blue figure rushing out the door. I lurched up, staggered against the dresser, stumbled around the bed. Stetson and Buckram had already left.

"Lemme at that punk!" Cobb Carver growled as he pushed into the room. I started to raise my fists, but he had the advantage now that I was drugged and helpless.

He hit me twice. Right to the plexus. Left to the head.

The floor got the last punch in.

Chapter 9

One Damn Thing . . .

My eyes were sticky and my muscles and bones were as dense as lead. Invisible hands roughly lifted me into the air. I was swung about through a mist, the details dull and scattered, like an especially bad bout of seasickness.

Below me, graveled earth tilted and spun. "Boy! I'm talking to you. Come here. Now!" I smelled a dog's breath, heard its vicious growl and huge jaws snip right at my ear. "How did he get in? You tell me! Right now!" That was Molly, but she was directing her fury at someone else, not me. I heard a dark mumble, then a brisk slap.

The air grew darker and damper. The brown shadows of two girls, lounging and laughing, surrounded by blue smoke, passed by. Egyptian queens with tall gleaming buckets towering from their heads.

A pink-and-blue-tiled floor swirled below and hollow fans hummed, driven by small engines.

My flight ended in a hard landing on a thin mattress. Springs and metal squeaked in protest.

"Miss Carver said feed him," a slurry voice said, with the sound of a tongue slopping about.

"Fuck her."

"I knew this fella," the ugly voice said. "He did me a kindness once . . ." A scornful laugh. "No, he did, really, on the ship comin' home . . ."

I went blank. When my brain lit up again, I had to force my eyelids apart, like peeling bandages off a wound. I saw a ceiling of wood and rusted plumbing strung by cobwebs. They had dumped me in a basement.

My head throbbed and my arm was sore where they had stuck the needle. A knot pulsed over my left eye. My mouth was cold, sticky mud and my stomach felt like it had been drummed on by a gorilla.

A pair of long-fingered hands and brown skinny arms floated down, bearing a large green plate, on which sat a sandwich and a glass mug of foamy yellow liquid. The hands set the plate on a brown wood stool. The waiter was the young mulatto I had seen that morning outside the Carver house. His giant dog was nowhere about. Close up he looked familiar, but I was too tired to think much of it. He took a step back and looked to where Chess Stetson leaned against the wall by a door, puffing on his long bent pipe. Stetson dismissed him with a nod. The boy dragged his eyes over me as he left.

Buckram was sitting nearby on another stool under a ceiling light shaded by a rotting cone. The shadows concealed the hole in his face. Stetson studied me with feline insolence, arms folded, smoke trailing from the polished pipe bowl, like a grubby genie who had leapt from his bottle not to grant my wishes but his alone.

I sat up, my joints feeling tight. They had dressed me in the clothes I had picked earlier in that sad little bedroom. They were indeed too small. Flexing my shoulders, I glanced around the basement. There were two walls of junk behind me and to my right. There were boxes marked SALON, brimming with frilly women's things; old bedframes and mattresses; empty burlap bags with the words BARLEY and HOPS woven into the fabric; small tanks, funnels and copper tubing, five-gallon jars and jugs. Stale aromas of beer and whiskey mingled with perfume and sewage.

"Hungry?" Buckram turned into the light, so I could see him smile on his good side. But for the scar on his forehead, he looked like a baby-faced bulldog, none too bright, but a good one to have in your corner.

I reached for the beer but stopped, shifting my eyes about.

"Nah," Stetson laughed. "Go ahead. Drink up. Chow down. No more mickeys, not now."

Buckram grabbed the glass, sipped some beer and licked the foam off his lips, his tongue slipping into the shadow that hid his scar. "Carver beer, good beer!"

he sang, words from an advertisement. He toasted me and set the mug back on the stool.

Carver beer actually tasted like cat piss. I rushed it down and damn near inhaled the ham sandwich, warped and dry as a cardboard pencil box. At the end I belched loud enough to offend my mother's family from Thanksgiving through Christmas. Then the three of us looked at each other for a long sour minute.

"All right, what the hell's going on? What do you want from me?"

Stetson caressed his fine black mustache with his thumb, glanced at the bowl of his pipe. He slowly drew a wooden match from the pocket of his black camel hair jacket, struck it off his thumbnail and waved the flame over the bowl.

"Blackmail." He puffed away, shaking the match out.

"Yeah, I get that. But for what?"

"Dago Loosner."

He watched for my reaction. I fought to hide it as the truth behind the situation struck me. My first case. The file I promised myself I would review Monday morning.

"He's goin' on trial Tuesday. You're the prosecution, right?" He pointed the pipe stem at me. "The one who's supposed to send him up."

"You want me to throw the case."

As he nodded, my belly dropped as I tried to remember what Brady had said to me while I was afloat in my romantic fog. Something about Loosner being one of the few Volstead violations we were prosecuting ourselves, as a message to out-of-towners to stay out of the San Francisco rackets. Brady called it "a cinch." All I had to do was read off the file in court. The name Bat Falcone had come up, but I would not have to worry. Even the legendary Bat would not dare "mess with us."

"We thought Loosner was Bat Falcone's man."

Chess Stetson shook his head. "He's ours."

I also remembered Brady's edgy smile as he handed me the file. "You're losing your cherry, kid. Don't blow this, got me?"

"If I go through with this, I'll lose my job." Wet as he was, Brady was neither a forgiving nor patient man. He did not give second chances.

Stetson shrugged. "Maybe. Maybe not. Molly Carver says you're smart enough to figure your way out of gettin' fired. But if you do get fired, you're still young. You'll find another job." He grinned. "Maybe you can come work for us over here."

"And if I pull this off and don't get canned? You'll destroy that photo?"

"Don't be stupid. We'll have other favors. You'll be our San Francisco cat's paw, Bacon. It'll be worth your while."

Worth my while? I felt pinned like one of my father's butterflies. I would have to leave San Francisco, all the connections Uncle Lloyd had called on to land me this "soft" job, the law schooling he had paid for, all for nothing. The wastrel nephew would ride the train back east in dishonor. "What would Mother and Father say?

We always knew you were a good-for-nothing . . . Your father spoiled you, spoiled you *rotten!*" Sneaky whispers would spread all the way from Oregon Corners up Red Mill Road to Mohegan Lake, downhill to Peekskill and downriver to Manhattan. "Tut-tut, too big for your britches, eh, college boy? There's still that job at the hardware store!"

Worst of all, though, would be the dishonor I would feel towards myself. Sure, I was a black sheep, but the one thing I had never done, and would never do, was throw a fight. Whatever game I played, whatever I gambled, I played honest.

For now, though, the Dago Loosner problem was three days and another world away. I was right in the middle of someone else's problem and it did not look good for my new associates from where I stood. They were under siege and I was trapped with them. If I did not get out soon, I would not be alive to worry about my job or my honor.

"Where am I now?"

"Not your bother. The only place you want to be is on that ferry back across the bay."

"When does that happen?"

Chess Stetson paused. Not to torture me but because I had asked a question for which he had no prompt answer. He wiggled the pipe in his hand.

"After we fix a little problem."

"Are you even sure you can get me to the boat? Or solve your problem before Tuesday? From what I know, Bat Falcone is no little problem."

I looked at the floor between my knees, tempted to spit in contempt. But a hand suddenly stole under my chin and snapped it upward. Stetson stared down his needle nose, his eyes cruel slits. He pushed his thumb hard into my chin.

"What the fuck you know about it?" He let his thumb off my chin so I could reply.

"Okay, okay, I *heard*. About Bat Falcone. He may be from way up north, but I've heard of him. You're from right across the bay and I've never heard of you at all."

"What have you heard about Falcone?"

Stetson dragged his thumb along my bristled chin as he stepped back and folded his arms. I started telling some tales I had heard a month ago from a group of out-of-town county district attorneys and state and local cops who had come to San Francisco on a semi-official visit. I tailed the party to the back of Blanco's Restaurant on O'Farrell and wound up sitting in on a late-night poker game until three in the morning. I started out winning, but the more they talked about Bat Falcone, the more my playing faltered as my ears perked up.

Bat Falcone was the giant at the top of the beanstalk: a man of mystery and power. Before Prohibition, he had been a small-time smuggler and dealer in stolen goods and, it was rumored, Oriental slaves. Then came Prohibition, and like others criminally inclined, he had turned the law to his advantage and became a lawless force in Northern California. From a single winery in a corner of Sonoma County, he took over other wineries. Unlike some of the other growers, he was not satisfied with tending his own grapes. He was a Napoleon who wanted much more. And he set out to get it. He began smuggling in whiskey from Canada and distilling his own and building his own illegal breweries. Now he commanded an army of gunmen and thugs. All thanks to Prohibition.

The legends said that Falcone had been born fully grown. No one knew why they called him Bat. Was it because he only emerged from his cave at night? Or because of the baseball bat that he carried with him to use on smaller operators and businessmen who failed to tithe what was called the Bat Tax? Meaning if you did not pay your tax, you got the bat.

As I talked, Stetson's face remained impassive, except for the occasional tiny smile creeping under his mustache, as if he also knew these stories. By the time I finished, he had sunk back into reptilian composure.

"So, Paulie boy hears chinwag from some yokels at a hotsy-totsy San Francisco feed bag. You paid their tab for their bullshit, right? We've been dealing with that greaser since when you were in knee pants." Behind his scorn, though, his bravado sounded shaky and hollow.

"If he's going to hit back, maybe now is the time to get me out of here so—"

"So you can bring in those state cops, like you said? Fat chance, Bacon. Remember, you're the one in the corner with the dunce cap."

"But what if I catch a bullet? Your plans to get Loosner off will come to nothing. And don't forget I am *somebody*, even if I am just a junior attorney. I turn up dead and—"

"We don't care how big he is," Buckram piped up suddenly. "We took the Heinies in the Somme. He's nothin'."

Stetson ignored his partner as he returned to his place by the door, stooping under the low ceiling. His pipe had gone out. He fumbled for another match from his pocket and dropped it. As he knelt to pick it up, he gave me a hard look over his left shoulder. They were vulnerable and he knew it and he knew I knew it. And if they were vulnerable, I was vulnerable. I licked my lips, took a short, deep breath and went on with my case as he rose and leaned against the door.

"I'll do what you ask. I'll get Loosner off. But if I get killed here, it won't happen, you understand that? Furthermore, even I do get out, if you lose your war or it goes on—"

"Hey!" Buckram protested. "We just said we're gonna win!" He looked at Stetson. "We are, ain't we, Chess? We're gonna win."

I picked my words carefully. "Maybe it's all fairy tales, but what Falcone did to your boss, that was no fairy tale. That was your boss I saw lying there dead, am I right?"

"Cobb's the boss," Buckram objected, but Stetson shot him a look: *No, not true.* My earlier impression was correct: There was no longer a captain at this helm. He had been murdered the night before.

"Honestly, Mr. Stetson," I said, "it's not fair to drag me into the middle of a war that's not my affair. Especially one that—well, pardon me for saying— doesn't look good for your side. Look, you got him back last night. Like I heard you say this morning. You evened the score a little. Maybe it's time for a truce."

Stetson laughed. "You're somethin'! You oughta count your lucky stars you still got that big pretty head on your shoulders." Stetson threw the burnt matchstick on the floor and then fished a pistol from his pocket and aimed it at me. "You keep yappin', I might put an extra hole in your face."

"Please!" I raised my hands, though I knew he was bluffing. "They won't let you get away with killing me, even if I am just a junior attorney. You really don't want a war if you can help it. I've seen what can happen. I was in the war, like you."

"You were on a *boat!*" Buckram jeered. He rose, grabbed the ceiling light, shined it on his face, forcing me to look at his ghastly wound, with his teeth and gums showing. He waved his other hand. "The whole time! Goin' back and forth! That's where you were!" He looked at his partner. "A medical steward on the boat comin' home! The only weapon he carried was the thermometer he jammed up my ass." He let the light fall and sat back down as shadows swept over his face.

Stetson laughed as I fell mute with embarrassment.

"So, we got us a real battle-scarred doughboy." Chess tossed his pistol into his left hand and held up his right hand to show his amputated middle finger.

"Tell him about that hole in your face, Bucky."

"Shrapnel bomb at the Argonne." Buckram waved at his face. "Burst outta the sky, like Fourth of July. Got me all over. Hardly knew it happened. A guy nearby, he got sliced up like a jigsaw puzzle. I still got metal in me." He smiled affectionately at Stetson. "Woulda died if you hadn't drug me out of that trench." The two men's eyes met in the middle of the room, warm and shining, as though recalling a shared paradise.

"A lot of Heinies paid for that face." Stetson grew boastful. "I made 'em pay. Counted 'em off as they fell like tenpins. More than fucking Alvin York, I know it." He snorted. "But no headlines, no medals. They just made me a corporal. Not white enough I guess."

Buckram's face reddened around his scars. "And you were on a *boat*." He spat on the floor as I shrank into a little mud ball of shame, a state in which I remained for some minutes, until I noticed what little light there was outside was fading into an uglier gray.

"How long have I been here?"

"A while."

"How—?"

Suddenly there came a knock on the door. Stetson turned and opened it slightly. The huge fat cop I had seen last night outside the ballpark filled the slot, his tiny tin badge glinting on his massive chest.

"We got the driveways blocked and more men on the roofs."

Stetson glanced at me, then said, "Outside." He left, closing the door behind him. Alone, I would have put my ear to it, but before I could even think of that, Buckram spoke up.

"No, you don't remember me." He smiled, favoring me with his good side. "I was on a hospital ship comin' back from France." His smile grew beamish. "The boxing matches you held up on deck. You lifted me out of my bed one day, wheeled me up top, then you got in the ring and beat hell out of a guy. You took 'em and threw 'em even harder, lifted him right off his feet. Then you wheeled me back to my bed." He snapped his fingers. "Never forgot that. One of the best fights I ever saw. Nah, you don't remember me. I was in bandages." He shyly waved his hand at his face. "You still boxin'?"

I shrugged. "No. Just refereeing here and there, on weekends."

I hoped he would stop asking questions, but he went on. "How come you quit? You fought like a champ."

"I didn't like hitting people that much. I like my nose, got afraid of breaking my hands, getting slaphappy." I shrugged and laughed. "Maybe I'm a coward like you say."

"I didn't say that." Buckram's ruined face darkened. "You shouldn't say that about yourself. A man should never shit in his own hat." His eyes glittered as he stood up. "I got stuff to do," he said with a gulp and left the room, locking the door behind him.

I waited a minute, then stood up and promptly bumped my head on the plumbing. The clothes they had stuffed me into nearly tore at the seams as I crept to the door, stooping like an old man, and put my ear to the wood. Outside, a chair creaked, a voice sniffled. I looked through the keyhole. Buckram was sitting with his face in his hands under one of those helmets I had seen those women wearing. It was a hair dryer. The outer room was being used as a hair salon for the hookers.

I next set about taking the measure of my prison.

Chapter 10

. . . After Another . . .

The door was made of heavy redwood and impervious to fast jimmying. I looked for another door out. With so much junk crowding the room, the two walls to the side and back were invisible. Somewhere behind the jumble there might be another door leading out.

I looked out a small rectangular window high on the open outer wall, set at eye level. A mud plain stretched away to a low brick wall. Beyond that, fog. My heart beat faster as I realized the air was shading from gray towards night again. I had been out for a long time.

The window looked barely wide enough for me to squeeze through, but it had been painted shut and barred. I searched my jacket pockets and found the monogrammed handkerchiefs from the dresser drawer. I used one to wipe the grime off the glass. A pair of heavy shoes plodded by less than a foot away, a rifle barrel making a third leg.

From my guess, I was in the basement of that three-story Victorian, with the Carver residence behind me and the third house on the far side. Women's voices and laughter filtered down from upstairs, the guttery merriment I had heard around French seaports, brothels and San Francisco docks, voices cooked by hard booze and cheap tobacco. On the floor right above, a Victrola phonograph started playing what sounded like a Negro woman singing "Bring Back the Joys." I had heard the record before but could not recall the singer.

If I were the kind prone to depraved irony, I would have laughed: Cobb Carver, the mayor of Butchertown, was also the town's chief whoremonger, his house of ill-repute right next door to his family abode. Here his daughter had learned the art of fooling a foolish young man. I shuddered wondering at how far things might have gone. What sort would send his own daughter to finishing school in a cathouse?

I pushed my face against the window to look left. There stood Big Cobb himself, next to one of the touring cars, a red one, now being used to blockade a side driveway. Molly stood next to him, both their backs to me. Cobb looked rounded and stooped. Molly wore a very proper and respectable square-shouldered brown suit, the style secretaries around the office and women in business wore. Her hair sat on her head like a helmet.

Next to them loomed the giant cop with his elephant gun. Chess Stetson stood in front of them, arguing, his stony face now very plastic. The German shepherd walked by, this time right to left, leading two guys, each carrying a rifle and a shotgun. My eyes followed them as they passed by where the young mulatto had suddenly appeared on the brick wall, hands folded in front of him, his head down, likely just back from scouting for approaching danger. The mastiff sat nearby, silent and still. Even if I had been able to force my way through that window . . .

I turned my attention back to the conference. Stetson nodded in my direction as he argued with Cobb and Molly. My name had come up in the debate. I normally did not mind being talked about but this time I did. Maybe Stetson had taken my point about calling a truce. God, I hoped so. Only some peace— even a temporary one—would assure my escape. And I would bring real police in right then and there to break this up and cart them all away in the paddy wagon. My excitement at the prospect faded, though, when I remembered that compromising photo of me in bed with that floozie and the headline sure to follow:

YOUNG CITY ATTORNEY
CAUGHT IN FUNHOUSE!

Well, whatever happened, it still beat the hell out of dying in this basement.

The argument outside went on. Molly did most of the talking with her shoulders up and jeweled hands slashing the fog. Stetson kept looking at Cobb, not caring a tinker's damn for anything the boss's daughter had to say.

Finally, Cobb lifted his head and spoke. A decision had been reached. Molly nodded firmly in approval. She had won. Stetson strode way, his fists clenched. As he crossed in front of the window, he shot me with another of his bullet-eyed stares. He knew I was watching, saw me silhouetted against the basement light. He shook his head, then walked out of sight. I looked back to find Molly also staring in my direction. My fate had been decided. I was doomed.

I spun around and leaned against the wall. It would be war. Fine. To hell with them. It was up to me alone to escape. I grabbed the ceiling light by the cloth-covered cord and tried to shine it through the junk piled against the wall, hoping to espy a hidden door. But then a key slid into the door from the salon. Looking for a weapon, I impulsively grabbed a piece of coiled copper tubing used for distilling spirits. As it shook in my hand and light poured in from the salon, I thought maybe I should have grabbed a chair.

Cobb Carver came through the door, Molly right behind him. Cobb carried the Luger, finger on the trigger, barrel aimed at my belly. He would not shoot me, but he guessed correctly I would sit like a dog. I threw aside the copper tubing and raised my hands again.

Cobb's eye would be swollen shut for days and his manly pride was probably bruised for evermore from the thumping I had given him that morning in his very own house. The beating he had given me in return had failed to slake his thirst for revenge. Molly looked dogged down, her face white and pinched like a dirty bedsheet. She was indulging the old man's rage.

"You got a big mouth, punk," Carver said with a wheeze. "You wanna get back home alive to fancy town, you keep it shut, see? I saw your nose turnin' up the minute I laid eyes on you. You think 'cause you're from the big city you're better than us? This here's our world and you're nothin' in it, see? You don't make friendly with Chess Stetson or any of my boys. No one around here cares shit about what you think you know. I'm the king, see?"

I shrugged. The words leapt out before I could stop them. "The king of nothing looks to me."

He stepped up and pistol-clipped me across the side of my face. This time I was ready to roll with it, crying out, staggering back, collapsing onto the pile of junk, pretending to be more hurt than I was. Cobb stood over me, pointed the Luger in my face, his voice growling from inside the hungry black barrel.

"I'm the still the goddamn king." He swept his arm around the basement. "I made this town and I make yours. The gas that runs your cars, the paint on your walls, the steaks and pork chops on your linen tables, the reams of paper you write your reports on, it's all made here and I own every acre under it. You don't ask who makes your fancy doilies. You don't want to know, 'cause you're all soft. You wouldn't want stuff anymore, would ya? Wouldn't want the steak if you have to kill the bull yourself. My name oughta be on this town, goddamnit."

His eyes shifted as he wheezed and coughed and grew old and tired again as his attention slipped and drifted away like a kite. Molly stepped in and took his arm, saying, "C'mon, Daddy. We have work to do." She tugged him towards the door.

"Molly."

"Paul, you'd better keep—"

"I'll do what you want. I'll get Dago Loosner off."

"Fine. Keep your nose out of our affairs."

"I want to know something."

"What?" She really believed she owed me nothing at all—no explanation, no apology. I was a tool and was supposed to lie silently in the chest until brought out. But I had to ask. I wanted her to speak her true intentions.

"Did you feel anything for me? Or was it all make-believe?"

"It's family. My family. I work for our business." She lifted her chin. "You were easy. Just another sucker with his tongue out, like the men who pay to see the girls upstairs. Pull his rope, he'll follow." She sneered. "You should've gone home like you were told."

I tried the doorknob after she closed it, but it was locked. I knelt, peeked through the keyhole. Their shadows slid along the wall up the steps, out of sight.

I worked swiftly as possible, moving the junk from the back and piling it in front of the door to the salon in case they returned. I was halfway to the wall when my hands grabbed hold of a pair of two-tone shoes. I tugged on them, but they were attached to a pair of black-stocking feet. The feet were attached to a pair of legs in cream-colored pants, which were attached to a blue-jacketed torso with a pair of hands and arms stiff at the side. And finally, at the top, the crushed and shattered skull of Danny Carver.

I staggered back, biting my hand, blurting out words I thought I would never speak again.

"Please, God . . . Please, Jesus, help me . . ."

But it was better to stay alert and on my feet. I shined the ceiling light towards the back again, satisfied there was no door in the wall beyond the mutilated body in front of me. I turned and threw aside the shabby metal bed—

The first shot rippled from far off through the dusky air, a pistol crack. Seconds later another pistol shot from only yards away, like a responding signal. Falcone's men had breached the walls already, right under the Carvers' noses. I turned to see a man's face slam to the ground in front of the basement window, one eye blown out, the face splattered with blood, the other eye staring right at me with the same vast confusion I had seen in the eyes of that dead Chinese.

The killer's feet, wearing heavy boots, walked right past the window. Then another gun went off, this one from far outside. More gunfire. Glass shattered and a woman screamed from somewhere in the house. The ceiling shook and dust fell as everyone upstairs hit the floor.

The shooting picked up speed and power—shotguns, pistols, rifles—bullets and pellets thudding into the house, shattering glass, driving me back from the window, back to fighting my way through the junk towards the door on the other side.

"God the Father, have mercy on your servant . . . God the Son, have mercy on your servant . . . God the Holy Spirit, have mercy . . ."

From outside gunfire flashed like summer lightning. The air turned smoky blue. A wounded man's roar dwindled to a boy's pain-racked voice pleading for his mother's solace. The outside door into the salon crashed open. Footsteps. The doorknob started to turn behind me. I threw the bed in front of the door with the other junk to block their way. They were hammering at it now full force.

Finally, I found it, the other door out, a large, round oak dinner table the only obstacle remaining. My desperation made it feel light as pinewood . . . but when I finally got it out of the way, that doorknob rattled like metal bones. I backed away, my hands going up, as the door flew open. A Remington pump gun poked through right at my belly. Buckram's ravaged face floated into the room.

"C'mon, Mr. Bacon! Let's get outta here!"

I dashed past Buckram into a dark, narrow room. I tripped as the Remington exploded behind me, exploded twice, and a man screamed in agony. I spun to see Buckram jump back. "Whooo-wee!" Then he turned crouching. "Hurry up, Mr. Bacon! . . . Man, feathers flew like a turkey!"

I flew up some steps and out into the driveway between the Victorian and the main house. The girls from upstairs ran past in a ragged line, their flimsy silk dresses fluttering. More gunfire came from behind to my right. Buckram herded me behind the coosies. An explosion boomed, again from the far side of the Victorian, followed by the smell of burning wood and paint. Buckram guided me right, across the front of the Carver house.

One of the girls collapsed in front of me, fell like a sack. Instinctively, I slowed down to help her. It was the girl who posed with me in the photograph, her dull face now twisted with agony as a black pool poured from under her. Buckram bumped into me, gave me a hard shove.

We crossed in front of the main house, heading for the last house. Bullets cracked and zipped around. I glanced back to see Buckram crouching behind a garden wall, firing at the invaders.

Now was my chance. I turned right, took off down the alleyway towards the rear, comparatively quiet, completely empty and open. I did not hear Buckram yelling until I reached the end.

But I was not as clever as I thought, because there came Chess Stetson out of the night, the devil with his strange gun smoking in his hand, his face savage as his cruel eyes saw me.

"Where the fuck you think you're goin'?"

"Outta here," I said. Both my fists put him down— right to his gut, left to his head. He dropped out of sight, spitting vicious curses.

I did not stick around for the count but ran off, crouching low. Sure enough, his machine gun chattered and bullets whizzed by inches away. A ball of feathers exploded in the chicken coop. Another alley led between the coop and carriage house. At the end of the slot I collided with a slat wooden fence, fell on my ass, got right back up. My pants ripped at the seams as I crawled over the fence.

The gunfire started to fade. I tripped over a sack. The sack moaned. Another wounded man. I ran across a gravel courtyard circled by bungalows, dashing from shadow to shadow, hoping everyone had forgotten my very existence. I stumbled on through smoke-filled shadows towards a misty glow up ahead.

I slowed as I made my way down another alley and out onto a broad boulevard. I had no idea where I had landed until the looming curve of the ballpark appeared through the ochre fog. I was on San Pablo Avenue, near Park. It was Saturday night, but the whole neighborhood looked like a Sunday, deserted, closed up, every speakeasy, gambling house and brothel darkened. Word of trouble had gone out. The revelers were all staying away.

All except for the occupants of a large Pierce-Arrow touring car, a Series 32, puffing away a half block to my left, its bow towards Oakland.

I should have scurried back into the shadows, but they were still shooting at each other behind me. Up ahead to my left, a Key train clacked from somewhere, ringing its bell as it approached the stop. This train would get me to the quay and the ferry that would take me home.

The only obstacle was that car. If it was an obstacle.

I worked my hands into my tight pants pockets and put my head down. I tried to pass for just another guy, a working stiff on his way home from the factories. Maybe a little drunk. I was so tired, it was not hard to fake. I thought myself invisible, as I did while running for my life down that slaughterhouse catwalk the night before.

The Pierce-Arrow let me pass. I strolled like I had all the time in the world. I drew ahead of the car. My chest loosened. I breathed easier, but the bad air was a soggy woolen sock yanked over my head. I sneezed once, twice, three times. I peeked out from where my face was buried in my sleeve. The car was rolling along, keeping pace with me.

Up ahead the train stuck its nose across San Pablo. I picked up my pace. *Boy, long day at the plant. Gotta catch that train!* The car's engine gunned to life, the rubber tires crackling on the pavement as it leapt forward, made a U and charged right for me.

The train had stopped up ahead. I started to run but tripped, fell to my hands and knees on the tarry walk. The car stopped on pinpoint a couple feet away. The black eyes of another two-eyed shotgun slid out the passenger window and to stare me down a foot from my face.

The broad, tan face smiled down from behind the gun, black eyes wide and curious as they had been last night. There was the neat, trim Van Dyke beard, the glittering diamond ring on the finger, the aroma of sweet-smelling Cuban cigars. Hard footsteps ran up from behind as I stood on my knees, hands up, the fish caught on the hook.

"*Madre dio!* So it's you again!" Bat Falcone said with a hearty laugh.

Chapter 11

Bat Out of Hell

As the Key train chugged away towards the ferry dock, Bat Falcone's men lifted me up, slammed me against the car and searched me down to my groceries. They tugged on my shorts where they were poking through the seat of my pants. Someone spoke in Italian. Then they laughed. This was the humiliation that crooks received from San Francisco coppers. I had seen it. Now it was happening to me. But at least those poor punks knew they would likely make it out alive.

They tied my hands behind my back good and tight, dragged a burlap bag down over my head. The rear car door opened and they shoved me in like a sack of apples onto a hard plank floor covered in rough canvas. They had taken out the back seats to make room for crates of bootleg. And saps like me.

Voices jabbered coarsely back and forth, swimming from Italian to Spanish. Bat Falcone barked orders in both tongues in an elegant and fluent baritone. I listened hard, but aside from obvious words—*sí, bueno, mañana*—I understood nothing. Their talk sounded pretty and fluid, like music. Except they were likely debating life, death and where I might land between those two poles.

Doors slammed, the engine roared and the car leapt forward, the force rolling me against the back. They made a fast right, rolling me left, then a quick left, rolling me right. I tried to keep track of the twists and turns, but I was floating on a sea of motion sickness. I felt every damn bump as I fought the urge to whimper, cry and plead. The more fear they smelled, the greater their appetite to maim and kill, as I knew from being both boxer and referee.

Finally, I sniffed out a clue to our direction. That oily cloud of gas fumes I had been driven through last night and this morning suddenly suffused the air as we passed over metal plates. We were heading north over Gasoline Creek.

After an eternity the car slowed and stopped. I tried to cooperate as they pulled me out, but they shoved me about regardless, dragging me up a sidewalk, my toes stuttering over concrete, then up a flight of steps. A door opened. I smelled spicy red pepper, burnt meat, beer and sour whiskey mash. "This way, *cabrón*." We went up creaking carpeted stairs. A baby cried from nearby. They had me in some sort of house, hotel or apartment building. Down a short hall, then right. A door clicked open, hinges creaking.

The door slammed behind me. Bat Falcone briskly snapped orders. They untied my hands from behind and tied them in front of me, tight again. I was shoved into a lumpy cushioned chair. The door opened and closed, leaving me in damp silence as voices rumbled out in the hall. Then the door creaked open. Footsteps softly crunched across the carpet. A slow-ticking watch approached, each tick echoing like a church bell.

An angry demanding voice cried out in Italian. "No, no," Bat Falcone said. Then the voice repeated it, his voice rising angrily. I heard a scuffle: grunting and feet shuffling on the creaking floor. *Tick . . . tick . . . tick . . .*

"God the Father, have mercy on your servant . . ."

Then the struggle ended. A man started weeping.

Bat Falcone snapped another order. The burlap bag was ripped off my head, taking pieces of my skin. I yelled, then got slapped on the back of my head. The world looked like milky water. A match struck nearby, followed by the billowing aroma of a good cigar. A heavy and sweaty presence loomed behind. A gun barrel hovered at the corner of my eye. Guns are cold, brutal things, but this one shook with rage, with the desire to drive a bullet into my brain.

They had me in the corner of a small hotel room, the furniture frayed and worn by thousands of transients. A big double bed took up most of the room. There were two windows catty-corner on each side.

Bat Falcone stood at the window to my right, smoke forming a thought above his head.

"*Madre dio*," he sighed. "What kind of a shithole is this? Does the sun ever show its face here? My men tell me, 'The sun never shines in Evansville!' And I say, 'You mean it is like up inside your asshole?' Ha! Now here I am and I see they are right! Does the sun ever even rise here? Maybe it covers its face as it flies over because it cannot bear to look at the filthy world below. We have ugly places up north, ugly like a pig's ass, but this? What possessed men to make such a world?" He shuddered. "I swear this cigar has not left my mouth since I arrived Wednesday. Else I would faint like a woman, walking around inside this giant devil's fart."

He turned from the window and sat heavily on the bed. He then slowly lifted his feet up, reclining regally against the headboard. He picked up the baseball bat I had seen him carrying last night from where it lay on the bed, hefted it and looked it up and down. He then looked at me as he set it down without comment. A bottle of red wine with a couple of wineglasses sat on the bedside table. He carefully poured wine into both glasses partway, a well-practiced pour, then nodded at the man to my left as he set the bottle down. "Maurizio, one for our guest *per favore*."

Maurizio stepped around me, his brown eyes squinting with hatred, teeth bared like a shark's. He held a huge .45 automatic inches from my forehead. He was shorter than I but tightly built, a wound-up little rooster who could handle himself. He wore a light-brown camel hair coat, whose sleeves were caked with blood to the elbows. I could smell it. It was just beginning to dry.

Falcone watched with an inscrutable smile, his lips making pink flower petals in the center of his beard as Maurizio brought the glass over and forced it between my lips, sending most of the wine down my chin. "Easy, easy! Don't drown the poor *bambino!*" I know little about wine, but I know bile from grape juice, and this tasted like the former. But that was Prohibition for you: No matter what faucet you turned, what barrel you tapped, what cork you pulled or popped, the drinking was most always bad.

"My own label!" Bat Falcone proudly lifted his glass.

I nodded politely, licking my lips, smiling as much as fear would permit. If Bat Falcone believed his wine was the best in the world, then, like Carver beer, it *was* the best. I would sing it from the hilltops! Once again my polite upbringing was saving my life.

We studied each other for a minute. Bat Falcone weighed well over two hundred pounds, solidly packed. He dressed as he had last night, with rustic elegance. His black suit was roughly tailored but fit him well. Though not a city man, he took care with his appearance. A diamond-stick tiepin on a fire-red silk tie gave off the brightest light in the room. His shoes were polished like a mirror, the laces tied like gift bows; even the soles looked polished. A new-looking porkpie hat neatly decorated a nearby dresser. Next to Falcone, Cobb Carver looked like a Dickensian guttersnipe. And though I grew more afraid the more I liked him, I also recognized an important quality about him, one to keep in mind if I hoped to stay alive.

"This is the second time we've met. Again, unexpectedly. Given what the Carvers did to me last night and tonight, the number of my men they have killed"—he nodded at Maurizio—"this man's brother for one, while sacrificing their own, all to rescue you. Bringing slaughter to the slaughterhouse. You must be one valuable hombre. Last night I did not care. Last night you were a mistake, a turd floating in my wine barrel. Now I see you again and I ask, who are you?"

"Nobody," I croaked.

Falcone nodded at Maurizio. Maurizio's fist set off painful fireworks in my head.

"Do not be stubborn and coy with me, *bambino*. Maurizio's little brother had the back of his head blown off this morning. Maurizio found him lying in the gutter. Now he wants blood. Maybe I should let him drink yours. By the time he is through, there will be nothing left but your cries."

"I didn't kill him," I croaked, remembering Buckram's hand brushing across the back of his head. "I haven't a damn thing to do with this."

"You think that matters now, after all that's happened? You ever have a fever where you did not care about anything but ending it, no matter what it took? Have you ever been in battle? No, you are only standing around, caught on the wrong side of the fence. That's all the reason he needs. And believe me, it is a need that sooner or later I will let him fulfill, even if the sufferer is an innocent lamb. He has the fever only killing cures."

And so I closed my eyes, told him my name, where I came from, including my address, and how long I had been there; how I earned my living, how long I had been doing it; where I came from, my navy service. Then, blushing, I summarized the events leading me to Butchertown.

When I opened my eyes, Bat Falcone was staring at me in amazement, his gleaming be-ringed hands folded on his stomach, ash bending down from his cigar. A perfect blue circle from his perfectly pursed mouth formed a wreath around his Van Dyke, then broke apart as he spoke.

"You came all the way across San Francisco Bay . . . in this fog . . . to this shithole . . . for *pussy?*" He paused again. "In those horrible clothes?" He threw his head back and laughed, slapping his huge thigh.

"These aren't my clothes. You saw how I was—ow!" Maurizio twisted my ear like a watch key, shouting, probably calling me an obscene liar.

"No! No! This *idiota* speaks facts!" Falcone waved his hand through his laughter. "Look at that baby face! How could you not believe it? *Povero bambino!* So tell me, Signor Bacon. Who was your dresser? A blind man? I don't remember how you were dressed last night, but oh, excuse me, this is too funny . . ." He wiped away his tears.

"I got these from Danny Carver's bedroom. I think you knew him. The mayor's daughter and I were on our way to a dance hall last night, heard gunshots and found him on the street. Danny Carver, Molly's brother. His face . . ." I waved my hand over mine. "Gone. How could you—"

Bat Falcone sat up, swept his feet off the bed to the floor, his smile turning into open-mouthed shock.

"Wait! Danny Carver? Danny Carver's dead?"

"Yeah, he's dead!" I heaved an exasperated sigh. "Another gent showed up, picked up the body, and they all left me standing there."

Bat Falcone looked at me as though I were one of Mr. Wells's Martians, smoke drifting raggedly out of his mouth. He looked away and sighed.

"So they thought . . . *that* is why they attacked us last night. Not to rescue you." He sighed. "*Dio, dio, mama mia*, this is too, too bad."

"You mean—"

"No, Signor Paulino." His eyes rolled up in his head at the most obvious fact in Creation. "I—we—did *not* kill Danny Carver." He pointed his finger at his head and spun it in a tight circle. "Not I."

He drew hard on his cigar. "He is dead and they accuse *me*." His large square forehead puckered like a tin roof. As I tried to absorb this myself—was he lying or not, and why?—the phone on the bedside table rang. Falcone plucked the receiver from the cradle.

"*Sì?*" I was unable to follow the conversation. He caressed the edge of the ashtray with his cigar tip, his voice rising. Finally, he said something that sounded like a curse and neatly slapped the phone back in the cradle.

Maurizio asked a question. Falcone shook his head and looked at me, full of pleading and wonder. "Who are these bloodthirsty stubborn people?" Then he went on. "I arranged *incontro privato* with Carver, a meeting of just us two. No, we have not been *amico*, that is true. In fact, it was my plan to snatch him, as they say, hold him as coin for certain business negotiations with his papa. Obviously, those two local *bastardos* I hired arrived after he was dead and found you instead, *Signor la Rimanenza!* The leftover! Idiots! Well, you do look enough like that poor fucker from a photograph we had. This dirty fog makes it seem God formed us all from the same mud."

He rolled the cigar between thumb and forefingers. "You said the girl and man ran off with the body, left you there alone, for us to find you. Then later you escaped from us, brave, clever and yes, lucky. Most men would have cowered. Shit their drawers. How did you manage that anyway? I sent a man to, um, look in on you."

"He was shot before he reached me, through the belly." I went on with my story but skipped over the man I killed on the stairs, even though he was one of Falcone's enemies and it may well have been to my advantage to admit it. But something kept me quiet on that.

I told about the two drys who picked me up the next morning and let me into Cobb Carver's house, a twist that intrigued him as much as it did me. He queried me on who the preacher was, but all I could say was that he was maybe a relative or friend of the family. I skipped the blackmail part, too—I did not want to give *him* any ideas on that score—said they locked me in the basement, where I was a prisoner until the battle started again.

"Really?" He sensed I had skated around a hole or two. "Not only am I amazed that you came all the way over here but also that the mayor's little girl found you that interesting. I understand that she's not exactly ladylike."

"Even a witch looks beautiful by candlelight. Like you said, the fog."

Falcone looked at his cigar, tapped its ash into the tray.

"How many men does Carver have?"

"I don't know." Maurizio stretched my ear like it was taffy. "Hey! They didn't exactly let me take roll call!"

Falcone nodded for Maurizio to let go. "Make a guess."

"Maybe a dozen or more? They talked like they had men all over. They own the police, at least what there is of them. They have a big stockpile of weapons, good ones from what I saw. Brownings and such and some newfangled machine gun. A couple of them were front-line doughboys. Killed a lot of Germans."

"As did some of mine."

"The Carvers think they can fight you and win," I said. "At least the old man does."

"And you doubt this?"

"I know who you are. I've heard stories about you." From there, I briefly repeated some of the tales I had shared with Chess Stetson.

This pleased him, as I expected. He grew large with flattery as he puffed happily on his cigar. "Yes," he said when I finished, "and the Carvers are a fungus eating my grapes." Then he gave a sad sigh. "So! What to do with you?"

"Well, sir, I would like to be on the next ferry back to the city."

"You would, eh? Uh-uh. I think not. Not until my business here is finished." He slowly bared his teeth, jabbing the cigar. "Until *twice* the blood is spilled."

He barked orders to Maurizio. I listened closely, heard names like Sausalito, Santa Rosa, Healdsburg and other northern towns. He spread his arms and pulled his hands towards his big chest—*Bring them to me*, the general calling his troops together—then shook his fist, his voice rising to a shout, his face swelling.

"*Sí*," Maurizio said, and reached for the phone, but Falcone waved him off, jabbed his thumb over his shoulder at the door. His man objected, but Falcone shrugged him away. I picked up the word *bambino* as his brown eyes swept over me.

Bat Falcone had much more to say and could more than handle me alone.

Chapter 12

Persuasion

When Maurizio left, Falcone disappeared into the bathroom. I pondered escaping again, studying the knots that bound my hands, but even if I managed to wiggle free, where would I go? I sniffed the air. Butchertown's stink was less pervasive here. We were close, though, maybe just across the city line in some East Bay elsewhere, at the edge of the plume.

I closed my eyes to think. To say Bat Falcone was not as crude as Cobb Carver would be an understatement. In addition to his dress and deportment, he looked younger and in better health, no doubt thanks to country living. He also held a tighter rein over his crew than Cobb Carver held over his. He had saved me from death at the hands of one of his men. He remained their captain, their *padrone*, wherever they went. I hoped things would stay that way. I had made him like me, at least a little. I had to persuade him to like me more.

I had just turned my thoughts to Danny Carver's murder when the toilet gargled and roared. Falcone emerged from the bathroom like royalty, buttoning his coat, a fresh cigar in his mouth. The pipes played a rattling fanfare. He pretended to ignore the peon at his feet as he strode to the window and peered carefully through the curtain, murmuring to himself in Italian.

Finally, he peered sideways, as though surprised to see me. "No, no sending you home, *mio bimbo*. You are our guest until the battle is won, until the blood stops flowing. And it will run like a swollen spring river, redder than my wine."

His great hands shook, his anger bending the cigar between thumb and fingers, as ash bombed the carpet. "I fought in the Philippines as a young man. I thought I would never see such things again: so many men dying in so short a time. Mostly the natives. They fell in sheaves before our rifles. Now it's *my* men. Eight of them. Every one of them has a wife, children, a mama or papa who must be told, who must be comforted and compensated. A brother who must be avenged. It will be like Bat Falcone has pulled the trigger on them himself. I will be blamed. And so every life must be accounted for." He jabbed his cigar like a pointer. "*Every* single one. Doubled. Sixteen for eight, thirty-two for sixteen. Do you know why? So those animals understand it must never happen *again*. So when they think of me, they will see blood. And when they see blood, they will remember me. Bat Falcone. I will turn them from pigs into sheep."

I took a deep breath as he turned from the window and sat on the bed. I decided to put my foot in things again. Talking had got me into trouble. But it got me out of trouble as well.

"Is that why you came here in the first place?" I asked. "To fight? To kill? To spill blood?"

"Huh? No! I came first because I need access to a place from where I can sell my wine and Canadian booze to the south and east parts of the state. A staging area. I came for business. Not blood."

"Couldn't you go elsewhere? Go through the towns east of here, sell your wine, beer and booze from there." I tried to sound reasonable and pleasant.

He smiled, stroking a grain of sand out his right eye with this thumb. "You don't understand. Maybe you cannot, drowning in booze as you are in San Francisco. You think the whole world defies the federal government, but that is not true. While Prohibition has made me rich, it has made its believers happy, at least for now. They believe they are succeeding. They believe they will be victorious. I certainly hope so.

"There are many counties and towns all over more than eager to obey the law of this land and do whatever they can to keep their people sober and dry, and men like me from doing business by providing them with what they really want. Berkeley, Oakland, other towns, they are sewn up like a wineskin by the law as their people thirst. I cannot even touch the borders with the front tires of my trucks without being arrested. I have to find whatever weak spot I can." He gestured towards the window. "The only weak spot is a few blocks away. On the shores, up and down the bay front, I can park my boats for refueling, off-load my merchandise onto trains going east and south. East of San Francisco, this is the only wet spot on the entire map, all the way to Reno."

"I understand that, sir. Completely." He tilted his head in curiosity. "I can tell you're a very smart and wealthy gentleman." I flowered on more flattery. "They don't speak of you as a bloodthirsty man but as reasonable. A businessman. I can tell by that suit."

"My papa once said never listen to wisdom from a man dressed in borrowed clothes." Falcone laughed. "His words will also be secondhand and frayed."

We both laughed. Alarmingly, I found myself warming to him even more.

My alarm was justified, because his smile vanished like a blown-out candle. He sprung off the bed and thrust the glowing tip of his cigar an inch from my eye, baking my cornea. My eyes watered.

"I warn you, Signor Paul Bacon, if you try to fool with me, I will cook your eyes in their sockets and make you eat them like hard-boiled eggs."

He withdrew the cigar and backed away as I blinked furiously, hot tears running from my stinging eye.

"Mr. Falcone," I snuffled on as he sat back down on the creaky bed, "I saw Danny Carver dead, shot right in the face with a shotgun. A big shotgun."

"But not by my hand. Nevertheless, eight of my men are dead as a result. What else is left but war?"

"I completely believe you wouldn't do such a thing. I *know* for sure you didn't kill him, or your men wouldn't have mistaken me for him. Surely the Carvers didn't kill him either."

"Oh, but maybe they did." He curled his lip. "Maybe the rest did not want peace as he did."

"True or not, they *believe* you did it. They'll keep raising the ante, like they did last night. They won't stop unless they hear the truth and understand the odds are against them."

Another virgin handkerchief appeared in his large, soft hand. With surprising tenderness, he came over and wiped tears from my face and let me blow my nose. Then he threw the handkerchief in the wastebasket with another laugh.

"So, the white boy from the big city thinks Bat Falcone cannot handle a gang of scrawny pigs in this grease spot."

"No doubt you'll win, sir. No doubt at all. But will it be worth the cost? From what I've seen of them, it might end as one of those Pyrrhic victories. You've lost eight men. While killing sixteen of theirs, you might lose eight more. Eight more men to mourn. Eight more families you have to deliver bad news to. Good blood after good blood. Where does—"

"I will not run, young fool. Keep up your stupid chatter and I will stake you out like a goat so they shoot you dead!"

"I'm not saying you should run. I'm saying you oughta go back to square one and negotiate. As you intended to last night."

"With what?" He swatted away my words. This time he decided not to use my eye for an ashtray. He lifted the bat from the bed. "Usually all I have to do is show this and they roll and whimper. But these pigs . . ."

"With your superior force, sure, you would wipe them out, but what would be left? Did you see what downtown Butchertown was like Friday night? The whole world was there, money everywhere. Tonight, Saturday night, it's a ghost town. They might not come back for weeks. Empty businesses mean the money's stopped coming because people are too scared. This war has taken the fun out of everything, and when the fun goes, there goes the money, unless you're in the weapons business. It hurts everyone: the speakeasies, cribs and gambling joints. The factory owners will suffer too if the workers stay home 'cause of all this. Everyone gets hurt in the pocketbook and they'll do something about it. Those drys who picked me up this morning are at the state capital by now and they'll bring the state militia back with them. Before you know it, both the state and feds will shut all this down and make it a dry town like Oakland and Berkeley. You'll be locked out again, maybe for good. All that blood spilled and you go home in total defeat *if* they don't throw you in the clink."

He shook his head. "But you said the Carvers will fight to the death."

"Cobb Carver, yes. But I'm not sure that he's really in command. He seemed senile, like a sick old bull. His son, Danny, he was running the ship. But now he's dead and I doubt the old man can take the wheel again. I'm not sure who's really running things. But one of them talks like he knows who they're up against. At least I think he knows you."

"And who would that be?"

"Chess Stetson."

At last, the magic words had fallen from my lips. With a beaming smile, Falcone rocked back, clutching his hands together, almost applauding.

"Chess Stetson?" Jewel tears sparkled in his eyes. "*Madre mio!* So, that is where that boy went to! I thought he died in France!" He eagerly poured himself a glass of wine. "Chess toiled in my vineyards many years ago, before the war. A smart *paisano*, head like a tack, tougher than two barrels of nails. Would do anything, sometimes overdo, quick to spill blood. He's high in the herd, you say? He is exactly as he looks. A snake. With a hawk's wings. A dragon."

"He was Danny Carver's lieutenant. And now he wants to be captain himself. I'd give him fair odds. All that's between him and the ship's wheel is an old sick man and his daughter."

"That *puttana* no longer tickles the balls, does she?"

"Molly Carver? Hell no." I was speaking honestly now. I had never felt so damp, sour and dead towards another person, man or woman. "So, if you and Stetson were friendly before, could you be friendly again?"

"Ahh!" Falcone aimed his cigar at me. "I see your point: I already have a friend on the inside, right? Someone more *amico* to negotiate with. I would not have to kidnap him."

"Someone who could help you take over without firing another shot. Or losing another man."

We sat in thoughtful silence. I felt a thimbleful of relief. My gamble had paid off. Bat Falcone was proud, vain and he was a businessman and a pretty good gambler, like me. I had played on all of these bets correctly. In the tug between his business sense and his thirst for revenge, business was winning out. He looked like a man who realized he had a big pile of chips and held even better cards. I already felt the ferry deck under my feet, heading back across the bay—

"We will walk carefully." Falcone spoke from behind blue smoke. "I will send someone ahead to open the negotiations." Then he waved the smoke away, smiling broadly, his eyes a-twinkle. He again pointed his cigar right at me.

My guts sank to my shoes. By "someone" he meant me. This I did not expect. I thought the mere suggestion of peace talks would earn my immediate release. Instead, my big mouth had talked me back into the middle of things. Bad things.

"Signor Falcone, I'm just a punk in the basement to Chess Stetson. Please understand me. Except for Molly Carver, I don't have a damn thing to do with this."

"Really?" Falcone looked amused. "Cobb Carver whores his own daughter to get you to come to Butchertown to make you a guest in their basement?"

"They were trying to bribe me," I fibbed. "They're trying to set up business in San Francisco, like you've been doing. Wasn't going to work on me, though, nope. Listen, I'm not much of a negotiator so—"

Bat Falcone rocked with laughter. "You talk me into making peace and then you tell me you don't know how to talk? Signor Bacon, never be falsely humble. It is as sinful as being an empty braggart. You are bright and articulate, even if you are unwise about the world, especially women. That is your youth and you might as well grow out of it. You've persuaded me away from war for now, and it only makes sense that we send you to persuade them—"

"But old man Carver hates my guts. He'll shoot me on sight."

"Would he now?" Falcone nodded. "That would certainly conclude negotiations."

He stood up, picked up his baseball bat and strode about the room, occasionally pausing to take a swing at an imaginary ball.

"Bacon, you are the bird, the one who sees the shape of the land below. You have a feathered silver tongue and a mind like a fox, fast and clever. You will go far as a lawyer. And that is why I'm sending you with the white flag as my representative, my negotiator."

He stopped, softly tapping the bat in the palm of his hand.

"You have persuaded me and now I will persuade you. Carry my flag of truce. If you survive the trip over, you'll have a talk with my old friend Chess. Maybe he likes you too, in ways you do not understand." He winked. "Tell him what you told me. Remind him his old *padrone* is not a greedy man. I don't want all of this shithole. Just a little. To ship my wine, brew my beer, distribute and sell my whiskey—good whiskey from Canada, not the piss they distill around here—to the factory workers." He paused. "Those are my initial terms. The rest we can discuss at a subsequent meeting, both sides together."

"What happens to me afterward?"

"You go back to your own noisy city."

"And if I refuse?"

"Then I send you without the white flag." He stood back and swung the bat right at me. I felt its breeze brush my face.

"Then I'll carry your white flag for you. I'll talk to 'em."

My chances were better with the flag than without it, though not by much. The Carvers might answer by sending my bullet-riddled—if I was lucky—body back across the street. My tired mind sought some other way out, but all I had were my fists and my mouth. My fists were tied and my smart mouth had just dug me into a deeper hole.

Bat Falcone crossed back to the window, frowning through the curtains.

"I don't understand. Why do they fight so hard for this hell? Even at my vineyard to the north, during the rainy season, even with the fog, we have faith that the sun will return. The clouds, the fog, they are a veil over God's face so He can rest. Those stories about me living by night are mere fairy tales, my friend. Every morning I awaken my whole family to watch the day come and hear the birds raise their voices in song. I gather them in the evening to feast, to drink a toast to the sunset and thank God for the day. That is a life worth fighting for.

"Such things cannot happen here. The sky is a dirty carpet laid over a rotting floor. The people live like gophers. Even God cannot see through the hell smoke. There is nothing for Him to come out for, not even a little church or a storefront to sing His praises." He stopped to cross himself. "I would burn all this down to the ground, wash the soil, plant vineyards and orange groves. The world that was here before had to have been better than the one that is here now."

There came a knock at the door. Falcone turned. "*Avanti!*" Maurizio entered. They talked Italian for a while. I heard the same place names, but that was all. Maurizio suddenly grew agitated, probably frustrated at the news that his boss was going to attempt negotiations with his brother's killers again.

Then Falcone gestured at me as he kept talking. At the end, Maurizio walked out in a smolder: whatever his hatreds, he would obey his chief, at least for now.

"Time for bed, my child," Falcone announced. "You need rest."

"A room with a bath I hope."

"We will try to get you some clean clothes." He pointed his cigar. "A man should always be well dressed, not in toddler's clothing. Especially one who stands for me."

Maurizio returned with two more men. They dragged the burlap over my head again, untied my feet and dragged me out to the hall, then one floor down. Maurizio gripped me hard, spitting curses, spraying the burlap with saliva.

They took me to another room, where they ripped the burlap away again, taking yet more skin. Single bed, tiny bath, a thick layer of dust. The bathroom window was too small to escape through. Two of my guards sat either side of the bathroom door while I squeezed naked into a tiny rust-stained tub, my knees to my chest. I slowly bathed myself in lukewarm water that gushed from rattling pipes before fading to a trickle.

I tried to think useful thoughts, but I was blank with exhaustion. After all I had been through, I was about out of ideas. Every single one of them had turned to manure anyway.

Where they got me clean clothes from, I don't know, but they must have borrowed from two different guys.

They were nice enough and the white cotton shirt and tweed vest fit fine, but the tan worsted trousers were a bit small. My two guards tied my hands and feet again, tightly and carefully, and then shared a bottle of grappa. It tasted like someone had washed their hands with it. It mattered little, though. One glass put me right to sleep.

I awoke in darkness to snoring, an opening door and pale-yellow hallway light. I sat up, my mouth like caked flannel, my head throbbing. One of my guards was sitting with his head back, snoring like a bull, as his buddy came in, slapped him on the shoulder and turned on the lamp.

I asked for the time, pointing at my wrist. The second guard flipped open a gold-plated Elgin pocket watch. The engraving in flowing script on the inside cover read, "To my son, Paul. From Father, November 16, 1916."

"That's my watch!" The guard laughed. "That's mine!" I repeated, pointing at the watch, then at me. "My papa!" He glanced at his friend, his eyebrows up. They said something that made them laugh even harder.

The watch had said eleven o'clock, morning by my guess. They brought me bread, butter and more of that lousy grappa. I ate, then slept some more.

I woke up to find Bat Falcone towering over my bed, bearing more dry bread, a plate of cheese and an apology for "being late." He had to drive all the way into Oakland to attend Sunday Mass, he said. "Butchertown must be the first circle of Hell!"

As I ate, he chased the guard from the chair and asked how I was feeling. I demanded my watch back. I was mad, mad enough to be called crazy, but I had been pushed around enough. I wanted something of myself back, even if it was only a small piece.

"Your men stole it from me Friday night. It was a gift from my father before I shipped out for the war. He engraved it for me. It means a lot to me, as your own father's gifts mean something to you." I paused, lifting my chin. "I won't help you. I will not say a word on your behalf unless I get it back. You can do what you want to me, but I won't lift a damn finger for you. Not without my watch."

Bat Falcone slowly nodded. "Sergio!" he yelled. Sergio came in. He was the one with the watch. His chin up, Falcone held out his hand. "*Mi orologio d'oro!*" Sergio handed the watch over without a peep. Holding it by the chain, swinging it back and forth as would a hypnotist, Falcone lowered it into my shirt pocket as though bestowing a great favor. Then he sat back, lit a cigar and lectured me on what would happen.

"Change not a word, not even a breath!" Then they untied my hands, handed me a tweed jacket that miraculously fit just right. ("With your precious monogrammed handkerchiefs in the pocket," Falcone assured me.) They brought me a blue tie. They even polished my shoes. My spirits lightened. I felt better than I had all weekend.

They blindfolded me, marched me out and loaded me into the back of a car, one with its rear seats still intact. Soon we re-entered the poison cloud of Butchertown, bouncing over stinking, choking Gasoline Creek.

They stopped, pulled me out, walked me a little ways and yanked off the blindfold. We were in a murky alley between two dingy one-story clapboard houses.

I jumped as Maurizio appeared suddenly at my shoulder, cradling a Browning. A scrap of white paper fluttered down from above and landed at my feet. I stooped over to look at it. It was a small white butterfly that had fluttered in from somewhere and then died, unable to turn back once it realized its mistake. My father would have known—

Maurizio yanked me up. He shoved his face in mine, spitting in angry Italian, drawing the flat of his hand across his throat. Then he stood back and kicked an imaginary soccer ball.

"He hopes they cut your head off and kick it back across the street. If they don't, he'll be happy to do it himself."

Bat Falcone stood nearby, holding out a piece of lead pipe about four feet long with a white flag dangling from the end. It weighed heavy in my hand.

"Speak carefully and well, my friend. May Saint Gabriel keep you safe!" He crossed himself. "Because as of now I cannot. Now go!"

Maurizio aimed his rifle at my belly with a vicious grin, daring me to refuse. I had not slain his brother, but what did that matter? He was blood crazy. Any death would do. Even the death of a useful ally.

I walked out onto the street through the fog, my feet dragging, my knees bent and my bowels heavy as wet sand. I raised the pole in both hands and called out in a scratchy voice, "Hello!" and "Don't shoot!" and "We want to talk! Please don't shoot!"

A wrecked automobile came into view. One of its tires had been blown off and its doors punctured with dozens of bullet holes. I stepped in a black gooey puddle. A derby lay nearby with two holes in its crown, one small, the other big as my fist, its edges crusted with gray matter.

Three men, hatless and in long, heavy coats, two carrying shotguns, one a Browning, crept sideways out of the fog. One aimed his shotgun at me, while the other two swept the area around. I announced that I was from Bat Falcone, that I was unarmed and wanted to talk to Chess Stetson. I repeated his name twice, three times, like an open sesame.

"Chief!" One of them backed away into the fog. A huge shadow rolled out to meet him, that big fat cop, lugging his trusty elephant gun, the kind of weapon, I realized, that could destroy a man's face. Someone behind him said something about a "ferry buoy." Another two gents appeared. They searched me all over. I protested when they took my watch, but they told me to go mate with myself.

The fat cop led the way, the three gunmen following. I smelled cordite, burnt leather and oil as they herded me around the car wreck. The Victorian came into view, its rear corner charred, its clapboard shingle siding pulverized. The ground was blackened and carpeted by shell casings. More dark, muddy stains, pools of blood that would never dry in the damp air.

I looked up from one of these pools to find Molly Carver waiting like a mourner by a grave, dressed in her smart-looking, high-collared brown wool business suit, arms folded under her breasts, now hidden. Her eyes were stones, her mouth flat, jaw set. I had met female government lawyers like her, but none were as tough. In her way, she looked as much a dry as Louise Wheeler, but she was forged of cold steel. She would not pretend to apologize to me this time. She would show no regret. She would show no mercy.

Chapter 13

The Negotiator

Chess Stetson was nowhere around. A sense of doom fell on me like a tombstone. Cobb Carver was absent, too, probably slumped in his threadbare throne or in his big feather bed, his hands pawing the air, his old brain treading murky water, feeble emperor of a grimy empire.

Molly Carver appeared to be in an absolute rage at finding me underfoot yet again. The way she wore that fitted suit, I figured she might have been a tomboy when she was a girl. Since they got the vote, women seemed to be stepping up and out all over the world. That seemed to be true here as well. But I could not bestow my admiration on her as I might on others, not here in Butchertown.

They herded me further into the property, onto the driveway next to the family house, away from the guards. The chief stood behind her, his white-dough face hung with two rolls of bristly jowls. He carefully leaned his humongous shotgun against the house and unhooked a black leather billy club from his belt. He started slapping it calmly, rhythmically in the palm of his hand—*slap . . . slap . . . slap*—his eyes like black beads. I had seen that look recently in the eyes of some San Francisco cops before they went to work on a Tong member in the basement of the Chinatown precinct house. I had stood open-mouthed outside the circle as they beat the poor crying man like a drum, like jazz syncopation. I had felt both frightened and ashamed. Soon, I would get a taste of—

"What are you—?"

"I guess we can't stay away from—"

"Shut up! I'll ask! You answer!"

Slap went the billy club.

"What are you doing here? Why aren't you back across the bay?"

"Or dead?"

"You got fucking nerve," the chief said. *Slap.*

"What are you doing working for Bat Falcone?"

The flagpole hung heavy in my hand. I let the end thud on the damp dirt and leaned on it, my other hand on my hip, trying to convey savoir faire.

"He grabbed me on the way out of town after last night's gunfight. Thought I was one of your mob. I had a hell of a time persuading him otherwise. He sent me over to talk to you, since, well, you and I are already acquainted. He had a dozen guns on me, and one of his troops wants to kill me to avenge a brother of his *you* killed. So yeah, I'm helping out. It looks like my only way home is by him through you. I'd like to get out of here without running through a hail of bullets."

"What does he want?"

"The first thing he needs you to know is that he didn't murder your brother." I added an exasperated sigh.

Molly flinched. I glanced at the chief to see how he would react, and react he did: he stepped around and kicked my cane out from under me. I fell hard on my right side, on my hip. He stood over me and raised his sap, his rotting teeth showing. He would hit me with all he could, until long after I was dead. I rolled up like a hedgehog.

"Wait!"

The chief stopped at the top of his swing. "You sure?"

"Yes." She spoke louder than necessary, louder than a man would. I unrolled and started to get up, but she jabbed a finger at me. "Stay there!" I almost said "woof woof," but I was better off not being a smart guy at that moment. My right hand clawed around, instinctively looking for a weapon, but my flagpole had fallen out of reach and, with that troll standing over me, his club raised and ready, it was better to play the mouse.

I sat up, crossed my legs Indian-yogi style, my hands gripping my knees, and lowered my head, waiting for their questions as cold damp seeped through the seat of my trousers.

"So that's all he has to say? He's innocent? We're supposed to believe that?"

"I guess I do."

"You do? So what? What do you know?"

"A couple minutes after you took off and left me all alone, a couple of other guys came by in a Ford. I got scared and hid in an alleyway. They stopped, got out and hung around a few minutes, like they were supposed to meet somebody. But that somebody didn't show and they left. Falcone says they were his men, looking to meet your brother. It doesn't make sense they'd come looking for someone they'd already killed. I guess you folks were trying to negotiate some kind of deal or partner—"

"Bullshit," the chief protested. "Mr. Carver told Danny not to go. He said this is what would happen if—"

"Quiet!"

"Falcone said he was planning to kidnap your brother and negotiate his release with Mr. Carver, not kill him. But his boys showed up too late to make the grab, after he was already dead and gone. Falcone figured the night had been a wash. Your attack at the stockyard was a surprise to him. That's why he cleared out so fast. He didn't know Danny was dead. He didn't kill him. Otherwise, he would have had his men at the ramparts waiting for you." I sighed again, almost as though I were talking to a child. "You've killed eight of his men for no good reason at all. And got some of yours killed."

"So now he wants to negotiate?"

"That's it."

"Fuck him!" The chief growled. "That's bullshit! I say cut this punk up and send the pieces back across the street."

Molly gave me a peculiar look. "If Falcone didn't kill my brother, then who did?"

"I don't know, lady. I'm not playing Sherlock Holmes here." I winced as the chief raised his club again. *Stow the smart talk,* I reminded myself.

"Please, listen! You got a war on your hands!"

"We know that."

"But you don't understand. You're outnumbered and outgunned. After the last two nights, Falcone and his gang are out to finish you. He's called in his whole army from the north. He can roll over this town by force, kill every mother's son of you. I did you a favor by talking him into holding his fire and negotiating first."

I rolled sideways as the chief kicked at me. He missed, stumbled backward and almost fell like Fatty Arbuckle, though nowhere near as funny.

"Who asked you to negotiate? What did he offer you to lie to us?"

"I wasn't asked. I was told. Look, I'm negotiating for *me,* to get out of here alive. I figure my odds are better if you're not all shooting at each other. I don't like refereeing anyone's fight outside a boxing ring, least of all yours. You don't give a damn about me, I don't give a damn about you and I don't give a damn about Bat Falcone. I just want everyone to calm down and listen to sense. And then I want to go home."

She shook her head, biting her lip. I kept talking.

"The rest of Falcone's mob will be here tonight or tomorrow. How many, I don't know, but they'll have more than enough firepower. Maybe you won the first couple of battles, but you won't win this war. He's sworn to kill you all twice over. I believe him."

"We'll handle him," the chief growled. "Just like we handled all the others."

Molly gave the chief an almost imperceptible headshake, her eyes shivering, as though she could see Falcone's army storming ashore. "Whether he murdered Danny or not," she said, her voice cracking, "it makes no difference to us. We don't let outsiders come in and tell us what to do. We don't make deals. This place used to be nothing but Indians and Mexican farmers growing lemons and tending cattle. My mother's father took this place and made it new. He made Evansville. He made it ours." She took a dramatic breath. "It's going to stay ours."

"We can stand up to anything that wop has to throw at us." The chief laughed with dumb confidence.

"But Molly, are you sure? What about—?" I looked around for help. *Chess Stetson, where the hell—*

"You think I can't run things as my father would 'cause I'm a woman, but you'd be wrong. My brothers are gone, and I have to step in until my father's back on his feet. You may think this is a slum, but it's ours. My family's. Mine. I'll do anything to save it."

"Someone called for me," a familiar voice growled from behind.

I looked over my shoulder just as Chess Stetson's amazing face floated down out of the gray sky. Buckram stood behind him, along with another half-dozen characters, all of them armed.

I would have bet a thousand nickels that Chess Stetson had always looked evil, even when he was a sleeping baby. I imagined his parents creeping, tiptoeing across the room as he lay in the dark, watching from his crib with his narrow eyes. Were they still alive? What did he do to them? Even so, it was better to have him on my side, at least here.

Molly, meanwhile, had squared her shoulders. The chief let his billy club fall to his left side as his right hand moved towards his holster. His eyes flicked at the elephant gun leaning against the house. Three or four more armed mugs gathered behind them, from around the corner of the house. The atmosphere curdled. I felt trapped in the middle of a tense biology lab experiment, predatory cells splitting all around me.

"You got a lot of nerve comin' back here." A smile crept along Stetson's mustache.

"Falcone sent me. He remembers you. Said I should talk to you."

I repeated Falcone's message, that it was not he who murdered Danny Carver, and that he wanted a meeting and they had better agree to it because the rest of his army would be there tonight. I braced for the chief to start whaling on me, but they let me talk. Stetson showed no interest in how I had wound up there. As a messenger boy, I counted for little. That could have been a good thing. Then again, maybe not.

"I say make his head into a bowling ball, roll it back across the street!" the chief huffed with bloodthirsty pride.

"That's enough, Wagmore," said Stetson.

Wagmore? I bit my lip, stared at my lap to hide my smirk. *Wagmore?* I felt punchy, ready to laugh at anything. I had to be careful, though, or it would be my last laugh.

"What's ol' Cobb say?" Stetson's eagle eyes zeroed in on Molly. "He's still the general, ain't he?"

Molly met Stetson's stare. "My father says we fight."

"That's all she wrote then." Stetson turned to Buckram. "The general says we go over the top, then over we go." Buckram's scarred face remained still. Stetson called to the men behind. "You heard the lady, boys. Write your letters home, hoist one more." Then he stared down at me with his commanding sneer. "He's your mess. You take care of it."

He and Buckram turned away. Chief Wagmore drew out a .45 revolver and aimed it between my eyes, its black barrel a tunnel to eternity. The hammer cocked, that ruthless metallic sound like a door closing and locking.

"God the Father, have mercy on your servant. God the Son, have mercy—"

"Wait! Stop!"

Wagmore gaped at Molly. Stetson and Buckram stopped and turned.

"Put it down," Molly said. Wagmore lowered the gun.

"We'll meet with Falcone. See what he wants."

"Miss Carver, your pop ain't gonna—"

"He put me in charge, said to use my judgment. I'm using it. You want to tell him different, then tell him."

Chess Stetson smiled with calm satisfaction. Then they all turned their attention back to me, started peppering me with questions about Falcone. I answered as honestly as I could, emphasizing how they kept me either blindfolded or tied up in cars and small, dark hotel rooms and how I barely knew a word of Italian or Mexican. Stetson scoffed when I related Falcone's complaint about having to drive all the way into Oakland for Sunday Mass. "Guinea bastard ain't changed. Got his fat, greasy hand in everyone's pocket, even God's."

Finally, they asked me if Falcone had proposed a spot for the next meeting. He had not, in fact. This was to the Carvers' advantage, and they, of course, would seize it.

Stetson immediately suggested the Hollis Street bridge over Gasoline Creek. Just hearing that name made me sneeze. They all agreed to this plan immediately, then dictated the message I would take to Bat Falcone.

Finally, they let me up. As I got to my hands and knees, I saw the flagpole a couple feet away. Wincing, I grabbed it, used it to get to my feet with maybe too loud a groan, but no one seemed to notice. Molly ordered Stetson and Buckram to come to the house after they had sent me back, then turned away without a word. Chief Wagmore and his boys followed her around the corner of the house, the mulatto boy trailing behind.

Stetson spun me about. His troops made way as he and Buckram walked me back to the curb. I limped along between them, using my flagpole like a cane.

"You shot at me, you bastard," I said.

"You ran, you chickenshit." Stetson paused. "In France it was my job to shoot guys who tried to run when the whistle blew."

"I bet you enjoyed it."

"Don't look like you can run much of nowhere now," Buckram mumbled. "Wagmore bust you up? Or was it that Falcon fella? Most everybody runs when they get the chance. Sometimes wish I'd run."

I asked Stetson if he believed Falcone's claim to be innocent of Danny Carver's murder. Instead of calling it a lie, he shrugged, as though the question no longer mattered.

It was odd how they seemed to shed so few tears for their fallen leader. Stetson had shown up on the spot after Molly and I found the body, striding coolly in, as though not one bit surprised to find his boss lying there; as though he had been waiting in the shadows. And there was another nagging detail, one I could not yet tease out. An oily black chill seeped through me. I let the question die on my lips.

The wind had picked up into a stiff breeze and the fog thickened. Visibility was only a quarter of the way across the street now, from a dirty shore across a foul sea. In the gloomy distance the smokestack glowed like an eternal flame.

They sent me limping off on my metal cane without a word. As I reached the middle of the street, it hit me how little I had really accomplished towards my most important goal: getting out of Butchertown alive. I was being passed back and forth like a piece of paper. Sooner or later someone would crumple me up and throw me in the gutter with the other dead.

I stopped for a second, alone in the fog, both sides of the street invisible. Maybe I should have—could have—taken off then. But then the fog lifted to reveal Bat Falcone's gunmen, ready and waiting.

I hobbled on, calling out hello, clumsily waving my lead-pipe white flag as its blunt end thumped on the tarmac, begging them not to shoot, telling them that I had an answer for their boss and please don't shoot, all I want is to go home.

Goddamnit, just let me go home . . .

Chapter 14

Possum Paul

As I reached the other side of the street, Maurizio and one of his pals closed in on me, sideways and slow. The pal pointed a Remington .30-06, his face empty. Maurizio, gripping his shotgun, wore a brown grimace. For a few slow seconds I was alone with murderous itchy underlings, no master around to pull on their leash.

Maurizio growled something. "He's asking if they worked you over," his partner translated. I grunted affirmatively. Then he spoke some more and his partner added, "Good. Your night is just beginning."

Maurizio yanked the lead pipe from my hand, throwing it aside. I again fell hard on my side with a loud grunt, nearly bruising my elbow, plunged in a ground fog of paint fumes rising from the cracks in the tarmac. I was damn good and tired of seeing the world from the ground up. But I had to keep the act going.

Maurizio shook his head, surprised that I had returned in one piece, again speaking his stewy Italian. His partner asked me, "Why send you back alive?"

"I have a message for Signor Falcone."

"What message?"

"I have to tell him myself."

Maurizio moved to drive his gun butt into my skull, but his partner intervened. They ordered me to my feet. I held out my hand but they refused to help.

"Look," I complained, "the least you can do is let me have that stick, all right? I'm hurt!" I finished on a high note of pleading: they need not fear me, broken and crippled under their guns.

Maurizio picked up the flagpole and teasingly held it out at arm's length, a small man lording it over a fallen giant. "This bag of shit's too big to carry anyway," his partner said. I pulled myself up, using the pole, then thumped and gimped along ahead of them, a poor cripple whose bounding strutting youth had ended. *See where the path of sin leads you!* my aunts would have cawed, their fingers wagging from the shadows.

Among the fumes of paint, oil and tallow came the odor of a cigar as we entered the alleyway. A tiny orange light guided us in like a buoy to where Bat Falcone leaned against a tilting telephone pole. His right eyebrow arched as I limped up to him.

"So!" He blew smoke in my face. "He's alive. *Bellissimo!* That means we will talk."

I passed along the Carvers' message. He listened without expression. He then asked if I knew the area around the Hollis Street Bridge and Gasoline Creek. No, I only knew it stank of oil and gas. He called out and four more men appeared. He spoke rapidly to them in Italian, waving towards Hollis. They ran off.

He then asked if the Carvers believed his claim of innocence. I shrugged: I had made the case as best I could, but the funny thing was they seemed to have hurried on from Danny's death. I told how they had tried to stop Danny from leaving the ballpark to meet with Falcone on Friday night and I had sensed strong disagreement among them in how to deal with the invader. Police Chief Wagmore had all but accused the late Danny of being a traitor, with no one objecting. He wanted to fight to the death, like the old man. As for Molly, she seemed determined to fight with her father at first, but then Chess Stetson showed up and then, just when Wagmore was about to put a bullet in my brain—

"*Donne, donne!* Always changing their minds!" Falcone shook his head, gravely amused. "Are they seeds on the wind, or are they slyer than we think? The girl wears her papa's pants, walks in his big shoes and swings his cojones, like one of these 'flappers' from the East with their short skirts who wear their hair like hats, their faces painted like whores. Now they want to be boss. Is this what you young people are bringing us? Where is it all leading? I pray to the Virgin that world never comes to pass." He grunted dismissively. "Even so, *la strega* knows on which side of the hill the vines grow best, I give her that. But she does not quite hold the reins, as if a woman could.

"They stand as one only so long as I threaten them. If I stood far enough back, the filthy dogs would devour each other and we would only have to hose their blood from the streets. But that could take too long and I am not that patient. This is not like growing grapes.

"So, Signor Bacon, you've done an excellent job, as I thought you would. Tonight will be a repeat of the same: you will go ahead of me out on the bridge, a tribune bearing my colors. Then, if you remain standing, I will follow. I need a little time to consider the terms of their surrender, which, as my *consigliere*, you will help me deliver.

"Now, now, do not be so bashful, young man. As I've said, your mind is quick, your tongue is like silver, and I will pay you well for your work. Why return to that miserable hive across the bay? Come and live among sunny vineyards. We would have to teach you to speak some Italian, a little Spanish and maybe some Portuguese to deal with the workers here. It would be worth it to both of us. I promise you a comfortable life among my vineyards."

He waited for my yes. I struggled to find breath to reply.

"Please, Mr. Falcone. I'm done with this. I can't do any more for you. You'll have to work it out from here. I've started your peace for you and now you gotta do the rest. I'm a junior DA for the city of San Francisco. That's all I want to be. I don't know these people, I hardly know you, and I don't know this business or this territory. Please! Let me go!"

The brown in Bat Falcone's eyes turned fecal. With a silent headshake he turned away. I had made another fatal mistake. As he walked to his Pierce-Arrow parked nearby, Maurizio called out to him. Falcone called him over and they spoke for a minute. Maurizio started to argue with him again, and again Falcone cut him off. Then Bat Falcone got in his carriage and rode off into the fog.

Maurizio returned, looking morose, as Falcone had again thwarted his desire to kill me. I was still the dog he wanted most to shoot. His pal, standing right behind me, asked a question. Maurizio replied, looking away after his boss. Then his pal said, "Back to the hotel with you."

I saw the night before me: I would die later instead of now. They would store me away, then repeat the ritual of a few minutes ago: send me out on the bridge alone, this time without the white flag, maybe force me to carry an empty gun. I would draw first fire. It was not hard to see. That would be my last favor for Bat Falcone, the last favor I would do for anyone.

It was time to skedaddle.

Maurizio, standing in front of me, was looking away sullenly after his boss. Someone called out to his partner from behind. His partner turned away to answer.

Now I could remove my lame disguise.

I swung the lead pipe into both hands, slammed Maurizio full force across the side of the head. I glimpsed his feet flipping up as I spun around and plunged the pipe end square into his partner's solar plexus. He grunted, dropping his rifle as he doubled up. I brought the pipe down hard across the back of his head. His knees and forehead hit the ground as one, his rump in the air.

I dropped the pipe and ran lickety-split. I sprinted like a rabbit down the street, towards the clacking trains and droning foghorns, the thrill of escape pouring new energy into me, driving away my aches and pains. Run west, scared young man! Run for home! I recognized San Pablo Avenue up ahead. A left turn, then two, maybe three blocks to the Key train stop.

I pumped my knees to my chest as I rounded the corner and charged down San Pablo. I glanced left as I crossed the street running by the Carver compound. No one coming that way, not yet. The Oaks must have been playing away that afternoon because the stadium stood silent and empty. Park Street, too. Because of the troubles? Whatever the reason, Butchertown belonged to the ghosts.

Soon my chest started to burn as my lungs struggled to absorb the bad air. I slowed, coughing violently. I made out the Key train stop up ahead. Or was it just a mirage?

I staggered up to the train stop. It was real all right. But there was no train coming from east or west. I looked for a printed schedule, but there was none. I listened hard but heard little through my gasps. My lungs burned as though I had inhaled an entire box of nickel stogies. I clasped my hand over my chest, slumped against the stop sign and swore then and there to quit smoking for good.

I was standing on a plain of concrete and cement that stretched away into the fog, visibility about twenty feet maximum, as poor as anything I had seen crossing the Atlantic. The sky to the northwest glowed like bourbon. The foghorns from the bay grew louder, the train whistles closer. "Come on! Come on!" I looked around for an alleyway, a doorway, a ditch, a culvert to hide in until the train came, but all was flat and open.

Then I realized: this was *Sunday*. Sunday night. Would trains even be running? I could not remember. I patted and squeezed my pockets, dug my fingers deep inside. Not a penny on me for my fare. I would have to beg for a ride. What if they said no, kicked me off, left me there? And what if there were no trains at all?

I glanced behind me, expecting to see Bat Falcone's car racing out of the fog. I peered ahead, towards the Oakland city line, somewhere out there in the gloom, maybe only five minutes away. There I might find a copper walking his beat. They had to know what was happening here, had to be guarding their borders. At least I would be safe. Better to be a moving target than a stationary one.

I looked east once more, then headed south. But I had taken only a few steps when I heard the sound I was waiting for—an engine growling from the east. The train to the ferry! And just in time!

But hope disappeared. It was not a train but another type of conveyance. Electric train engines did not backfire. This one did. *Pop pop pop!*

An old Model T, tilting on one side, limped out of the fug on a street running right alongside the train tracks.

Voices shouted from the fog to the north. They would be invisible until they were on top of me, bursting through that foul curtain, baying like hounds.

Whee-honk! The Model T rattled and growled as it aimed for the curb. In it sat two familiar profiles, one of them the stern silhouette of a woman's hat, with its short, flat crown and narrow brim. The Ford stopped a foot away. The preacher leaned from the passenger seat, wearing a wry sneer. *You again?* Irredeemable Drunkard. Failed Prodigal. Denizen of the Gutter.

"Paul! Get in!" Lou Wheeler, her crucifix swinging from her breast, seemed not to have lost faith, however feeble it may have been. I saw a glint in her eye as she spoke to the preacher.

"It's a sign from God, Tag. It has to be!" She looked up from under her dark brow. "C'mon, Paul! They're coming! We'll get you somewhere safe!"

They were drawing closer, killers obsessed with using me, obsessed with killing me. An angry roar like a giant black wave rose around us.

I leapt into the backseat and off we went.

Chapter 15

The Believers

The car leapt forward, stumbled across the avenue, straight towards the curb. The preacher jabbed his finger forward. "Follow the tracks!"

As we hit the curb, my knees hit me in the face. No street ahead, only a narrow dirt alley with a warehouse on one side and rail siding and the Key Line tracks on the other. The car careened down the alley, rattled and rocked between warehouse and tracks, the hard rubber tires bouncing over the rail ties. The cement-block wall covered with graffiti rolled by like a magic lantern show. A huge pair of eyes watched us, a thrilling vulgarity ballooning from the caricature's painted grin.

A harsh beam of light caught us from behind. I looked back into blinding glare. Damn me, the trains ran on Sunday after all. And the one I needed was chugging along right for us.

"Stay right!" the preacher shouted. The train screamed by inches away, its musty windows empty but for a few drowsing heads. As the rear platform neared, I struggled to stand up and leap from car to train like Tom Mix. But we were shaking badly and I was not Tom Mix. I would have fallen under the train wheels and so ended this story in a most gruesome fashion. As I collapsed in my seat, the train, my best and last hope for escape, clattered on without me.

The car's frame had been welded out of cheap tin, but it had been tightly bolted over a strong chassis and a mulish engine. It would not fall to pieces, like the ones in Hal Roach pictures. The ride nearly chipped my teeth and ripped my ligaments apart, but Lou proved herself a capable, strong wheelman and kept a straight course.

We bounced out onto a broad avenue of damp, flat mud. The preacher directed us north, back into Butchertown. The potholes were many but shallow, making the ride somewhat smoother. Then he gestured right. "In there." We steered into a dead-end alley about twenty feet deep, a foot or two wider than the car, with dirty brick walls crowding in on three sides.

Lou stopped a few feet from the end, switched off the ignition, turned off the headlamp. Muffled silence fell. Minutes passed before gray light and the sound of wind, foghorns and train whistles crept in. Behind us, outside the alley gray mist blew.

Lou spoke first. "Is everyone all right?"

I stared at the preacher. "Where do we go from here?"

The preacher scowled, as though my question were impertinent. "That might depend on where you've been. Don't sneer at me, Bacon. We coulda left you there."

"We'll go when things calm down," Lou said. "There's been some shooting."

"Yeah, I tried to tell you that yesterday. A lot more than some." Normally, I was not so brusque, especially with someone like Lou. I had been denuded of both my fancy clothes and my good manners.

"Don't be so ungrateful," the preacher said.

"Ungrateful? *You* sent me into that lion's den so I almost get my head shot off and you call *me* ungrateful? You misled—hell, you lied to me."

"What happened? Tag?" Lou looked at both of us. I was about to tell her what he obviously had not, but he cut me off, his hand raised in sudden contrition.

"You're right, you're right! I'm truly sorry and I repent. I should've given you the whole picture. The thing is I didn't see it all myself. In one sense, though, I didn't lie. You asked to see the law in Evansville, and that's the only law around here. That police station on Park has been empty for years. I figured they'd feel a little obliged to help you out. I guess not, considering what happened the night before." He smiled insolently.

"Evansville has always made its own law. There ain't no other, not even God's. Especially not His." He hacked and cleared his throat. "Yeah, I sinned against you. All for a joke. It was aimed at them, though. Not you."

"You used me for a joke?" A sneeze ballooned in my head and I pulled one of those handkerchiefs from my pocket. As my head cleared, I saw the crudely sewn monogram and remembered a stray remark Molly Carver had made the last time we talked, four words racing by: "My brothers are gone . . ." I remembered how tall Danny Carver appeared that one time I saw him alive, at the ballpark and, later on, stretched out on cold ground, and how those clothes I had put on yesterday—

"Whoa, I get it. Molly Carver mentioned 'brothers.' I thought the initials on this handkerchief said JC. but they're TC. You're the other brother, right? She's your sister. You're Danny's brother, Cobb's son. You had the key to the house. That was your bedroom they stuck me in, not Danny's." I sighed. "No wonder those duds didn't fit."

The preacher hooted. "Ho! Now he gets it. The name's Tag Carver by the way. So, what else did big sister spill about her little brother, the shameful sheep of the family?"

"That was it. I had no idea until now. Molly froze up when we saw that Temperance parade roll in Friday evening. Now I understand why. That was you in front, waving that big black Bible." I swallowed hard. "Say, do you know your brother's—?"

"Murdered. I know." A muddy tear cascaded down his pale cheek, the first real mourning for Danny I had seen. He turned away, lowered his head. Lou produced a handkerchief and leaned over, planting gentle dabs on his cheek then laying her hand on his shoulder.

"Awful. Awful. I didn't know until yesterday morning, after I dropped you at the house. Falcone, that son of a . . ." He suppressed his curse with great effort.

"So," he said, after recovering, "how did you like my family?"

"I never talked to your brother, but your father and sister are, well, colorful, if you don't mind my saying. I also didn't get to meet—"

"I don't mind a bit. Characters are what they are. Yeah, you're from polite society all right, like Lou here. Your kind talk the King's English. Dot your *i*'s, cross your *t*'s, never say shit even if you got a mouthful." Lou pursed her lips with disapproval, but he ignored her.

"I was in the navy during the war. I know all those words and maybe some you don't."

"But you're too polite to call evil by its right name to its face, right?" He paused. "What about Bat Falcone?"

"What about him?"

"He's the devil fire we just pulled you from. I saw him drag you into his car last night after that little rumpus. Amazing."

"Little rum—?"

"We've heard shooting." He rubbed his hand over his cheek as though nursing a sore tooth. "I didn't think things could be any worse than when I left, but they are. Blood and fire rain down like at Sodom and Gomorrah. Lord Jesus, I came back to stop it all, save my family from this Pit, lead them out, show 'em the Light, like Jesus led the dead through the Gates of Hell. For months I heard God in my heart: 'Go home, Tag!'" He pointed at his heart, then at Lou. "She heard the call, too. But we also sin in what we don't do, right? I didn't listen. Why didn't I listen?"

"We haven't lost yet, Tag. We're not through here. We're not defeated. God's still with us!" She glanced at me with a hint of that long-ago smile. "Remember I said I knew Paul from back east? I didn't mention that he's the son of a priest." She looked straight at me. "That's what I meant by a sign from God."

"You mean like a Catholic?"

"No. Episcopalian." She made a face.

Tag frowned, mystified as though she had called me a Martian.

"Weak-tea Catholics."

"More like near beer." I gave a cheeky grin, but they speared me with prim-aunty stares at my poor manners; while you might jest about some things, you never joked about the Cause.

"We don't gotta know his upbringin'. It's recent news we need."

"We're on a mission, Paul," Lou said. "To save this town from the Devil. Maybe you'd like to join us." She raised her lovely chin, fierce with the determination I had seen in my aunts when I returned from the navy to find—along with other bad news—the country being smothered by virtue's wet blanket.

"To shine a light where darkness rules." Tag stared up at the blank sky.

"So it rules no more."

"Only the blessed light of Jesus."

"For ever and ever more."

"Amen!" They slapped their hands together, their faces beaming. I blushed. Even my father found this Holy Roller singsong hard to take. *Too much protest*, he would say, playfully mangling Shakespeare.

"And now you're with us. Whatever your sins before, you can repent of them now. That's why God sent you here. To save you, too. Now's your chance." That she and her boyfriend had misled me was beside the point. "God brought us together again for a reason, Paul."

Tag sat back against the passenger door. "I know you've been negotiating for my brother's killer and with my family, jumpin' from frying pan to fire." He replied to my stupefied look. "Faith gives a man eyes to see far—"

"Excuse me." I hacked and spit over the side of the car. "We oughta get our asses—excuse me, leave right now. Oakland's just a short ways—"

"Did Jesus run from the garden that last night?" Lou broke in rhetorically. "He faced torture and death, but he fulfilled prophecy, carried his burden to the end. We will do no less."

"What exactly do you have in mind?"

"You know a thing or two I don't, Bacon," Tag Carver said. "You've been in town as long as I have. You step out with my sister, find my brother murdered, then we find you in the gutter next morning. Later I drop you at my house and Bat Falcone grabs you that night. You've had a couple of ripping days, the man at the center of it all. The more I know, the better our chances of bringing peace and victory."

From where I sat, he had no chance at all, and to help emphasize the point I once more repeated my tale of woe, eliding his brother's terrible injuries and the man I had killed.

"You said nothing about the shoot-out at the cattle pen when we picked you up yesterday."

"I didn't want to involve you."

"He was trying to protect me," Lou said.

"I thought of it as police business—"

"Right, I made that harder than I should've. I knew you'd tell them who let you in. That was little Tag playing ghosty. 'Buh-boo! I'm home everybody! Buh-boo!' Like a thief in the night, the Gospels say. Too tricky by half. If I'd known about Danny and what you'd been through, I wouldn't have played the jester. So you slugged it out with my pops and won?" he went on cheerfully. "That's better than I ever did. Good with your fists, fast on your feet, eh?"

"Not enough of either to get me out of here. By the by, Pops looks to be in bad shape. Your sister's trying to run things but—"

"Keep talking. Please."

So I did. Talking to Tag Carver was like talking to a man through a curtain. He would hardly look at me. His rough manner clashed with his priestly collar and black suit, a dichotomy I never encountered in the starchy world I came from. (He was right about my people's reverence for the King's English. It took a year of navy training to learn to say "ain't" and drop my g's.)

"It's a miracle you still walk among the living." He picked lint off his suit.

"That's not the only miracle." Lou shivered. "Ten years and thousands of miles."

"I know of Bat Falcone. I heard the tall tales from behind the kitchen door. He kills my brother but lets you live? Yeah, that's a miracle. You must be valuable, at least to him."

"I managed to escape in time, that's all. Bat Falcone's a charming sport all right. Talks a long streak. But to be honest, I don't think he's your brother's murderer."

"What? You believe that wop gorilla?" Carver hissed with indignation. "You saw that baseball bat he carries, didn't you? You saw what he does with that thing."

"Except your brother was killed by shotgun blasts, two of them. I saw the results, saw them take the gun away. Look, I'm not saying I believe him, but—"

"What else did he say?"

I described Falcone's desire to wipe out the Carvers, both to avenge his men and to punish the enemy for being so ornery, until I persuaded him to negotiate.

Then he had me act as messenger boy, then . . . "It was time to go. He pretty much wrung me out."

"You resisted his offer to act as counselor for evil." Lou nodded stoutly. "You talked him into making peace. You see, it means something. Even if it is a wrong peace."

"I was a scared animal. I wasn't thinking noble thoughts."

"You *thought* you only wanted escape. But the path led you to we who do God's work. See how God's hand guides everything? Believe it. This here's your path."

I felt little reassurance. I could not read God's Mind, as my priestly father had warned. Nowadays I doubted there was even a Mind worth reading.

"So that butcher pretends to want peace, eh?" Tag Carver shook his head. "He doesn't want peace. He's just buying time, jockeying for position."

"Tag, listen. Maybe he does want peace."

Tag stared at Lou, astonished and annoyed at her naïveté. I decided to put my two bits in.

"She may be right about that. I think he's sincere about not sacrificing more of his men. And anyway, your sister agreed to a parley. Like I said, she's running things, or trying—"

Tag's jaw dropped. "They—what? She did? Parley? When? Where?"

"Tonight, eight o'clock. On the Hollis Street bridge over Gasoline Creek."

"A-*ha*. Ambush. I know that neighborhood. Used to play cowboys and Indians there with my brother and his pals. It's a maze of factories, right by the oil refinery. Blind alleyways all over. Got left behind there once. Took me all night to find my home. Perfect."

"Falcone's boys are scouting the rooftops. He was gonna stake me out like a goat again."

"Who'll be the sacrificial lamb now?" Tag laughed.

"Don't ask me. I'm wondering how serious everyone is about making peace. Falcone's a practical sort. He's also a Catholic—"

Lou sat up. "Really?"

"Really. He may be just hedging his bets—"

"It won't be a lasting peace, that's for sure," Tag said.

"And why not?" Lou asked.

"It's the peace of thieves. There's no love in it, neither human nor God's. It's a peace that lets 'em keep picking each other's pockets and selling their poison without getting killed. Money's all they really care for. And the Carvers are not gonna let some outsider like Falcone tell 'em how to make it or spend it, while taking his piece. And they won't let him raise no pope house."

"The situation looks a little muddy to me," I said. "With your brother gone, there's some dispute about who's captain. Like I said, your sister—"

"You mean Chess Stetson?" Tag grinned. "I know him. Another bad one. He killed his own pops, you know that? For the money. At least that's the story."

"He said Danny was going to meet with Falcone when he got killed. I believe him. Your sister agreed to meet tonight, but she's working for your pa, and I know like I know the sun don't shine in Butchertown your pa wants war. He's still the admiral. I'd put my chips on an ambush, at least on his part."

"What would you wager if the three of *us* were there, to meet them on the bridge?"

Lou's words rang like a bell. She was trembling. Tag and I paused. She went on, her voice rising.

"What would happen if we brought God to the table? In prayer, praise and song. We'd make it the peace of God. Maybe Bat Falcone can't raise a church here, but we can. We can make all the difference! This could be the first Temperance miracle!"

"So, we show up like when Jesus walked on the water?" Tag sank into deep thought. "All their eyes watching."

"No. More like St. Paul on the road to Damascus. God speaks and they fall. He will stay their hands against us. They'll repent of their sin. They'll see what they were, what they are now. But most of all, they'll see what they can be with the Lord by their side." She gave me a dreamy look. "Remember I told you Paul was raised by a man of the cloth. He knows all the hymns and prayers better than I."

I groaned silently, staring into the brick wall two feet away, praying for it to crumble and make a hole for me to jump through. I had not been inside a church in years. The Lou I had known years ago had died and arisen as a humorless maniac, her vivacity and joy soured by fanaticism. I had seen what happened to busybody Holy Rollers when they intervened in life on board crowded troopships, especially when trying to break up the near-constant brawling by invoking the love of Christ. Oftentimes they got the worst of it, just as the Gospels warned—mustard seeds on stony ground and all that—but were as baffled as kittens afterwards, wondering why so few wanted the perfect loving peace they offered. It was not until we organized the fisticuffs, refashioned them as boxing matches, with gloves, rules and referees, that the seas calmed and I got my promotion to steward.

I looked to Tag Carver, expecting him to be in sensible agreement—he seemed to be a man of the world, like me, immune to such heavenly delirium.

"It would concentrate their minds," he murmured. "Give them a point of light to stare at. Like when you stare for a long time at a candle. The whole world disappears, even the darkness."

"Three in one, we'll be His face, all eyes upon Him."

The hush grew loud. I raised my voice in objection. "Listen, folks, I'm sorry, but I really think we'd be smart to drive right out of here and fetch some real cops to straighten this mess out. The government, somebody." They sat deaf as stone. "You promised to take me somewhere safe! At least do that!"

"You weren't always so timid." Lou sighed heavy with tragedy. "You were so brave when we were young."

"You're wearin' diapers on your head," Tag Carver scoffed. "You think you're sensible, but this ain't a sensible situation. You really think the government and the cops give a dime if a couple packs of mad dogs devour each other? That's how they'll see it. You know they're pushin' the whole country towards Temperance. They're even poisoning the liquor they sell themselves to scare people off the stuff. So what if some bootleggers die? This war fits their plan. They don't have to lift a finger." He shook his head, contemptuous as a crow. "For a guy who was in the navy in the war, you sure don't know much. You're more a Lamb than a Bacon."

He smiled at Lou, reached out, gently laid his hand on her arm.

"No. She speaks truth. It's gonna take a miracle. By God's hand. The Lord's the last, best and only hope this Hell has. It's the only way to erase the name of Butchertown."

"Fine then." I stood up, sensible like my Aunt Edna. I dropped one leg over the side of the car. "You're the big crusaders here, not me. You want to walk into the middle of that fight, go ahead. I'll cheer for you and bring flowers to your funeral. But I'm an assistant district attorney for the city of San Francisco and my boss expects me in the office tomorrow morn—"

But as my foot searched for solid ground, Tag hissed, "Shh! Wait!"

A car engine grumbled by right outside the alley. Light splashed across the entrance. I pulled my leg back in and crouched down in a big ball. The red brick glowed. The engine grew louder, then faded away. Then another car passed, its purr rising over the other engine, this time on our side of the street. My eyes closed; I hoped their eyes would remain closed to me.

Then a strong hand grabbed my arm. I looked up to find Lou and Tag leaning over the backseat, staring ferociously down at me from a foot away, their faces ablaze.

"Paul, we need you. The three of us make a trinity, like we learned in Sunday school, remember? Father, Son and Holy Ghost. You, Tag and I. Wherever two or more are gathered. *That's* why you're here! This is what it means for us to meet again. Remember when you saved the day, when that boy fell through the ice and you were there for him? That time has come again. Time for another miracle. It can't happen without you." She paused, leaned closer, her hand trembling, eyes brimming with tears.

"I need you, Paul."

"Where'll you go by yourself, chum?" Tag Carver asked. "They're out there and they'll shoot you down. Like a dog. Take it from me."

His homily closed with a sour smile.

"Butchertown's no place to walk alone."

Chapter 16

Pas de Trois

As I slumped there in the backseat, another car passed by, almost slowing to a stop this time before driving on. My nuanced practical arguments made for a weak soup. Carver had a point: this was an insensible situation. Who could say God manifested in the likes of us would not bring real peace? So far, my big mouth and bright ideas had done nothing but stick me in one jam after another. I swore that if I escaped from here I would beg Aunt Ethel to sew my lips shut for good, a thousand stiches if need be, my head tucked under her Singer sewing machine as she piously hummed her favorite hymns. while crowing, *This'll teach you, young man!*

"So the meeting's at eight." I futilely searched for my watch before remembering it had been filched again.

Tag Carver looked at his. "It's almost five. We sneak in just before they do. We have three hours." He snapped the watch shut. "We'll rest until then."

Lou released my arm, putting her hand to her mouth, coughing delicately. "I need somewhere to freshen up." I blushed. Tag, unfazed, waved down the alley.

"There's another alley, a slot really, twenty feet to your left as you go out." Lou seemed unoffended. She knew the rough life. Carver and I both half stood like gentleman as she opened the car door, banging it against the brick wall.

"Move careful, look both ways and go all the way to the end!" Tag whispered. "There's rats all over, man and animal."

She crept down the alley flat along the wall, her back and shoulders straight and perfect. At the opening she peeked and peered both ways, then slid around the corner out of sight. My heart clattered. I wanted to follow, stand guard over—

"You think your San Francisco's some wide-open sin city," Tag broke in peevishly. "Think you've seen it all. But Hell has lots of small neighborhoods like this." I tried to ignore him, kept watching the alley, but he continued pounding my back with his talk.

"Your shining city's no patch on this burg. My grandpa Evans built this town so he could do all the whoring and gambling he wanted without paying a dime in tribute to Caesar; then my Daddy brought the factories in and brother Danny added liquor to the stew. They're the law here. The Carvers have been paying graft and kickbacks to the factory bosses, the county cops, state boys and feds since forever. 'We'll be damned for our sins as proud as roosters and we'll let you make your gold and your trifles here, too.' There ain't no churches, no Wobblies or Bolshies in sight thanks to the Carvers. That's always been the deal.

"The furnaces of this Hell forge the pleasures of your puny heaven. And your heaven, the heaven of *things*, is forever stained 'cause of it. But so what, so long as those shiny things keep comin', right? You got no vision in you, no fire, no righteousness. Only righteous fire will cleanse this place."

Finally, he stopped his revival-tent ranting. "What was she like when you knew her?" The sudden shift drew my genuine attention. His small mouth was pursed in a smile. "When you were in school together?"

I paused, searching for the right words. "Spirited, funny, sharp. A bit of a suffragette. Fun to be with. She could sing."

"Oh yeah! Voice like a flyin' velvet carpet. I know it."

"The boys all jockeyed to step out with her."

"Did you?"

"Step out with her? Close but no cigar." I remembered the taste of that one kiss. I could have said "wicked" too, because it was a wicked kiss as she—

"She lost her baby, you know. And her husband."

I stared at him.

"She married a drunkard."

"I heard she ran off with a guy named Eddie Jones."

"That's it. They came out here hoping the sunshine would dry him out, but he just got wetter. She became a souse, too. They had their baby, a boy. One day Eddie went out to buy more liquor, drove in front of another car."

"That wasn't smart."

"No, especially when he tipped over in front of a streetcar. Drove right over his head. Amazing they let just anybody drive these things. When the police showed up at the door, they had to kick it down because Lou was passed out drunk; little Eddie Junior was screaming in his crib, hungry. They took her to the morgue and made her look at her husband. Then they declared her an unfit mother, took little Eddie away. Afterwards she smashed every beer and whiskey bottle in the house. Been smashin' 'em ever since. She's working to prove herself a dry and fit mother and get her boy back. Nope, she's not your happy, funny schoolgirl no more."

His eyes hardened into black pebbles. "You think us drys are a bunch of nosy, ignorant biddies, Bacon, but believe me, there are sides to this crusade you'll never understand. We've seen the world from down under the gutter. We know. You'll know too someday."

"So long as folks like you are reading my thoughts for me, I guess I'm in good hands." I kept watch on the street, but he kept talking.

"I was blind too when I left here, took the gutter out on my hands and knees. Not long after Prohibition started. Crawled my way down the coast blind drunk. Then one day I woke up in a Temperance shelter in Los Angeles with this angel hovering over my cot. I sat right up like a jack-in-the-box. Oh, yeah. City of Angels. Here's one. Later she sang 'Gather at the River' for us. I saw God's Heaven then because only Heaven could make a voice like hers. I was baptized that afternoon. I can still feel the water closing over me, like warm honey, while she sang. For the first time I really saw the world. Before Lou, the only women I knew were my mother and sister and my father's whores right next door. Born and raised in Hell's furnace, that was me.

"I didn't know there was so much sun and blue sky. And everyone around her was so kind. That really got me. All the kindness and forgiveness. So I got to my feet and stepped out of the gutter onto the path, into the Light, under God's sky. I took a mail-order course to earn this collar. You got to know it, friend. You got to see it. I saw it 'cause of her. And now here I am, like the prodigal, but returning as witness and preacher, returning to forgive instead being forgiven. All because of her. I wouldn't be here but for God pushing me, through her. Oh, I fought it, but she reminded me family is family. And I had a duty to return home, bringing, sharing the Holy Light of God! To lead them out, all of us together, a family broken by sin reunited by God."

I squirmed, moved and embarrassed, though unsure for whom. I had occasionally found myself trapped on ships and trains with guys like him. And he seemed so naked, brave even, to spout such talk. He made me feel cramped, small and petty.

"Lou says that the summers where you lived smelled of woods, grass and flowers." His eyes narrowed, his voice taking on an insinuating tone. "Is that right?"

"That they did." I warmed to his invitation to nostalgia, remembering more of that afternoon by the brook in the woods behind the school; her leaning against the tree, saying *yes, yes and yes*. A mysterious blue glow surrounded us as she spoke with her words, her eyes her mouth.

"Every season had its own special light and aromas. Even winter." I smiled. "And how they changed from one to the next, like a painter slowly painting over a canvas, like from underneath. We were . . . blessed you could call it. Sometimes I think every kid should grow up in the world we did. Like Tom Sawyer, you know?"

"No! I don't know!" Tag Carver exploded at me over the backseat, thrusting his pale face into mine, saliva spraying. "None of us do. We live like this. In shit!"

A loud silence.

"If you weren't going to like my answer, why did you ask?"

"'Cause I knew you were gonna talk stupid."

"That's not very Christian."

"But you quit the flock, didn't you? You're like a traitor, worse than the sinners around here. Yeah, you are. The rules are different for you. Lou's right. You're soft and slippery. You'll run first chance you get, let me and that beautiful girl walk out there alone among the devils."

We spoke no more. My fingers were prying the rips in the cracked horsehair seat when Lou at last slipped back around the corner, sideways along the wall, her step longer, skirt swinging looser than before.

We stood again as she slid awkwardly back behind the wheel. "I went all the way to the end." Tag winced as he eased out of the car. He headed out, favoring his right side. Lou watched him, her eyes steady, lips moving in silent prayer.

"Is he all right?" She frowned, signaling I had asked an impolite question. "He looks hurt."

"There was a riot Friday night. A drunken mob attacked us as we marched into town. They pushed him through a window. He'll be fine. God has steeled him with suffering."

"You probably scared them a little with that hammer of yours."

She turned her back, holding her head high with piety. *My superiority requires that I ignore you in my perfection.* I fumed for a while, until I got an idea how to crack that smug shell.

"I still remember our first kiss. The only one. In the woods behind the school—"

She snapped her head around. "That did *not* happen!"

"I still remember the taste. The air was moist and warm. You wore a soft-violet dress, with the bow and the ruffles, and that smile of yours. You were looking up and—"

"I did *not* let you kiss me."

"I don't recall you resisted. If you didn't like it, you should have slapped me."

She huffed up with starchy dignity. I pressed my offense.

"The only thing I'm sorry about is not kissing you again. And again."

"I thought you were a hero." She turned slightly, her voice hoarse and low. "You pulled that little boy from the pond, saved his life. You seemed so different from the others."

"Then I fell off my pedestal."

"Right on your head. Two weeks later you get caught behind school, drinking alcohol and smoking; you ran dice games, staged fistfights, took bets on turtle races. *Turtle races!* Trespassing, poaching! You were so common. And a rector's son. Your father must have been mortified with you carrying on like a cheap criminal. Now I find you where everyone said you'd end up—in the gutter. You're just the same. Glib. Careless. Irresponsible." She shook her head in devout exasperation, my three aunts rolled into one beautiful package. "What your parents must think of you."

"I have no idea what they're thinking anymore. No one does."

She turned slightly. "What do you mean?"

"Influenza. Took them both right as I was coming back from the war, while I was waiting in quarantine. Didn't find out until I came home and found the curtains drawn and a black bow on the front door. I thought I'd surprise them. But I got the surprise. I should have seen it coming. I'd seen it already on ships, in hospitals. I saw it from the window on the train coming up the river, coffins piled along the tracks, kids romping on them like they were homemade forts. Thought I was special, like you did. Thought it would miss me, like so much else had. You know something else? My mother and father would have been overjoyed to see me home safe, that I know. That's the only thing I know anymore."

She lowered her head. "I'm sorry, Paul. I didn't know."

I touched her shoulder. "No apologies necessary. No forgiveness needed. I'm more concerned that you haven't taken me someplace safe like you—"

"I had moved away."

"Yeah, I heard you eloped with Eddie Jones. Tag told me what happened. I'm *really* sor—"

"He did?" She grabbed the steering wheel as though to rip it out. "That's nobody's business! I forbid you to speak of it! You hear me?" As I reeled back, she gave me the dirtiest of looks. "All right. Very well. So long as everyone's gossiping, telling secrets, here's one: Tag's mother died from drink. So there."

I considered the news while recalling those clean squares on the tobacco-stained walls of the Carver house, where pictures had once hung.

"That explains a couple things."

"Does it now?"

"Like why you both turned Temperance."

"It's not only about us. It's about the world." Her implacable pride returned.

"Maybe the whole world doesn't want to be saved."

"What people want and what they need are two different things."

"You oughta ask them first—"

"They don't know. They need to be told. And shown, as I was." She gripped the steering wheel as though she would drive the car right through the wall.

"Maybe it wasn't such a swell idea giving women the vote."

"Don't be impertinent. You think once we got the vote, we would just put on our aprons and go back to the kitchen and make babies? You thought we'd stop there? Let you keep running our lives from the saloons?"

"I withdraw the comment then. But this Prohibition business—"

"Doing right never ends. You think I'm deluded? We've just started. The argument is over. Temperance is the law of the land. We are winning everywhere. We will do anything it takes to enforce the law and see that it is obeyed. It may take time, but we will succeed.

There are no two ways about this, only one. You see it or you see nothing."

"You really think you can arrest everyone?"

She bowed her head. "If it saved one child, I would lock the whole world in jail."

"Lou, that's—"

"I'm not a girl anymore!" She turned around once more. "This is who I am. It's our way here or the world out there. You have to choose."

Surrounded by brick walls on three sides, I was talking to a fourth wall. We sank into private sulks. After a few moments she turned around and her face lit up, brighter than it ever had for me. Tag Carver was limping back to the car. He eased into the passenger seat.

"I went three-quarters of the way in." He glared. "You'll be back, right, Lamby-boy? Don't forget where you are. They'll make bacon outta Bacon. Oink-oink baa!"

I hopped over the back of the Ford, slid down the alley, close to the wall. Lou hissed, "Why did you tell him? What gave you the right . . . ?"

I stopped at the corner. To the north, sour fog. To the south, the same. West, across the street, a one-story brick building. A lemony-white blob hung low in the sky. *Ahh! That would be the sun!* Hope surged in me. Then a milky spasm of windblown smut rose and drowned it. The only steady light came from the smokestack to the north, a lighthouse on a burnt shore.

I crept left until I stumbled into the aperture. My sinuses burned and the tart haze of human waste almost knocked me out. We were by no means the first to use this little cranny as a privy, an alley a little wider than my shoulders. I stopped halfway back. Then the sneezing started, bursting out of me once . . . twice . . . three times . . . I placed my head on my forearm to keep it from hitting the wall. Soon I lost count, my head empty, my brain churned to mud.

Finally, the sneezing stopped. I closed my eyes as I relaxed, leaning a hand against the wall, my eyes closed. I needed to think about what would come next, how I would talk those two crusaders out of their doomed and loopy scheme.

But I knew they would not be persuaded. There was only one way to stop them—and here I took a breath: by force.

By force.

So obvious, so simple. I would take the wheel, stage a one-man mutiny. I was bigger and stronger than the both of them. Putting down Tag Carver would take one punch. Louise would be more complicated. Much as I had resisted, I had been raised a gentleman, and a gentleman never struck a woman. *Ever.* For any reason. Under any circumstances. But my world did not know of circumstances such as these. Were they carrying rope? I could tie Louise up and stuff the two of them in the back of the car, with Oakland just a short drive away. Away from Butchertown.

My bedeviled mind swirled. If she did not love me now, she would love me even less afterward. I would not be her hero, though I saved her life. I recalled her as she was that day by the brook, felt the rough bark of that birch tree under my hand. Bright colors, the tender aroma of woodland flowers and the perfume of a woman's soap mixed with spring air. Lou glancing up, saying, "Look!" And there it was, a butterfly on the trunk overhead, its blue wings open.

"It's God!" she cried, and I looked down as she looked up, her mouth open—

But then my fancy drained away and I returned to my present reality: a muddy, urine-scented alley. I neatly buttoned myself up. Real men did not waste time on faded fancies. Two days ago I had gone over the edge of an abyss and was still falling. But now I had a plan to stop the fall. I had a mission to carry out. No, I would not run, as they so smugly assumed. And maybe someday she would understand and be grateful.

Now filled with purpose, I straightened my shoulders and flexed my hands, like I did before stepping into the ring.

But as I turned to go, I found myself staring into the dead eyes of a double-barreled shotgun held a foot away. A brutally scarred face stared unblinking down the barrel.

So this was it. My death pushed toward me.

I closed my eyes and waited.

Chapter 17

Knight Takes Pawn

"I'll kill ya this time," Buckram promised, jerking the shotgun barrel upward.

My hands rose obediently as I exited to the street. Buckram stepped to my right. To my left, Chess Stetson leaned insolently against the wall, a .45 automatic in his right hand, his other hand poised on his belt. His charcoal suit fit like snakeskin. He looked unfashionably sleek and panther-like, but men's fashion would have been better for it. He might have been big in the movies, tying Pearl White to the railroad tracks, twirling his mustache and chuckling as he strode away. Douglas Fairbanks would have run like a chicken. Even Lon Chaney would have shrunk under his stare.

"Wondered what Falcone's boys were runnin' after. Your sneezin' gave you away. What are you still doin' here?"

"Trying to go home." I heaved a sigh.

"Not your day, sailor boy. Hell, don't think I ever met a man with worse luck, not since France." He stepped back and waved for me to follow. "Where you been hidin'?"

"In that pisshole." I avoided glancing behind me. They had no idea that Louise and Tag were nearby. I felt mild relief at first but also realized that they would be unaware of what was going on. *I knew he was a coward. He couldn't even wait for first cockcrow.* And then they would carry out their crazy plan, out onto the bridge, in blind faith, driven by their dream.

Stetson and Buckram walked me to their car, a block away. The car was a closed Ford coupe, roofed in greasy gray cloth. I put my hands behind my back for the ropes, cooperating as much as I could, as Stetson pushed me firmly into the backseat. From there they drove me through empty streets, tense with silence, to the last place I wanted to be: the Carver compound on Adelyne.

"Why we stoppin' here?" Buckram asked as we parked a block away.

"Don't want them knowin' we're home."

I almost fell as I exited the car, but Stetson caught me. They marched me down a mud walkway and across another street a block from the Key station. As we reached the compound, a ghostly growl came from the shadows: the mastiff who had almost bit my head off watched from a few feet away. We passed through a gate in front of the green house on the far left. "Close it quiet," Stetson whispered.

"Why are you—?" I whispered, but Stetson put a warning finger to his lips. We reached muddy marble steps, leading up to two ornate iron-gated doors. He unlocked the one on the right. We entered a grimy vestibule. The inner door was pocked and splintered with bullet holes.

"Wipe your feet." Stetson glared down at my shoes. I scraped hard, almost doing a shuffle dance. God knew what I had tracked out of that alley. Buckram joined us in our cell, easing the gate shut behind us as Stetson unlocked the front door.

We entered another inner vestibule. "Shoes off." *Very well, Mr. Fussy Gangster.* As I turned away, he picked up my shoes, looking at the heels. Bleaching would be next.

I entered a carpeted hallway, then turned right into the living room of a large apartment that covered the entire first floor. The place was spanking clean and neat, even with rifles, shotguns and other weapons leaning in corners and sitting decoratively in polished maple gun racks on the walls. The aroma of tobacco hung heavily. The wallpaper, decorated with trellises strung with carnations, was coated in oily, light brown. Otherwise, the place gleamed immaculately. I sensed a woman's touch, imagined Stetson's wife or girlfriend working away in the kitchen.

Stetson nodded for me to sit in a flocked blue-flowered sofa that looked shiny new and more suited to my grandmother's house. It seemed very soft and deep.

"You wouldn't mind?" I turned to show my tied and tired arms. Stetson scowled as though my request were absurd, but I insisted. "I'm too beat to run anymore."

He grinned. "You fooled Falcone with that lame dog trick, didn't you? You won't fool me."

"Even if I did get away, I'd just bang into him again. I hurt two of his men, pretty badly I think. He probably likes me about as much as your boss does."

"He ain't our boss no more," Buckram said.

"Shut up," Stetson growled.

Buckram blushed and pouted, staring at the floor. "Don't like you talkin' to me like that, Chess."

We compromised. They retied my hands in front of me, one over the other, palms up. I could not do much, except maybe wash my face. For this, I also asked permission, adding an Episcopalian "please." Buckram stood guard as I bent over the sink in a tiny bathroom. The water was lukewarm and dirty, the soap like dry stone.

As I exited the bathroom, my eye caught a framed document on the wall:

PROHIBITION BUREAU
PERMIT CA-1A
LICENSE TO SELL SACRAMENTAL WINE

A permit to purchase and use wine exclusively and solely for ritualistic and religious purposes is hereby granted to CHESS STETSON, Rabbi, B'nai Chabad Congregation, Oakland, California, on this date, October 23, 1921.

"I didn't know you were a rabbi," I said as we returned to the couch. "How did you—?"

"Any idiot can get one of those," Stetson grunted. "Danny got one. So does Cobb. Just tell 'em you're a rabbi, slip 'em a tenner. What's so funny?"

"I can't see all you guys wearing yarmulkes."

Stetson found this funny too and we were both laughing by the time he sat me down. As I feared, sitting in that couch was as good as being hog-tied. I was looking up at my knees, could see every thread in the slacks Falcone had given me. I closed my eyes as Stetson ordered me to relax. A minute later I sensed his reptilian presence coiling by and opened my eyes to see a cut glass filled with amber liquid on the side table. I gave Stetson the hairy eyeball.

"What?" Stetson stared down his nose, his long bent pipe hanging from the corner of his mouth.

"I was warned not to drink the liquor around here."

He shook his head with a big grin. "That's Canadian. We took it off one of Falcone's trucks. Nah, don't worry. I need you awake." He put the glass in my hands, poured himself a shot from a nearby bottle and then, to my amazement, raised his glass in a toast. Our glasses clinked. I sipped with both hands. Warm whiskey toasted my raw throat, making me sweetly fuzzy.

As I took a third sip, Buckram kicked through a swinging door in front of me, carrying a plate piled high with ham sandwiches, and wearing—I swear—the brightest, floweriest, goofiest apron I had seen since my last Christmas at Aunt Isobel's, all ruffled along the edges with wide blue trim, and bright-red roses winding and splashing across the front. I half expected him to kick up his heels and burst into Gilbert and Sullivan. I spluttered as the whiskey went up my nose.

"You all right?" Stetson frowned through the smoke rising from his pipe.

"Yeah, I'm fine." I wiped my nose on my sleeve.

"You're supposed to drink it, not inhale it."

Buckram beamed proudly, posing with his arms wide. "Ya like this? I sewed it myself!"

I started sneezing again as Stetson took the glass away. He wiped my nose, and then Buckram, his attempt at a smile making his scar even more grotesque, offered me a sandwich. It was about as yummy as burlap, but it would do. Soon a glass of Butchertown beer appeared. Yum! Liquid gold! My well-bred hypocrisy once again kept me among the living.

"So," I finally said. "What do you cards want from me now?"

Stetson pulled out a small maple chair from a side table and sat at an angle to my left, relighting his pipe with a mechanical lighter, glancing sideways at the floor. Buckram sat at the table, where he munched on a sandwich in small bites, his good side to me. I was relieved not to have to watch him chew on his bad side.

"I like how you get down to business."

"I know the drill by now. I'm alive because I'm useful. So long as being useful keeps me alive, I'll be useful."

"What did I tell ya?" he called over to Buckram. "His mind skips like a stone across a pond." Buckram shrugged, happily absorbed in his meal. Stetson fixed his narrow eyes on me, leaning forward, suddenly seeming like an amiable businessman.

"Our old boss—that's the late Danny Carver—he took a trip east a year ago, visited Chicago, New York. He met this Jew, name of Rothstein, a gambler and businessman, kind of like we are. Kind of like Bat Falcone too, but a lot higher up the ladder. A bigger fish in the biggest pond of all. Danny came home talkin' about how Volstead was changing everything. It's more than booze and beer comin' out of those pipes. It's money. Millions. We had to start thinkin' about the future, do more than just build backyard stills and small breweries, run whores and gambling joints and bust up strikes for the factory bosses, cattlemen and the like. We had to do more than eat and shit the money we take. We had to make more of our own booze and beer. Make it better and sell more of it to more people, take that money and put it to work. We gotta grow our way out of Evansville. We gotta be businessmen. Think big. Make a system."

"Like Henry Ford, you mean."

"Bull's-eye. Now this town's a crossroads for the whole East Bay. Oakland and Berkeley are dried up tight, but no matter how dry they are, there's a million wets who want a drink. We're the beer spigot, the big speakeasy for the whole East Bay. That makes us the transfer point to markets in the interior of the state. Anyone who wants access from the north and east has gotta come through here. Or else we steer 'em this way. That's what Falcone's been trying to do ever since Prohibition, without paying us toll, without us getting our share. For a couple of years we've been stickin' up his trucks and boats or siccing the law on him. Sometimes he kills one of our guys in retaliation or tries nibbling into our territory, building his own distillery and warehouse, like that one at the stockyard."

He paused, his eyes glinting, pointing his pipe stem.

"The one we shot up Friday night. You know about it. You were there."

I sank deeper into the couch, my scraped knuckle, the fist that killed Johnny Pyle, exposed. I could not hide it. How did he know?

Stetson tipped the whiskey bottle into my glass again and handed the drink to me. "Don't deny it, Bacon. You didn't just hear gunfire. You were smack in the middle. Why you lied about it we'll take up later." He yawned slightly as he poured himself another and sat back. I glanced over at Buckram, who was looking over at us chewing away, his simple face crumpled with curiosity.

"He was at the stockyard?"

Chess ignored him. "So, Danny says it's time to change how we do business around here. We and Falcone got common interests. We both want to make money, a lot of it, without too much fuss, including killing."

"So he did intend to go into business with Falcone."

"That's right. Create a syndicate for the whole northern state, both sides working together. Maybe even work our way into the 'Frisco market."

"Old man Cobb Carver isn't onboard with this, is he?"

"Old Cobb's been a happy pig in shit the past thirty years. A man ossifies as he gets older. Tomorrow's always gonna be like today. But his boy Danny thought different; he saw tomorrow comin'. Got me seein' it too."

"So he and Falcone set up a meeting for Friday night. Why didn't you go?"

"Falcone insisted it be just him and Danny, by the northwest corner of the ballpark."

"Where we found Danny. That was a trap."

Stetson's eyes narrowed. "We were supposed to be nearby, in case. But then Cobb suddenly calls us back for some bullshit about that prohi riot on San Pablo. But then he forgot what he wanted us to do and by the time we got back, well . . ."

"Even so, Falcone didn't kill Danny. I explained that already."

"Maybe." He sat back. "If we had known otherwise, we might never have attacked the slaughterhouse." He grinned. "And you'd still be there, probably ground into sausage at the rending plant. Or a hot dog in a bun with mustard at the ballpark."

"That's not funny!" I remembered how that hot dog had burst in my mouth, its peculiar-tasting juices trickling down my throat . . . and now the flavor returned, a moist, nauseating smoke ghost . . .

"Excuse me, I'm going to be sick."

Stetson yanked me out of the couch and back in the bathroom just in time. I staggered out a few minutes later feeling somewhat better, but barely.

"What, didn't he like my sandwich?" Buckram looked up unhappily as Stetson dropped me back in his precious couch and took his seat again. His face darkened, a punishing demon glaring through the smoke.

"After we run 'em off, we found that dead Chink in the office, blood everywhere." He reached down and pulled up my shoes, his long fingers hooked under the tongue. He turned them up so I could see the chess knight carved into both heels, a little worn, caked with gunk, probably from the blood I had stepped in, but still almost new. "We found a trail of bloody footprints made by these. They led to where we found our man lyin' in the stairwell with his neck broke."

"You mean Johnny?" Buckram looked up and over as he delicately patted his napkin on his mouth.

Stetson put the shoes down. He pulled my gold watch from his inside coat pocket, flipped it open to show me the loving inscription. "To my son, Paul . . ."

"This is your watch, inscribed to you. You didn't have it on you when we searched you in the kitchen yesterday morning. But you had it when we searched you today. That's because someone took it from you Friday night. Then you got it back after you run off last night. From the guy who took it from you the first time: Falcone. We knew someone else was at the slaughterhouse, but we didn't find him. That joker was you."

"He killed Johnny Pyle?" Buckram stood up, shaking in his flowery apron, tearing the napkin from around his neck, letting it fall to the floor. He took a step towards me, his pudgy fists clenching, his torn mouth stretching into a hideous grimace.

"It was an accident! I was dodging bullets, running for my life. We just ran into each other. I could've shot him with that gun I took off the Chinaman, but I didn't want to kill him. I got the first punch in. I never killed anyone before. I saw you coming and fell off the roof trying to escape." I was gasping. The air turned dark red and my head fell forward. I closed my eyes a minute, slowed my breathing.

Then suddenly a hand grabbed me by the hair. The roots stretched painfully as my head was pulled up. Stetson stared from a foot away. Buckram, right next to him, thrust his face at me. His scar looked like the twisted mouth of a hideous monster. A large bread knife trembled in his hand.

"Do we start on him now?" he asked his partner. "Let me go first."

Chapter 18

The Businessmen

Stetson released my hair and stepped back. Buckram lunged for my throat, his knife raised, but Stetson grabbed him when the blade was inches away, pulled him back and shoved him away.

"He killed Johnny Pyle!" Buckram spluttered, red with outrage, his neck almost pouring over his collar. "You promised we'd kill him slow!"

"Not this time."

Buckram backed away, quaking. "Goddamnit! God Jesus damnit!" Then he dropped the knife and stormed out in tears through the swinging door. The door banged back and forth, its spring hinges squeaking.

Stetson watched him go with a strangely tender look. But as he turned back, he became all hard sneers again. He glanced at the glowing ember in his pipe then at me, as though about to knock the ashes out in my eye.

"Am I done for?" I fought to maintain my dignity. Stetson would not kill me here, bloody his clean living room. I would die out in that chicken coop. Or at the slaughterhouse, where I would join the many sent to the rending plant. It would be hot dogs for me.

"That's up to you." Chess Stetson pulled out a pipe tool. "Don't like my boys gettin' killed." He tamped the coal down to get it burning as he puffed away. "For now I think he tripped. Call it the cost of business." He smiled grimly as he sat back down on his chair.

"Here's an idea to keep you alive: Evansville is the manufacturing center in these parts, churning out the goods for everyone around. But one thing they don't manufacture much of around here is brains. There was Danny. There's me." He winked and pointed his pipe at me. "But Danny's gone and now there's you. I like your mind, Bacon. You got a way of seeing things and a good way of talkin', though you talk a little too much and you're way too honest. But we can break you of that, like breakin' a horse. You're a lawyer, so—"

"Not yet I'm not."

"Close enough. That's all we need at this point. I'm tearing up the old offer and making you a new one."

I shrugged for him to go on.

"A sharpie like you is more useful over here than you are fartin' around in San Francisco. Over there, you're a shrimp, shark food. Over here, you'll be one of the sharks. Forget that two-bit blackmail we were pulling on you. This here's real business.

"Now, Falcone and I go back a ways. We ain't chums, but we ain't dumb. He now knows both of us, and I bet when he sees you and me together on that bridge he'll want to powwow. And once the parley's done, you work for the new combine. There's plenty of deal making to do, politicians, cops, businessmen who'll need stroking and greasing. There's unions and do-gooders that need to be brought into line or smacked down. You'll make a hundred times that chickenfeed you make haulin' the DA's water. Enough to buy your law license."

"And I'd be living here?"

"Of course," he said with a shrug. I marveled at how this shrewd thug seemed to think the whole world was one big Butchertown. "Just remember you work for me."

"What about Molly Carver?"

"What about her?"

"She's been part of this. She's no dummy, not at all. She agreed to the parley."

"Because the old man wants to stage his ambush and keep this war goin', so he can keep livin' the old way, that's why. She's just papa's girl. They're nowhere in this." He snorted. "The day women start runnin' things is the day we start flyin' to the moon."

We sat quietly. I was amused at being labeled "honest," an adjective that would have made Lou Wheeler—and many others—scoff. I understood his meaning, though—that I was legal, on the law's side, which, as I was still learning, did not mean the same as honest.

And to prove my dishonesty to myself, I kept quiet about the other game I knew was in play. Stetson was unaware I had run into Tag Carver again. For Lou's sake—I would not make her their quarry—I would leave Stetson in the dark on that. Even so, however, I needed to get an idea of his view of the matter.

"Molly told me there's another Carver around, a younger brother."

"Him?" He rocked back with mocking laughter. "Little Taggie Carver? What the hell's he got to do with anything?"

"He let me into the main house yesterday morning."

"Ah, he don't count." Stetson swatted an invisible fly. "Never did. Just a mama's boy, standing outside, crying for his candy. Too short for a man's pants." He grinned, toothy and hungry. "Nope, the Carvers are through. It'll be a whole new world. My mother's folks were Ohlone Indians; they lived here forever until my father's people ran them out. Then the Evans clan ran them off." He sniggered. "It'll be a homecoming."

"You fixing to bring back the grizzly bears?"

He laughed but did not answer. Maybe simple revenge would be enough. But for the Carvers, Chess Stetson liked how things were.

"If Cobb Carver wants to ambush Bat Falcone," I asked, "what's to stop him?"

He pointed his pipe stem confidently at himself. "I got more of the boys on my side than he has on his. Don't worry. I've got our backs covered."

"But what about Chief Wagmore and his elephant gun? Say, what if *he* was the one who killed Danny?" Stetson dismissed the notion, but I kept insisting. "That shotgun would do it. He shoved that thing right at me." I wiped my hands up over my face. "Boom."

"Wagmore *couldn't* hurt a fly. Flies are too fast and smart for the likes of him. Fat bastard won't fart without orders. He's out with the old guard." He looked incredulous. "You think old man Carver had his own golden boy rubbed out? Look, you only saw Danny in the dark. I saw him under lights."

"Meaning?"

"No shotgun slugs or pellets in him. No powder burns."

He let this hang in the air, leaving me to draw the conclusion.

"So, he wasn't shot. He was, what, hit with an ax?"

"We found a big sledgehammer near where he fell." He looked away, rubbing the stem of his pipe across his thin lips. "Or maybe it was Falcone with his baseball bat. When you met with Falcone, he had one, right?"

"But I heard the shotgun fire. Twice." I fought the smoking wooze in my belly. "I saw you carrying it."

"Yeah, the one I gave him to take to the meeting."

I recalled the sight of Buckram swinging a big something in the dark, not far from where Carver lay dead. And that big hammer in the utility room off the kitchen the next morning.

And there sat Chess Stetson, calm as a clam. Again, he walked into the scene so fast, like he had been lurking, watching, waiting to meet with Bat Falcone, once he had sent his boss into the Hereafter. But then along comes Molly and me, and suddenly he changes his plans, starts a war to deflect suspicion elsewhere, until he can get Falcone back to the table. Did that make sense? I was unsure. Nevertheless, Stetson was a man accustomed to war. To him it was something other than mindless slaughter.

Whatever the truth, my hands were tied in both senses. What else could I do but agree to be a biggish frog in this small, bloody waste pond? I pretty much knew the answer to no—hot dogs made with Bacon. I would pretend to agree for now, as I had for everything, try to stay alive until my escape.

"I'll be your lawyer then. I could use the money."

Outside, the fog was darkening. True night was falling. I suggested they turn on some lights. "They blew up the power station last night," Stetson replied. Then he barked over his shoulder, "Bucky! Candles!"

Buckram reentered moments later, apron off now, cradling both stick and votive candles in his hands. A soft orange-and-yellow glow suffused the room as he lit them all, completely ignoring me. Strange to say, his silence made me feel bad. Stetson checked my watch and murmured, "Six fifteen. Hour and a half or so." He leaned over and, with a wink, dropped the watch into my shirt pocket.

Suddenly a doorbell buzzed. Stetson drew his pistol from his shoulder holster, nodded at Buckram. Buckram hurried out of the room, grabbing a .45 from a table by the door, as Stetson took his position behind it. A half minute later Buckram returned. "Colored boy says it's all set. Old man Carver's shut down."

Stetson told me to get some rest, so I did, fluttering in and out of a doze. As I attempted to nap, Stetson and Buckram sat at the corner of the long table playing canasta. As they snapped their cards on the table, their bewhiskered edges softened. They were no longer a couple of tough mugs but more like everyone else. They chatted and bickered, as my grandparents did when they played cards on rainy summer weekends on the back porch in their house near Peekskill, a world I yearned to escape because it seemed so boring.

At one point I opened my eyes to see Stetson reach over and forgivingly pat Buckram on the forearm over some confusion about the rules. He left his hand there, squeezing his buddy's arm. Another glittering look passed between them. Again I noticed how fussed over the living room was and Buckram's pretty apron and one of Carver's soldiers growling, "He wants to talk to the ferry buoy." Clearly, I had misheard.

Oh brother . . . I pulled my eyelids shut.

Much too soon Stetson's big hand shook me awake. He let me put on my guilty shoes. Buckram bluntly turned his back as his friend motioned for him to help me out of the couch.

"What's with you?" Stetson asked.

"Nothin'. Thought he was one of the good guys, that's all."

Chapter 19

Come Walk with Me

Just before we went out the door, Chess Stetson untied my hands without comment. We stepped outside into smoky black air. Buckram led the way with an electric torch.

"You like it?" Chess Stetson asked. I was looking at the machine gun he was setting carefully in the backseat of the Ford. He handed it to me, his eyes gleaming. It was compactly made and surprisingly heavy.

"It's a Thompson. Just started makin' 'em last year. Danny boy brought it back from New York. That round part's the drum magazine. Heavy bastard, eh? That's why there's no recoil. Holds fifty rounds; fires 'em all in thirty seconds. Wish I had one in France. Beautiful!"

"Yeah, that's sure nice." I handed it back. He set it tenderly by my feet, as though it were a baby. I quietly moved the barrel so it pointed away from me.

With the electric power out throughout the neighborhood, we had only car lamps and the smokestack in the distance to light the way. Windblown trash rolled like tumbleweed through the lights of our headlamps. My eyes itched from the blowing dust. My mouth turned to dry cake.

We passed the shadow of an empty stadium that, Stetson said, had once been a dog track, built by the lemon growers over an Indian burial ground. It also contained a dance pavilion, likely the one to which Molly was taking me Friday night. The facility was going to be torn down soon. In the years since the meat packers and factories moved in and gambling had been outlawed statewide, attendance had declined, as it had at the horse tracks.

"They'll build another factory," Stetson said. "Make more dough than they do with that hoochie-cooch dog hall. We'll be here for 'em. You can help broker the deal."

As we approached the center of Butchertown, my sinuses swelled, my breath grew short and my chest started to ache. I burst into fits of coughing.

"We got used to it. You will too."

"Shoulda wore our gas masks," Buckram said.

Hazy blobs of yellow light appeared through my oily tears. They came from a long row of cars lined up facing us on both sides of the street. Stetson tapped the brakes as more lights appeared, flaming torches made from stinking pitch tar. We crept to a stop. An enormous touring car blocked our way. Stetson and Buckram swapped looks. I read them well enough by now that I caught their sudden unease like a cold. I looked behind to see another car coming up behind.

"Son of a bitch." Stetson reached behind and grabbed the machine gun. "You sure the boy said it was clear?"

"Yeah, told me himself." Buckram shook his head, his muddy voice shaking. "That's what he said, I swear."

Things were set all right, just not the way Chess Stetson assumed. I recalled wisdom Uncle Lloyd dispensed after we both walked out of my first poker game with our pockets empty: "'Assume'" is just another word for making an ass out of you and me."

A half-dozen gunmen marched towards the car. Stetson and Buckram slowly got out. I joined them with my hands up.

Stetson glanced at me. "Get ready to duck and run."

"Where to?"

Soon a familiar figure came limping down the center of the gauntlet—Cobb Carver, leaning on a shiny wood cane. Molly Carver, still in her brown business suit, guided him on his left, firmly clasping his upper arm, whispering into his ear. She stopped talking as they drew near. She adjusted the large leather purse strapped across her breast. Cobb's mouth hung half-open. His face looked puffier, the lumps from yesterday morning covered by more swelling. His eyes gleamed hatefully when he saw me. Only my bloody death could heal the raw humiliation I had heaped on him. I tried to act nonchalant, folding my hands in front of me with Richard Hannay aplomb, rested up and ready to leap from my corner for another round.

Then I got a sharp poke in the spine from a gun barrel. Three more of Cobb's gunmen stood behind us. Chief Wagmore lumbered up on Molly's left, his elephant gun sliding towards my face. Regardless of Stetson's contempt, there was always a first time for a guy like him.

"We oughta to get closer to—" Stetson began.

"This is as close as you get, Stetson," Carver growled. "You gunsels are stayin' put. We took your chums out. My men are all over you, you dumb freak. There won't be no powwow." He grinned. "That's what you get for takin' a nigger boy's word. He knows who's master of this plantation."

Stetson nodded at Molly. "She gave the order to—"

"She said what I told her to." Molly lifted her chin, her eyes narrow with feline pride. "I knew we'd catch you at somethin'. Goddamn traitor, like Danny, sellin' us out. My own boy. Sellin' everything I built to some goddamn spic."

Then he looked at me again, rising on his toes, breathing faster. "But first. This one. He . . ." He could barely remember who I was and what I had done. He only remembered that I was an itch that needed scratching out.

"Kill him now." Cobb Carver nodded at Wagmore. My knees went rubbery, my facial muscles cramped up as that steel black tube moved towards me. The gun shook in Wagmore's big sweaty hands.

What I did next either might have gotten me killed or hauled away in a straitjacket, but honestly, I was at the end of my tether, was sick of being pushed around, tired of having guns shoved in my face by crooks too dumb to know where the sun came up.

I knocked the shotgun barrel aside. Wagmore, used to throwing his massive weight around unchallenged, was completely taken aback. We struggled. And then the gun exploded. My eardrums caved in. The gun flew from both our hands. Wagmore staggered away as it clattered on the ground, right at my feet. I reached for it but was abruptly yanked back. It was Chess Stetson, quietly shaking his head, his lips pursed in warning: Not now.

He was right of course. Guns were closing in from all around.

"Stop it! Now!" It was Molly, openly interceding as she stepped up to me, the Luger in her hand. Behind her, her father drooped like a heavy old coat on a hook.

"We can make better use of him." She looked at her father. "Send him out on the bridge to draw their fire, all right?"

Oh Lord, this again: *Let's stab him. No, let's shoot him. No, let's put him in the frying pan. No, let's throw him in the fire . . .*

A tiny smile cracked Cobb's tomato face. This idea he liked.

"Chief, are the others ready?" Molly asked.

"All ready," Wagmore called over his shoulder, his voice quaking. His enormous gun was now back in his massive hands, but now he looked small and dim.

"You and me will walk Bacon here to the bridge," she said.

"Danny! Danny, don't go! Stay with me, son! I'm tellin' ya, you can't trust nobody." Cobb watched with constipated distress. Molly glanced around to see if anyone had noticed his confusion, but only Wagmore's slab face showed any awareness.

"He'll pay, I promise." Molly pointed the Luger at me. "The rest of you stay alert." She shot Stetson a hard look. "If Stetson makes a move, kill him. Otherwise, wait until I give orders or you hear shooting. You two follow us," she added, nodding at a couple of others. Wagmore stepped back and waved the gun to his left. I glanced at Stetson.

"Guess I'll see you on the moon."

He did not respond. To him we were already dead.

I walked a few steps ahead of Molly and Wagmore, my feet dragging as they did in dreams of sinking ships. Every second took a minute, every minute an hour. Wagmore's heavy breathing blew me along like a bellows from Hell.

"You sure about this, Miss Carver?" he asked. Molly shushed him. I glanced back the two gunmen following. "Keep walking," Molly snapped.

The street narrowed, the buildings closed in and the fumes thickened to spongy mist. The bridge appeared through red-brown air. It was a skeletal open-truss bridge, nearly a hundred feet long, plastered with "No Smoking" signs. Barely wide enough for two trucks, it faded into a mass of rusted fog on the far side. Gasoline Creek gurgled underneath, its banks dug out to create a wider, deeper channel to carry thick oily seepage out to the bay, the effluent that had laid that carpet of dead fish I had seen on the boat over. The smokestack disappeared up into fog, its fuzzy tongue of orange flame floating above. Trains chugged nearby. The foghorns called.

One match could set the air afire. I had tended to burn casualties on the hospital ships, had once pulled some from a sinking vessel. I now wished Wagmore had shot me after all.

As we stepped onto a plane of iron plates, Molly turned to Wagmore. "Wait here. Keep watch."

"Miss Carver," Wagmore protested, but she ignored him as she waved the Luger at me, herding me forward. The two of us walked alone onto the bridge.

"Are you going to shoot me yourself instead? Why? What have I done to you?"

"Paul, you're a goddamn fool."

"Yeah, I've had that thought a million times the last couple days. You know, it's funny; you don't miss your poor dead brother much. All that screaming you did over his body. You weren't grieving, not at all. You were just mad. Out of everyone I've met around here, your little brother is the only one who's shed a tear for him."

"So you've talked to the baby. What does he know? Nothing. Like every man I've ever known."

"This lousy air makes us all stupid." I paused. "Your brother was just another dummy like the rest of us. Is that what you mean? A chump to be kicked out of the way?"

"You think I killed my brother? You were with me when I found him."

"Yeah, you didn't swing the hammer, but maybe someone swung it for you. You and your pops and Chess Stetson are at each other's throats now, but maybe you were allies before Friday night. Maybe you didn't expect him to wind up dead, but maybe you wanted him out of the—"

"Oh shut up, Paul. You don't know what you're talking about. We have bigger things on our plate. Stop here."

We had reached the middle of the bridge.

"Just remember there's nowhere to run." Molly dug deep into her big purse and withdrew from its depths a large white cloth like a beach towel. It looked fabulously clean, almost glowing like phosphorous.

"What are you doing?"

"Still think I'm a dumb broad? That plan of Stetson's, where he negotiates with Falcone? That's my plan now. You're negotiating for me, Paul."

"What's your father going to say? He's expecting some big glorious shoot-out."

"He's losing his mind, you see that. There'll be no more gunplay. There's no profit in it, not for us, not for Falcone. If we work this out right, the men will do as I say. Once the deal is set and the dough rolls in, I'll be wearing the pants around town. I won't have to choose between being a drunken spinster or one of the whores next door. It'll be my town, like it was my grandfather's. Like it should have been my mother's. It'll be Evansville like it was. No one will ever call it Butchertown ever again.

"Play your cards right, Paul darling, and you could be a big man here." She gave me that sly, seductive, gamine smile, same as the night we first met, her eyelashes fluttering. "Maybe I'll even keep that promise I made; finish what we started, you know? I'll be more than good to you."

"Sounds like the air's getting to you, too." I rolled my eyes, shook my head. *What some people think of themselves*, as my mother used to say.

She snarled at me but then calmed herself and told me what to say to Falcone, an opening offer that resembled Stetson's, but with the proportions more generous to her side. Whether she cooked the deal up herself or stole it from Stetson, she proved she had the brains for this business, if not the status. Stetson had sold her short, as I had in my own way.

"Are you ready?" Molly started waving the white cloth back and forth, called out to Bat Falcone. She glanced at me. "Go on. Call him."

I cupped my hands around my mouth and shouted, my voice rapidly becoming tattered by the smutty air. We stopped, listened, then called out again, Molly waving the white flag. Stopping to cough, I tried checking my watch in the gloom.

"We might be a little—"

And then suddenly a voice pierced the fog like a golden lance, a voice in song, growing louder and closer, sweet and low and wine dark. I knew the song well.

... gather at the river!
Where bright angel feet have trod
With its crystal tide forever
Flowing by the throne of God?

A tiny point of light floated towards us, swinging low to the ground, to the beat of the hymn. The voice grew louder and the light clearer.

Yes, we'll gather at the river
The beautiful, the beautiful river ... !

Chapter 20

Shoot-out at Gasoline Creek

Lou Wheeler marched out on the bridge, stepping high to the beat of the hymn. Her flat hat was gone, her long hair loose and wild. An electric lantern swung from one hand, while a New Testament lay clutched in the other. Her crucifix shone brightly on her breast. She held her chin up, eyes half-closed. Her burgundy voice chimed like a bell.

And she was marching alone.

"Who the hell . . . ?" Molly waved and called out to the rear. "Hold it! Don't shoot!"

I leaned towards Molly, my voice low. "Louise Wheeler. She's betrothed to your little brother. This is the voice of God joining us at the table."

I peered into the clouds behind Lou. Tag Carver had to be nearby, hanging back, preparing some kind of savior's entrance, following Joan the Baptist.

But the hymn drew to a close and Tag did not appear. Nor did Lou seem surprised. What did make her gape was seeing me there.

"Who are you? Where's my goddamn brother?"

Lou ignored Molly's question. With trembling hands, she raised the crucifix over her head, shook the lanyard free from around her neck. Eyes closed, she lifted both cross and New Testament in supplication.

"In the name of the Lord, the Holy Ghost and the Son Jesus Christ. Wherever we gather, wherever we pray, you, Our Lord, are there with us. Through us, shine the light of your Love on this bedeviled world and take the poison cup of sin from their lips and bestow the wine of Heaven! Make them they lay down their arms, bury their hatreds as we bury the dead, turn their faces from drunken darkness to clear, sober light, to Your Love and Grace! For the Love and Grace of Jesus, to the peace of God and the breath of the Holy Spirit! Save them all, we pray . . ."

Then, as though in answer, lights burst from the far side of the bridge. A car engine growled. Bat Falcone's Pierce-Arrow rolled into view. As it lumbered onto the bridge, the plates rumbling under the tires, a dozen men wearing long coats and hats crept in behind in a line, sweeping their guns all around, their faces a blur.

Molly lost all interest in Lou, frantically waving her flag of truce as she walked past us towards the car. I sensed Wagmore's elephantine presence from behind.

" . . . to Christ our Lord. Amen." Lou finished her lonely prayer with a cough and looked behind her, then at me, her eyes wide. Before she could say another word, I leaned in.

"Where in hell is your dearly beloved?"

"He couldn't make it."

"Couldn't make it!?" I gnashed my teeth, my mind ablaze with a vision of Tag Carver's eyes protruding from their sockets as his windpipe crumpled under my bare hands. "What the hell kind of excuse is—?"

"He's hurt! Badly! I told you, remember? He started choking on this foul air. He's too weak to go on. I could, so I left him at the car. He's got somebody with him."

"I don't give a damn about that. He let you walk out here alone?"

She lifted her chin. "He couldn't stop me."

I grabbed her arm. "Lou, this isn't the answer to your prayers. These people think you're a lunatic. This is suicide."

"It's a sacrifice. You really think this world is sane?"

I pulled her closer. "Please, Lou. I don't want you to die, not in this manure pile. Listen. I loved you once long ago and I love you now." Then I added, "This won't get your baby back. He'll lose his mother for sure."

She struggled, spitting viciously. "You dirty son of a bitch—"

"Hey!" Wagmore's shotgun barrel poked between us, breaking us apart. "You're wanted, punk."

Molly was waving her flag at me from up ahead. A large familiar figure waited nearby. I heard my name called and so turned away from what I wanted to what I needed, to yet another agenda not my own. As I walked away, Lou raised her voice again.

Deep River, my home is over Jordan,
Deep River, Lord, I want to cross into camp-ground . . .

Molly lowered her flag as I approached. Bat Falcone had left his cigar behind. He was leaning on his prized ball bat with one hand, while the other was tucked in the pocket of his topcoat, where, no doubt, there was a gun. In a few short hours his wine-grower's rural elegance had wilted. His eyes were hollow and lugged heavy baggage underneath. His high fine mane had spilled in a lanky mess over his forehead. Even his beard showed streaks of gray. And he was not happy to see me.

"You again?" He pursed his lips, devoid of the benevolent amusement he had shown me earlier. I suspected the air had got to him, too. I had also run away and now had returned, rejoined with the other side. Both Stetson's and Molly's confidence in his trust for me had been misplaced. To Falcone, a man of honor, I was a mere opportunist.

"My man Gradus cannot walk thanks to you. And Maurizio limps badly now. If he were a horse, I would shoot him." He lifted the baseball bat in the air, studying it closely. "Perhaps vengeance would be served if I slammed this across your head, no? Maybe I will let Maurizio have the honor. After we're done here."

Molly started to speak, but Falcone cut her off with a hard tap of his bat on the iron roadbed.

"And now a girl in a man's clothes stands before me, as though she were the man; as though that were all the respect I deserve. Not even a princeling. A princess. From what Bacon says, with Danny Carver dead and the papa a sick old man, I suppose there is no help for it; however, if this is as much as you can muster, maybe I should go ahead and shoot down every one of you." He turned to wave behind him. "Do you play chess?"

Two men appeared out of the fog, dragging a third man, his head dangling, between them, his shoe tips stuttering across the roadbed. Behind them another soldier appeared from around the rear of the car, small, compact, and limping a little. Unlike the others, he was hatless. His face was a smudge in the gloom as he stopped behind another of Falcone's men, next to the car. I felt his eyes piercing me. Maurizio. I had added injury and humiliation to his grief, and now he was here to hack his pound of flesh from my hide.

The two men flung the man they were carrying down onto the roadbed in front of us. He groaned as he rolled on his back, his arms and legs spread-eagling. His grubby clothes identified him as a Carver man. Falcone walked up to him, put the tip of the baseball bat by his head and turned his face to us. It had been beaten to bloody pulp. Not as complete as the damage done to Danny Carver, but close enough.

Molly and I stood still as Falcone kept talking.

"If you play chess, you know it is countermove after countermove after countermove. You circle around behind me, I circle around behind you, and so on. Until what?"

Then he stepped back, raised the baseball bat high over his head. I shut my eyes as he slammed it down to crush the head of the man on the ground. The poor soul cried out. Then again and again. The man fell silent for good. Molly swayed and fell against me.

"One of us runs out of men." I opened my eyes. Bat Falcone was studying his baseball bat, now stained with blood. He inhaled a deep, angry breath as he lowered the bat, then burst into a fit of coughing. He stopped with his hand over his chest. "You will run out of soldiers, but I will not. You are outflanked. What pawns do you have left to play, pretty miss?" He sneered at me. "This one? He talks out both sides of his mouth."

It was time to step up regardless. I strode forward, snapping a bow, as though paying tribute to a deck officer.

"Signor Falcone."

"Careful with that large mouth of yours, *bimbo*."

"Please let me explain." I raised my palm, speaking in a tone of utmost respect, as I knew he expected, even as he doubted me. "I won't deny I've been trying to save my own hide, but maybe by saving my neck I may save many more, including those of your men, of which you've lost many in this unfortunate misunderstanding."

"Misunderstanding?" Falcone cackled. "I am attacked for a crime I did not commit. Nearly a dozen of my men lie dead and injured, including two by your hand, Bacon. This you call a 'misunderstanding'? This humiliation? This injustice? Further, I do not like this fence hopping of yours." He waved his hand at his mouth. "Which of your two mouths chatters now? Who exactly are you trying to save besides yourself? This hag?"

The air was taut with rage. Behind me, Lou was now singing "There Is a Balm in Gilead," her voice making the very fog shiver and brighten. Molly turned and yelled for her to shut the hell up, but Lou kept on without breaking.

Bat Falcone, meanwhile, had raised his face, listening, his eyes turning sad. "That is a lovely song, like something Negroes sing. *Mio dio*, you brought Lord Jesus with you into this Hell?" He shook his head.

"As I'm sure you know, Our Lord went to Hell for three days following His crucifixion and led the damned out through the gates," I said. Then I shrugged. "Hey! Music soothes the savage beast!"

At last Bat Falcone smiled a little and nodded. Then he turned grim again.

"Their fingers are on their triggers. Your last chance, Signor Bacon. Your words had better be sound and true."

"Please understand, sir, we must dance with the one who brings us. But maybe I can get the two of you to dance together, if you'll pardon the expression. It will bring peace and profit to both sides. There needn't be any more war."

"Peace is in everyone's interest, including yours," Falcone replied. "Only a fool wants to rule over an ash pile. We all know you're no fool. And Miss Carver is fully aware of what is at stake."

"And the Carvers have also lost many men. And some of their women—the whores I mean. They bleed and cry, as you and yours do. Am I right, Molly?" Molly nodded. "This woman's brother, Danny Carver, their boss, your equal, the man you were supposed to meet Friday night, was the first to fall."

"I had nothing to do with that!"

I tried to ignore the dead man at our feet, with his head crushed like a melon. I no longer believed Falcone on that, not after what he had done. But if he insisted on keeping up this front, I had to keep slathering the butter.

"You can understand their hasty reaction, though they were terribly mistaken, can't you? You are a man who understands another man's heart. But we all know now that you were completely innocent."

"I accept," Molly said slowly, her mouth churning as though filled with old pennies, "that you didn't murder my brother. We're really sorry for everything that's happened."

"So you're sorry. Whose tears does that dry? Since when does 'sorry' bring anyone back from the grave?"

"No one but the ghosts," I admitted. "But why send more living souls to join the dead? We must get on with things. There's still life to be lived. You have a home and family awaiting you. You came here for business reasons, because there's money to be made and it's a gateway to other markets for the booze, wine and other services you bring in from the north, services that many, many people want. You personally came here because the Carvers were blocking your way. You came to do business, not to fight a war. So let's get down to business."

"No, I did not come here to die stupidly."

"We won't block your way anymore," Molly said. "But we ourselves want to survive and prosper. In fact, we're proposing a partnership with you."

Falcone glared at her feminine effrontery, but I went on. "What's called a syndicate. I recall you said you were thinking of negotiating with the Carvers before all this." I briefly related what Stetson had told me about Danny Carver's trip east. "That's what he wanted to talk about. That will be the future, a future that will arrive soon. You haven't been able to sell in the markets to the south and east of here. The Carvers can help you enter that market before the Easterners grab it. They can also make inroads into San Francisco that you haven't been able to. Because they are small, no one notices them."

"The tiny mouse moves into the house the big rat cannot."

"That's right." I laughed. "Everything that's made for the Bay Area is made here, or comes through here, booze included. Every other city along the bay is a dry town, except San Francisco and here, and that's why Butcher—Evansville—matters. It's valuable to the both of you, and you should share it without spilling any more blood. This world may be small, but there's enough for all, even for a great man of great appetites such as you, sir."

"You flatter me!" Falcone laughed. He nodded at Molly. "What are the terms?"

I laid out the terms as Molly ordered. I feared he would walk away when I mentioned the percentages and was relieved when he did not. Instead he flipped them.

"No, seventy-five for me, twenty-five for them." He shook his head, wiped his face in growing discomfort. He broke out in another fit of coughing.

"How about fifty-fifty? Divide it up on a territorial basis," I coughed back. Beads of oil trickled down my throat. I wanted to get this over with before we all asphyxiated. I glanced at Molly, who now had the white towel over her mouth. I understood why the Carvers had chosen this spot: they were used to the climate and could stand it longer while watching their opponents cave in. Behind us, Lou's voice had started to crumble as she struggled to breathe.

Meanwhile, Maurizio, behind and to Falcone's right, raised his finger, as though preparing to object. *Please not now*, I begged silently.

"Look, might I suggest we continue this someplace where the air is breathable?"

"Really? The air is bad?" Falcone japed. "I thought I was inhaling tulips!" Jolly sarcasm showed through his discomfort. He nodded past us. "Perhaps the young singer could guide us out of this Hell with her lovely voice. It is good to have God with us." Then he looked at the body at his feet. With a regretful sigh, he made the sign of the cross, murmuring.

I started to feel optimistic myself. I turned to Molly, asked if we could get into the Oaks ballpark and talk there. She agreed with a sigh of relief. Both parties seemed to relax. The gamble had worked and I had made it work. Falcone turned behind him, raising his arm, waving his hand downward for his men to lower their guns. And so they did.

Except for Maurizio. His finger remained raised in dissent. As though to emphasize his point, he pointed it at the back of the neck of the henchman in front of him. A tongue of flame darted out from the finger. The air cracked. The henchman's head jerked forward. His knees buckled as he fired his BAR into the iron road bedding.

And so the peace ended. The air exploded with gunfire. I turned and tackled Molly, knocked her to the iron roadbed, covered her with my body. Bullets zipped and spanged all around. I curled up to make us both look like rag piles.

A huge boom erupted, shaking my skull. I glimpsed one of Falcone's men break in two, top and bottom splitting apart in a burst of gore, while another man behind him spun like a top, his long coat tails whirling like a skirt. Bat Falcone screamed orders from behind his car, which rocked under gunfire as its window glass shattered and bullets perforated the skin, making a sound like hammers on a muted xylophone. Under the gunfire and zipping bullets came shouting, screaming, crying.

I looked behind: Chief Wagmore was wrestling with his elephant gun, his tubby body lumbering about as bullets peppered him, raising puffs of black liquid dust. His fat bulletproofed him enough to let him stay on his feet for a while. Groaning, he slowly sat down, before one of his eyes spouted black and he slumped over on his back. Another Carver man ran from the darkness, waving a pistol. As he reached Wagmore, he slowly dove to the pavement, as though ducking under the fire, and lay still without having fired a shot.

More of Falcone's men emerged from the fog, raking the air with bullets, implacable, unstoppable. I was done for, I thought, but as I prepared for the end, there came a staccato rattle like a typewriter. One of Falcone's men slumped right, while another crumpled left, while a third danced like a string puppet before toppling on his face.

I looked back to see four gunmen emerge from the other side, spread out in a wide line: Chess Stetson with his Thompson, and Buckram with his BAR flanked the ends. The two in the middle also lugged BARs, their fingers locked to the triggers. They marched through the gun smoke, their weapons chattering, the gun barrels spurting fire with a cascading roar.

Three more of Falcone's men slumped. The rest retreated. As Stetson and his men drew even with us, it seemed time for Molly and me to get up and run.

But as we got to our feet, the air around us turned hot umber. To the east a couple hundred feet up the creek, a large tongue of flame leapt up into black air. Gasoline Creek had caught fire. The fast, strong current was carrying flames down the creek. Towards the bridge. Straight for us.

Tall as she was, Molly felt light as a feather and limp as an eel as I lifted her under my right arm and ran past Stetson, hollering out that the creek was on fire. I think he snapped me a *you're crazy* stare before quickly seeing my point. A few steps on I came across another lump on the ground, to my left. I reached down, pulled up Lou Wheeler. Our eyes met in the glow of the gathering fire. She looked as frightened as I felt.

I did not have to carry Lou; she willingly ran alongside as the heat of the approaching maelstrom swept over us, so bright I could see our frantic shadows melted into a shambling six-legged beast. Molly struggled and kicked, shouting for me to let go. I hung on until I felt the road soften under my feet. We were off the bridge. My grip on Molly slipped, and she was gone like a ghost through the smoke. I could run faster now. Lou stayed right with me.

The gunfire started to die down. Foolishly, maybe due to our exhaustion, Lou and I stopped to watch. A stray bullet plucked at my sleeve and we hit the dirt again as Bat Falcone's men counterattacked. One of Stetson's boys straightened up as his fedora popped up, blown into the air by a dark fountain erupting from his head. The other fellow crumpled where he stood. Stetson and Buckram retreated, angling off in opposite directions as four more of Falcone's men retook the bridge, marching to the middle.

Right in time to be caught by the towering flames rushing down Gasoline Creek, sweeping over the bridge.

Falcone's men froze in baffled terror, looking about, wondering where all the fire came from. The inferno consumed them, their screams and shrieks followed by pops from exploding ammunition. I heard an explosion: the gas tank in Bat Falcone's car. The air was scorching, the ground under us burning as oily smoke choked our raw throats.

The flames roared on down the creek towards the bay, waving in the sky like a foxtail, bathing the buildings all around in red light. Stetson and Buckram had vanished. Lou and I got up and ran as fast and far away as our feet would carry us.

Chapter 21

Pestilence

We ran until we could breathe without coughing, with handkerchiefs masking our faces, as we stumbled over ruins and tarmac, stepped in potholes, fell, got up and staggered on.

Finally, we could breathe again, though barely. We collapsed at an intersection of a nameless street and a dead-end alley. My lungs felt scorched. Every nerve and knuckle throbbed and the sound of bullets on steel echoed through my brain. Oily tears flooded my eyes. I had never felt so dirty. I wanted to keep running all the way back east. But I was stuck here. Stuck in Butchertown.

Lou crumpled beside me, a hand over her breast as her coughing subsided. Her runny eyes were half-closed, her mouth open, her skin running with sweat.

To the west, smoke had buried the smokestack and its guiding light. The creek fire was dying down as it flowed to the bay. The west wind had picked up, driving and spreading toxic smoke over the flatlands, up the hills. The sky was a clotted black.

"What happened out there?" Lou asked. "What did you *do*?"

"Me? I did what I was supposed to. I had them ready to make a deal. Then one of Falcone's guys comes out, shoots one of his own—goddamnit, no that can't be." I buried my head in my arms to think. "It had to be one of Cobb Carver's boys. He must have snuck through, missed the order to hold fire. Or disobeyed it."

"They're criminals, Paul. Devils and thugs. Who knows why they do—?"

"I don't give a damn anymore either. I'm through with this. I've been through with it since Friday night." I struggled to my feet. "And you should be, too. Come on. We're going."

I helped her up with new vigor. She pulled away as I tried to pull her close.

"We have to—"

"We're going, Miss Wheeler. There's nothing left for us to do in this Hell. There wasn't anything in the first place. We're leaving this shithole and calling the army in to straighten this out. That's all."

"We can't leave yet. *I* can't leave. Not without Tag."

I rolled my eyes. Oh. *Him.*

"He's waiting on the other side of the creek. He's injured, Paul. Seriously. I'm sure he's suffering. I persuaded him to come here and I can't leave him behind. Not again."

"We're gonna walk back through all that? We'll choke before we get there."

"We'll pray that it clears. Try to remember you were Christian once."

"Upon a time." I kicked a stone across the ground. "You should have taken him right to a doctor instead. Do you still have your lamp?"

She mumbled yes. Her hands rustled in her skirt. Something clattered on the ground, hit me in the foot. I bent down, scooped it up, found the switch, clicked it on. A yellow pool of light appeared on the broken ground.

She reached for the lamp, but I pulled away. "I've got it."

I aimed the light in what seemed to be a southwest direction and started out. But soon I realized I was alone. I turned the light back to find her standing where I had left her, fists bunched at her side, chin up, face ablaze, her hair wild and free with defiant abandon.

"You go on ahead then, Paul Bacon. I'll find him with or without a light. The Light of the Lord will lead me there."

She also knew I would not leave her there, would not let her go alone, damn her. I returned, waving the light about. Her eyes widened as I grew close.

"All right then. Which way? Let's get a move—"

"Paul, you're hurt!"

I winced as she touched the side of my head, caked with blood from a furrow dug by a passing bullet. Her fingertips felt warm and tender.

"You need that tended to. And your clothes!"

"It's okay. They're not mine anyway. I'm all right for now."

"There's first aid at the car."

"All the more reason to hurry. Lead on, mam'selle."

"We have to get to Adelyne, where we drove you yesterday, and go north."

We walked side by side, the light at our feet, picking our way over broken ground. We tried to hurry, but we could not hasten much, lest we fall. The black wind moaned monotonously all around.

"What the hell's wrong?" I said half to myself. "Every time both sides try to hash things out, something goes off and they're at it again. It makes no sense."

"This is Hell, Paul. Hell is not supposed to make sense, like Tag said." Her face was invisible, her tone plain and strong. "You think we're naïve? What did you expect from them? Killing, bootlegging, stealing and more killing: that's what they do, and what they do is who they are. That's all they do. Only God can save them from their depravity."

"They didn't exactly fall to their knees at your command out there, did they? Doesn't sound like God's got your back either." She became very still. I had offended her again. I also recalled how Bat Falcone beamed as she sang. But I let that issue fall.

"I'm not talking about our sense; I mean their sense. Money sense. Bat Falcone, Molly Carver, Chess Stetson. They're business types. They don't yearn for nature's green. It's money green they want. They live for what they believe is easy money. They even got big plans. It looks a rotten life to us, but it's theirs and damn the rest. So long as they're at war, they won't make a dime. Both sides know it. They want to deal. It may not be God's peace—"

"You're taking their side."

"I'm trying to understand how they think so I can figure out what's going on. That's not the same thing. Their peace is a place to start, God or no God.

"It's the peace of Hell and damnation. And you should be ashamed to be part of it."

I ignored her and kept talking. "The whole time I'm thinking I'm a duck caught between two warring sides. But maybe there's three sides to this, another party sticking its hand in. The one who gunned down Falcone's man on the bridge? He wasn't Falcone's. And somehow I don't think he was Carver's. He was from the side that doesn't want peace. That's where your evil is coming from." I slowed down further, almost stopping.

"And it all started with the murder of Danny Carver. Your fiancé's brother."

"By Bat Falcone."

"Uh-uh—"

"He beat a man to death on the bridge. I heard it. You saw it."

"It wasn't the same. I saw Danny Carver's face, or what was left of it, which was nothing. It took more than a ball bat to do that much damage. I first thought it was a big-bore shotgun, like that elephant gun that fatso cop had. But Chess Stetson saw Carver's body, too."

"That devil we saw pick you up outside the alley this afternoon—"

"Yeah, him. Say, I apologize for not coming back—"

"I understand." She touched my arm. "We came out to check on you and saw them take you away."

"Stetson said Danny Carver wasn't killed by a gun. His face was caved in by a big heavy object."

"That doesn't make Falcone innocent."

"But you don't know the whole story of what happened after Molly and I found the body." I repeated my kidnapping story, this time telling it true all the way through—I even confessed about poor Johnny Pyle. And she reacted as I feared she would, shrinking away, putting me even farther beyond salvation. But I pressed my case.

"The point is someone else murdered Danny Carver. And that's not all. You remember that gunfight last evening, Saturday?"

"We didn't believe you. At least Tag said he didn't."

"You were in town. You must've heard the shooting."

"I drove into Oakland in the late afternoon, picking up supplies. We needed food, water, bandages, things like that."

"Alone? Without calling the police?"

"Of course not! The police are useless. When I got back, Tag said there'd been some shooting but nothing serious. That's what he told me."

"Nothing serious?" My temper boiled over. "I was right in the middle of the goddamn thing! They threw hand grenades for chrissakes! The first man died right in front of me, fell right in front of the basement window. The killer walked right past me."

"Listen, can we not talk about this? Especially if you insist on cursing. You said it was out of our hands anyway."

"But I can't get it out of my head. You said something out there on the bridge."

"So did you. I hope you weren't serious."

"You said Tag had someone with him. Who?"

"The Negro boy."

"The kid who works around the Carver house?"

"I guess so. I don't really know."

"You know his name?"

"No. I see Tag talking with him, but they don't include me."

"Tag somehow knew I was a go-between for Falcone and the Carvers. The boy's been hanging around whenever I've been there. Like a spy. Something else bothers me. Stetson said he was going to take over the gang. It was supposed to be the two of us out on the bridge there palavering with Falcone. The boy was spying for Stetson. He said it was 'all set,' meaning, I think, that Cobb and Molly Carver had been pushed out of the way. Instead, when we got near the bridge, Molly and her pops sprung the trap on us. Stetson was the one who got set up. That fixed it so Molly and I were walking out there."

Lou did not reply as my thoughts whirled inside my head and out my mouth.

" 'Colored boy says it's all set.' Then Cobb Carver says later, 'That's what you get for takin' a nigger boy's word.' You know that boy has a quiet way about him, hanging like a plain curtain, then he's gone. You know many Negroes?"

"No, I don't. I see them around missions and flophouses, but they stay apart. We try to serve everyone, but they have their own missions."

I didn't know many either. I saw them clean up the golf courses, work as maids and servants for my father's wealthy parishioners. I saw them pushing brooms, working as jockeys and grooms at the horse track. Sometimes I wondered what they did after work and what their lives were like. I had read about the Civil War in school and about the lynchings and burnings in the papers. Even those who came back from the war wearing medals. Decorated war heroes who fought for their country, murdered just for walking around. You want to talk about evil? "Vile" is what my father called it. "Poor human judgment allowing the Devil's hatreds to stand in the place of God's love and justice. Never let it stain your heart. We have not raised you that way, understand? Never

let the mob's passions be yours." He called it a sin
against God and Creation—

Then Lou interrupted my thoughts. "Is that rain?"

"Huh?"

"It's raining!"

I held out my palm and felt nothing but mist
forming on my skin. Nevertheless a hissing sound like
soft rain rose all about. Then I looked at the circle of
tarmac illuminated by our little lantern.

A glittering black pool was spreading around our
feet. At first I thought it was a burst pipe sending a
sheet of liquid sweeping across the ground. But our
shoes were dry and the glitter was too alive, sparkling
and teeming, when it should have been a flat, dull
pool. The water hissed and clicked like falling pine
needles.

"Oh my Lord! Insects!"

"Cockroaches. Shit!"

In countless numbers. Like us, they were fleeing
disaster, an insect swarm an inch deep. I did not think
anything natural could still be alive in Butchertown.
But they were. And they were getting out.

We turned to retreat, but they were behind us as
well, beyond the reach of our light. Lou started
dancing, shaking her skirts as though they had caught
fire. I kicked around as they found their way under my
pant legs, tickling me through my socks as they crept
up my legs.

"That way!"

Forward we rushed, high stepping as though dashing through a puddle, our every step crushing insects under our feet. It took forever to reach clear ground. We stopped to shake the bugs out of our clothes, scrape them off our shoes. I took off my jacket and shook it. A few bugs had crawled inside my shirtsleeves. They bounced off the ground and clambered away. Lou muttered Biblical imprecations as she lifted and shook her skirts, dancing a jig in her high-laced shoes. "Pestilence . . . Lord, save us . . ." I did not feel like laughing at her.

Finally, she stopped dancing, her shoulders sagging, arms swinging wearily at her side, her face heavy with despair. "I've seen slums, but this is so much worse. How can anyone say there is no evil? How can we say we haven't sinned? 'The land shall be utterly emptied . . .'"

"'And utterly spoiled,'" I finished the quote. I took her by the arm and we went forward.

We pushed on. Around us dogs barked, cats squalled and vermin rustled in the shadows. Soon new noises came from up ahead: car engines, tailpipes backfiring, horns honking. Tiny specks of light appeared, looking low and sour as they moved left to right, close to the ground. The air turned a stinging acrid blue.

We emerged between two empty houses to find San Pablo Avenue stretching before us. The street was packed nearly curb to curb, mostly by people on foot

walking among slow-moving cars, trucks and horse-
and mule-drawn drays.

I had heard stories from doughboys on the ships
coming home about French refugees fleeing by the
thousands as artillery shells destroyed their towns and
villages. Now the stories were happening right before
me. Men, women and children carried only what they
could through the blue funk, bent, gray and shrunken,
their eyes cast down. They were fleeing like the bugs.
There was much coughing, muttered urgings and
prayers in what I now knew to be Portuguese.
Butchertown's citizens were abandoning the world
that they had made with their labor.

I felt like following them, out and away.

"They're leaving town." I leaned over to Lou as I
watched them. "We should join them. Maybe we can
be of—hey! Wait!"

Lou had flown off the curb, nimbly winding her
away through the stream, across the boulevard. I
rushed after her, jumping, dodging and sidestepping
the people going by, invisible to them all.

I found her waiting for me, standing straight and
severe. She made a grab for the lantern, but I held on
to it. No matter: Lou was going where she was going
and if it meant walking in total darkness, so be it. The
Lord would guide her. And, regardless, a gentleman
did not permit a lady to go walking alone by herself in
such climes. And so we marched on between rows of
dingy houses, until we reached Adelyne, where the
road was clear and the refugees were fewer.

We walked north. The area became familiar, even in the near-perfect night. Casting the light around, I recognized houses we had driven by Saturday morning. I stopped as I remembered more—Buckram in the Carver kitchen, brushing his hand over the back of his head, his eye gleaming like a dead-eyed hunter's. "*Boom!*" he'd said, the hunter so proud of his aim.

"Paul, what are you doing?"

"Remember that dead guy we found? Right about here." She shuddered as I went on. "You both prayed over him. Tag got out and knelt over him with his back to us."

"What of it? Come on!"

"Is Tag carrying a gun?"

"What? No! We're not those kinds of Christians!" She looked ready to banish me to the outer darkness to wail and gnash my teeth. But what did I care? We were there already.

"He looked like he was searching the body. Maybe for a gun."

"Don't talk nonsense." Lou marched on. I caught up in two strides. As we walked alongside, I asked about Tag's injuries with, I must admit, calculated concern.

"It didn't seem too bad at first. He got cut along here." She pressed a hand to her side. "It's been getting worse. But he's such a believer. He has such strength, like nothing in the world could stop him."

"How did it happen?"

"Like I told you, Friday night, during the march. A drunkard pushed him through a plate-glass window."

"You were there? You saw it happen?"

She shook her head. "We got separated in the heat of it. It was a mess with everyone fighting. I was nearly trampled. One of the revelers got me somewhere safe, out of the way." The first smile I'd seen in a while bowed her lips. "A sweet, drunken old man. Said he couldn't understand why God was against people enjoying themselves when He'd made the world such a hard place to live in. Actually tried to tell me the Bible praised wine drinking—but that's silly! Funny how people are. I'd almost forgot."

"Nope, not everyone's in the gutter, beating their wives and starving their children."

"The exceptions don't count, Paul. We can't afford to be distracted by details. The vision is all. We're so close to victory. The world is no longer being run by men in saloons."

"So, where's all this victory you keep promising?" I insolently waved the lantern around.

She ignored the impertinence, quickening her pace to separate herself from the sinner shadowing her steps. But this sinner was manly, tall and long legged. She would not get far.

"What time did you get separated? During the riot?"

"I don't know! Right about when it got real dark. We caught up sometime later. I'd given him the sledgehammer I brought because I couldn't carry it anymore. Then he lost it when he got pushed through the window. He's not a brawling hooligan, like *you*. Why are you asking—?"

"So he came back injured and without your hammer. When did you learn his brother was dead?"

"The next morning, after we left you at the house. The boy told him, he said. He came back to the car crying his heart out, crying that we'd come all the way back here for nothing. We were too late to save his family. He was ready to give up.

"But we weren't too late. There was still his father and sister. They needed saving more than ever. We had to stay the course and not yield to obstacles in our way. I mean, I encouraged him in this. It was my idea to come here, to march, to witness. Not to murder, not to kill."

Then she turned on me. "Do you understand? I know what you're insinuating, and you stop it, do you hear me? We're trying—*going*—to do good for this world! And you, you muddy our vision with clever remarks. You're worse than any gangster. You tolerate them, you practical men with your small minds, hard shriveled hearts and your sly arguments to do nothing. All from the tongue of the Devil. We'll say no more of it. We're going to find Tag and get him to a doctor. And then we go on as before. Without your distractions. Am I clear?"

"As the sky."

She shuddered as though breaking, her eyes closed. "Please, Paul, if you can do nothing else, help me find him and get him somewhere safe."

I nodded, my tone conciliatory, my face poker blank. "I understand."

I was no longer in such a hothouse hurry to get out of Butchertown. I had a goal more important now, a question that needed an answer. Lou Wheeler would lead me to it. I treasured her now as I would treasure a key.

Chapter 22

Shelter in the Wasteland

We walked on. Lou pulled out another handkerchief from yet another hidden pocket, and I found the last of Tag Carver's. We hurried across the east bridge over Gasoline Creek, past the clanking oil refinery, our mouths and noses covered. We had to move fast, but the more we hurried, the more poison we inhaled. I worried that we would even find Tag Carver alive and find the answer to my question.

Not long after the bridge Lou turned left onto a narrow dirt street that bumped away into pond-green smut.

"We drove down here." Her hankie muffled her voice. She removed it and drew a cautious breath, as I did. The air was only slightly clearer.

We walked in silence, my mood curdling. I was returning to the same pit from which I had just escaped. The air became saturated again. Up ahead the smokestack came into view, its fire crown dimmed but not out.

Then Lou slowed down, looking about. "Here. I left them here. Give me the lamp."

I shined the light around. The street had opened into a circular area, apparently used for parking and loading. There were several broken-down trucks about, their windows smashed, tires missing, leaning on their fenders like drunkards.

No sign of a prewar Model T.

Lou rushed back and forth through the light cast by the lantern, faster and faster, becoming a blur as she cried out for Tag repeatedly, moving in a circle, hurrying in and out of every slot and corner. Finally, she reached another narrow pathway, one that appeared to lead down to Gasoline Creek. She started down it a short way before retreating, her hankie over her mouth, shaking her head. She disappeared again. Meanwhile, I dragged the light from where the path started back to my feet.

The ground was a mixture of chunks of cement and tarmac and broad, shallow craters of damp dirt. I knelt and studied the ground like I did when hunting in the woods back home.

"Louise! Louise, come here!"

"Paul! Paul, I need that light." She appeared over me. "What are you doing?"

I rose and slowly started down the path leading to the creek. My chest tightened and my lungs started hurting. I backed away.

"See those hobnail boot prints? They lead down that path, to the creek, about where the fire started I'd guess. Then they return. On tiptoe, like he was running."

"What? Don't be irrelevant. Those aren't Tag's shoes."

"No, they're from that friend of his I bet."

I waved the light in a circle. "There. Tire tracks. They match your car I reckon. They look fresh enough. Here's where you parked coming in. And then you see them make a Y-turn and they go out."

"Paul, listen—"

"And here's more footprints. Your shoes. When you went out to the bridge. You see where your skirt's dragging? Then these are Tag's shoes, am I right? They look like the sort our kind of people might wear, smooth soled. The gait is uneven, and one print is deeper than the other. That footprint's dragging a little, like he was limping. Off that way. Here you see he came back. He's even more off stride. He waited until you were gone, then followed."

"He just wanted to be sure I was all right."

Then I froze: right at my feet lay a preacher's collar, attached to its bib, torn and soiled.

I picked it up and held it out to her, shining the light on it.

"One of the last things my father—the priest—said to me: 'Beware, this is the Devil's favorite disguise.'"

I threw it on the ground and kicked it away.

"Well, what about it? So he took his collar off. So he went walking and then they drove off—"

I grabbed her, pulled her to me, growling low to force her intention.

"I've had enough of *your* distractions, Miss Louise Wheeler. Your boyfriend—fiancé, whatever—beat his own brother to death with that sledgehammer. That started this war, and he's been doing his goddamn best to keep the blood running."

She struggled to escape, but I held on like a mad mean dog. "He's been keeping it from you, doing a good job too. You're so enthralled with your crusade you'll believe anything so long as it's what you want to hear. Oh, he's hurt maybe, but not that hurt. I just pulled that lame-dog trick myself today. It wasn't that hard to send you off to Oakland so he could stir the fire again last night at the Carver house. Then he did it again tonight. He let you march out on the bridge while he snuck in behind Falcone's men with that gun he took off that dead guy. Meantime, the boy threw matches on that foul creek until it lit. They didn't care if you died out there, see? Tag didn't give a shit. He's on his own mission and it has nothing to do with—"

She kicked at me and I shoved her away. She staggered but stayed on her feet, bent and shaking like a sapling in a storm, her eyes flaring, her mouth tight and turned down.

"You're the one who's the liar. A killer. You have blood on your hands, Mr. Bacon. You are one of them. Your words run with blood and lies. There's an explanation. I know there is. I'll find him and he'll explain it all and it'll be all right and I'll get him to the hospital. *You* stay away from me, from us. May you burn in Hell forever!"

She lunged for the lantern, but I easily stepped away.

"Very well then. God will lead me there. I don't need Satan's light to guide me."

And away she swept into the smoky night. I stood gaping, maybe for longer than was wise.

"Wait!" I started after her, my heart aching. I was not responsible for her growing insanity, but I felt accountable for her safety. I sensed Father and Mother watching from behind the curtain of darkness that hung all around. And if I ever got out of here and returned home, I would have to tell *her* mother and father what happened to their daughter.

I heard her footsteps ahead of me. They grew louder, sounding as though she were walking in one place. I heard her breathing, ragged and panicky. She ran like a flash through the light. She was turning in circles, a dervish, her face blank as a ghost's.

"Is that you, Lord? Hurry, Lord. We can't stop . . . something's happening . . . always happening. If I stop, something will happen . . . and it will happen because I stopped. Don't let me rest."

I caught her in my arms just before she hit the ground, slung her over my shoulder fireman style and staggered on down the road towards Adelyne.

The gassy air had thinned by the time I reached the bridge over Gasoline Creek, but I was nevertheless wheezing as I struggled down the street in search of shelter. We passed a bakery that smelled faintly of yeast, though the aroma was moist and sickening mixed with the poisonous atmosphere. A short ways on I spied the house that seemed least likely to collapse on us, a one-story cottage. The cement front steps crumbled underfoot. Both the screen and front doors scraped across the stoop as I pried and pushed them open with my feet.

I stepped carefully inside and shined the lantern about. The occupants seemed to have left it all behind, in a hurry too, though "all" did not amount to much: a moth-eaten couch with its springs curling out the fabric like nether hair; a serving table leaning against the scarred plaster wall. I kicked away a newspaper that caught on my foot. Stacks of old newspapers were neatly piled about, maybe used for cleaning rags or the privy. I felt the crust of dead insects on my shoe soles as I walked across creaking, warped wood floor. I took a deep breath, almost certain that yet another dead body lay awaiting discovery.

To my relief I found no such thing. I set Lou down at one end of the couch and searched the place.

Though it was a hovel, with its plumb off-center, the cottage had been kept remarkably neat, its dwellers making the best of bad environs. The walls were hung with pleasant pictures of flowers and landscapes. The kitchen seemed stripped bare of food, with only utensils left behind: copper pots, cast iron skillets and a rolling pin that would be a plausible defensive weapon. I picked it up, flipped it in my hand and held it at the ready as I searched the rest of the house.

In a small bedroom in the back, a lumpy king-size bed lay crookedly on a tarnished brass frame, its covers kicked to the foot. The inviting sight intensified my exhaustion. A cheap metal crib huddled in a dark corner away from the window.

I set the rolling pin on a bedside table and returned to the living room to find Lou as I had left her. I carried her into the bedroom and laid her down on the right side of the bed. She awoke in sudden panic, first beating me with her fists, then clinging to me, her head laid against my chest. "Where am I?" I shushed her, holding her close. "Tag?" she asked. I winced. "Where's God, Tag? Where did He go? Let's pray, Tag. Pray with me please. 'O Merciful Father, who has taught us in thy holy Word that thou dost not willingly afflict or grieve the children of men . . .' "

That prayer had taken root in my mind when I was an altar boy. The words spouted easily from my memory but stopped at my mouth. I was only able to join in halfway through, more for her sake than mine.

It seemed to work. She softened in my arms and stopped quaking. I laid her down on her side and held her hand for a time; it felt dry, coarse and calloused compared to other female hands. I had been in similar scenarios enough times and knew what to do. I should have been snorting and bucking like a stallion. But not here, not now. Butchertown killed all of nature's gifts.

I stopped to consider matters other than immediate survival. What the hell was she thinking coming here? She was thinking nothing, that was what. She had lit a pure flame for a fallen world that meant to guide her to her lost child.

I had no right to be posing on my own pedestal, of course. I had been thinking nothing in my pursuit of lust's arresting light. Both of us blinded to the darkness all around.

I massaged my forehead to stop thinking, else I would spiral down with her. I was the man after all, protector and sentry, rescuer and perhaps warrior, the role I knew least of all.

I moved to the other side of the bed, set the lantern on the floor, kicked off my shoes, lay down and curled up on my side, my back to her. Safe enough for now, I allowed myself a light sleep.

Something turned over against me and I awoke, like rising from an oily black pond. I sat up alert in dead darkness. Lou had rolled onto her back against me. A lightning urge to take her right there rose, but I rose faster. Confused, groggy, I blundered into a wall, my face smacking into a framed picture.

I found the lantern, turned it on, checked my watch. I had slept longer than I thought. My nerves humming, I searched the cottage again. Whatever awoke me was either invisible or still far away. I shined the light around, almost suffered apoplexy when I saw what appeared to be a dead child facedown on the floor. But it was only a rag doll.

I took a closer look at the pictures on the pale plaster walls, of flower prints and seaside views; family photographs, people posed in solemn, formal groups, dull and dignified, their clothes simple and neat. They reminded me of the empty spaces on the bare walls at the Carver house, of the portrait hidden in the dresser drawer in the upstairs bedroom, mother and child in a kindly fairy-tale world—

I snapped to attention, now fully aware of what had awakened me. Cars in the distance. I crossed to a front window and peered carefully out through grainy light as a large Ford passed glumly by, closely followed by a big touring car. Then a parade of cars and trucks, one vehicle following another, rumbling steadily by, a dozen, maybe more, all headed south.

Bat Falcone had escaped the fire. Now he was back and would not—could not—stop, could not be stopped. The rest of his army had arrived from the north. They could not see me watching from inside the house, but I stepped back from the window anyway.

The engines faded. I went out on the porch, down the steps, shivering as I wrapped my thin coat tightly around me in the clammy air, and looked down the empty street. Wind and foghorns howled together. I could not hear the trains: no clacking of the bogies, no whistles. It had taken the whole weekend, but Butchertown's little war had at last brought commerce to a perfect standstill.

I stood listening in a loud silence, the kind described to me by the doughboys I helped guide home, the one they heard in the trenches just before their commanders blew their whistles and they clambered up into battle.

"What is it?"

Lou had come out on the porch, looking in the same direction, hands behind her back, her head raised like a bird's, eyes alert, focused, fully awake.

"More trouble. Big trouble now."

"Armageddon." She nodded solemnly.

"Yeah." I attempted a pun. "We both oughta be a-gettin' out of here."

She sighed sharply, her blue eyes flat, her pupils frozen black pebbles. "Tag's there in the middle of it. Right now."

She stepped briskly down the steps, steely and determined. I approached her, my hands up.

"Lou! Listen, let's go and get some real help. I mean it! We can't do anything." Then I fibbed badly. "Tag will be safe. The boy's with him. He'll look after him."

She bared her teeth with contempt at my petty lie, a patronizing thing said to a child when the truth is too much.

"Lou. I'm sorry. Please—"

Her left hand swept up and around. I glimpsed the rolling pin I had picked up and laid down. My head exploded.

Chapter 23

Blood Fever

Lucky for me, the rolling pin struck a part of my head still unhurt. I crumpled with my hands wrapped around my skull as red-and-yellow suns burst and bounced off the walls of my cranium.

"Oh, Louise, for chrissakes . . ."

As the pain faded, my head turned into a glass snow globe, sparkling blue and white flakes floating about. Under my agony lay shame. I had tried to be Doug Fairbanks rescuing Mary Pickford. Instead I was only Barney Google taking another one on the noggin from Lizzie.

By the time I regained my feet, Lou was gone. The day was as bright as it would get in Butchertown. I started weaving my way down Adelyne, calling her name, not because I thought she would stop so I could catch up, but as a prayer to keep a lovelorn hero going.

Go on. Say it: *You sap, you should have run then and there.* I knew where peace and safety lay, and who could stop me? I had my best shot at escape. But did I take it? No. I had avoided the blood fever that was gripping Butchertown. But I had a different fever.

If I failed to do all I could to save Lou Wheeler's life, how would I live with myself? It hardly mattered that she was as mad in her way as Butchertown's criminals. If I ran, it would be into a life of nightmares, full of those why questions said to torture the sleep of survivors. True, a guilty conscience is a selfish motive, but there were worse reasons to risk my life. If I had waited for pure unsullied motives, I might not have survived childhood—when I pulled that kid from that woodland pond years ago, I knew Lou was watching—and I would have been no use to anyone. At the least, I expected no other reward. Not even her love.

I slowed as the first gunshot rippled from the mist; then Chess Stetson's Thompson chattered. A rifle cracked, a shotgun boomed. Gunfire swelled into a barrage. A big white flash erupted, followed by a big whump. A peppery gust of wind blew through my hair, stung my eyes. Men shouted and screamed in bitter blue fog. I sneezed and coughed furiously, my head cracking. Ahead, a puff of black smoke billowed into the air.

I found Bat Falcone's fleet of cars haphazardly blocking the street. They were mostly empty. I crept from vehicle to vehicle. The fire came from one of the large touring cars at the head of the line. Its front end had been blown into twisted metal, with engine parts, glass and metal skin scattered in shards. Flames surrounded two charcoal silhouettes in the front seat.

Two more dead men sat in two trucks, one driver draped over the steering wheel, while the other driver sat with his head tilted back, his gaping mouth a bloody hole. His passenger lay sprawled on his back in the street, his feet still inside the cab, a pulpy dollar-sized hole erupting from his left temple. The corpse shivered as though running with electricity.

A bullet zipped past. A rifle cracked from up ahead. They were shooting blindly now.

I retreated and hunkered down behind a Dodge to wait it out. *Zip-bang! Zip-bang!* Bullets made metallic popping noises, punched out windshield glass. Chunks of tarmac exploded in the air. I may have started screaming. At least I heard someone yelling "Stupid bastards!" and worse. When I came to, my throat was sore and my hands hurt as though I had been beating them on the fender of the Dodge.

Then the battle dwindled to a skirmish, drifted away west. My fury spent and my head clearer, I crept forward again from car to car, squinting through the smoke. Visibility was less than twenty feet.

I finally reached the Carver compound. The old flivver sat off to the right, sunk in a corner curb, empty and perforated. The big Victorian loomed like Dracula's castle behind the low brick wall. Down a side street, several bodies littered the ground. Wounded men staggered and crawled away, some arm in arm, some alone.

I snuck up next to the flivver. Guns banged away from behind the house by the side driveway. I imagined Carvers and Falcones peeking around corners, over walls, and from windows and doorways, taking potshots and ducking back down to reload, looking for a way to break through for a final attack.

There were people huddling down behind a garden wall at the corner of the house under a shattered window. Heads poking up, ducking down. Lou was with them. I slipped over the front brick wall, scuttled across the muddy yard and leapt over the garden wall.

And damn near into the snapping jaws of that giant mastiff. I smelled his foul breath and rank spittle on my face and scuttled out of reach. He barked furiously, violently jerking at a chain that barely held him in check.

Again I found myself face-to-face with a handgun, held by the Negro boy, who stared down the barrel with the same dead-eyed look he likely wore when he set fire to Gasoline Creek; when he shot down the man by the basement window.

A small bloody hand slipped in and pushed the gun away.

"It's all right," Tag Carver said. "He's with us."

Tag Carver lay slumped against the house wearing a grimy smile, his legs curled beneath him. His black suit was burnt and torn. A .38 revolver hung loosely in one hand, while the other clutched his side, blood oozing between his fingers.

Lou sat a distance away, her knees up, her face buried in her arms, trembling. The rolling pin she had brained me with lay at her feet.

"With you? Bullshit."

"Or are you here for your base urges?"

"Shut up with that!" I wanted to rip his little murdering head off with my bare hands. "This is all your doing." I nodded at the boy. "The two of you."

"You're damn straight, chum. And they had it coming, too! Every bitch and bastard! It ain't murder to kill murderers. It's eye for an eye. For what them and this rotten world took from me, I give 'em a million times fire and hell!" He shook his head at Lou. "She didn't get it. She was seein' Jesus on a cloud in his nightie. She thought she was leading the way, thought I wanted the same thing." He softened.

Lou raised her head, her eyes tired, her face grimy. She nodded miserably.

"You lied to me."

He softened. "No. Not at first. This whole crusade was your idea. I didn't want to come, not me. I said forget it. Stay away. Butchertown's cursed. But I loved you. And I loved how you promised with your songs and prayers and Bible talk. Your songs of cities on the hill and salvation for my poor goddamn family."

"I didn't know."

"Oh! You didn't know! You who knew more than the poor bastard that was born and bred here, you didn't know. You brought me here. And gave me the hammer of—"

Gunfire exploded around us. We ducked down as a man shrieked. The mastiff tore at its chain, its barks like screams. The post that held the chain had been drilled into the side of the house on a simple hook that was slowly twisting in its hole, the wood around it splintering. The barrage simmered down again. I could hear the wood creaking as the hook turned and the frightened beast howled.

"This was about your mother, right?" I asked. "I saw a picture of you two."

"The bastards poisoned her. My only light in this cave, and they snuffed her out with their poison. It was Danny that brought it, the first batch from the brand-new still he built after the law started, like some chemist trying out a new formula on a dumb rat. Gave it to me, said give it to her. So I did and she drank it. Then she died. Right in front of me. And the boy here. He was the only one around. It ate her insides. Everyone had gone away, Molly too. Just me and the boy in that house, watching her die. When they came back, Mother's face was all twisted like she was still screaming.

"They *didn't care*. 'Oopsie!' That's what they said. She was a souse with a bad liver and gonna die soon anyway. Better now than later. But they didn't know, didn't care, what they were doing to me. And so I left, I thought forever. And when I came back into town Friday I thought I was all done with it, that I had forgiven them, like Jesus told me to."

"But you hadn't."

"Uh-uh! But I didn't know that. I was coming from Paradise and wanted to bring it home, share the glory with everyone. I had this Passion play in my head, with all of us on our knees arm in arm: father, brother, sister and me, booze bottles and tankards smashed, beer and booze running down the gutters. The breweries, the stills, the opium dens and cribs torn down. Churches, schools and happy homes blooming from the soil. Everything this place isn't. I rehearsed it a million times, every detail etched in my mind, playing like a movie picture. I would make it happen just by being here."

"But it didn't happen, did it?" ▸

"Friday night we marched in like the saints. But what happens? The sinners fight back! What kind of screwy people fight against what's good for 'em? Butchertown was a hell for so long, I guess it looked like Heaven to them and we were invading devils. I'm a hometown boy but I didn't know my own town. I forgot who they were. But I got reminded fast.

"Just before the riot started, I took the sledgehammer off Lou's hands and then we got separated. I got the idea to track down Pops, get him and Danny to come and calm everybody down. Father and sons calming the seas, y' know? Like Jesus calming the waters. I could see a ball game was on and knew they'd be there, so I went. The crowd parted before me. I had no idea why. I was so excited, I forgot I was carrying that hammer.

"I saw Danny come out of the stadium and followed him at a distance. Then Chess Stetson caught up and gave him the shotgun before he went off towards Hollis. I caught up with him. He turned around and saw me. Things all flipped back to ten, twenty years ago: the big bully brother and little pesky brother. He still had that freezing stare I remember from when I was crawling: '*What* are you doing here? *Why* are you even alive?'

"You don't get that, do you, you damned rubes? You come from nice families, all peachy with Christian love." He rolled his eyes. "Forget all about Cain and Abel, dontcha? Even I know about them two.

"Danny's cold eyes, they melted all the fine words I'd stored up, all the talk of Jesus, family and God's love. He stared at me like I was another Butchertown bug. Even God would have gone dumb. Danny was ice through and through. He was the smartest, but no one liked him. Only whores would go with him, and they didn't like him much either. And he wasn't happy at all to see his baby brother. 'Goddamnit! You!' Told me to shut up and beat it before I even opened my mouth. Hadn't changed a goddamn bit. Still a sneer for everyone, even the big hats from San Francisco. Down on me most of all. Still called me Taggie-boo with that snigger, 'cause I would never be a man like him and Pops. Be a real Carver. I could've been shakin' the world by its tail, covered in God's glory, but I was still just a good-for-nothing mama's boy to him. The baby underfoot. 'Mama should've aborted you. Maybe I will someday.'

"I got so knotted up. He kept sneering at God, at the cause, at me. I shouted back, tried to make him face up to what happened. To what he did. How he poisoned her. How could he not care? How could he make excuses? How could they just take her pictures down like that the very next day? Leave nothin' but blank squares to remember her by, so we were no longer children born of woman?

"I started shrieking. But he just laughed, said I was more useless alive than Mother was dead. 'Whatcha ya gonna do, Taggie-boo? Hit me with God's whuppin' big hammer?' He slapped me like he used to. He couldn't punch me with his fist, like I was a man. Slapped me like I was a girl or a child. He put his hand on my face, shoved me to the ground, told me to get out of town or he'd make me crawl out like a worm in front of all my Temperance friends. 'I'll make all you do-gooder worms crawl.'

"Then he turned away. Forgot I had the hammer. Maybe he thought it was too heavy for little Taggie-boo. But I jumped to it, like Samson knockin' down the temple. The hammer felt like a stick in my hand. He turned 'round as I ran at him. I caught him on the shoulder as he raised the shotgun. His first shot missed. I didn't feel the second. I hit him alongside his head, knocked him down. He saw it coming, lyin' there, his eyes big and wide: little brother swingin' his big whuppin' hammer. A thousand times I dreamed of crushing that sneer out of his face. And then my dream came true." Tag Carver smiled. "Crushed it again and again!"

"Then I was running. I didn't notice I'd dropped the hammer, didn't know I'd been hurt till I found Lou again. I said I'd been pushed through a window. You believed it, sweetheart." He snapped his fingers. "Like that. From there lying got easy."

"But you had no right. God didn't send us here to kill."

"He shoulda stopped me if it was that important to Him. Why did He let you give me the hammer? Why didn't I feel I'd done wrong? Why did He let me go on believing I'd done right? He shoulda stopped me! Why did He let us make this world such a shithole? He coulda done something!"

"Why didn't you stop yourself? You knew it was wrong."

"But I didn't feel it." Tag pounded his heart.

He turned back to me.

"After the riot we saw Stetson leading the gang up Adelyne. We followed 'em to the stockyard. They went inside and the shooting started. Lou got scared, wanted to leave then, but not me, no. We had to stick around, be there to help the wounded and the dying. We were *Christians*. It was our Christian duty. That's what she wanted to hear, so that's what I said.

"We spent the night in the car, north of town. I knew I was getting away with murder. Danny had been on his way to some meeting or other and my old man thought he'd been killed by whoever he was supposed to palaver with. I guessed who it was: Bat Falcone, our old family nemesis. It hit me that I'd thrown gasoline on this two-bit feud, made it into a raging fire. Little Taggie-boo brings the Apocalypse." He tapped his head. "I saw Butchertown lit by Hellfire. Sodom and Gomorrah. Keep the fire burning, purify the ground. Then we sow the seeds for the Kingdom coming—"

"All right." The more he talked in that singsong, the more it made sense. "I can see it's burning."

"The next morning we found you lying in the same kind of gutter Lou and I crawled from. Couldn't make you out, Bacon. I could tell you'd been in the fracas, but I couldn't see you on my father's side. Or on Falcone's. And then I saw those looks pass between you and Lou—"

I pointed at the pistol in his hand. "You took that off that dead fellow."

"I really prayed for the poor bastard. For his death to keep the fire alive. I meant to take you into Oakland, too. But then you let it slip that you'd stepped out with my sister and something had happened. You'd been abandoned. I knew what that meant. You were involved. I could make you part of my plan. Their heads were all spinning. I knew they'd spin even crazier if I threw you back among them. This time I knew the score. I was the man on the inside. They were on the outside, the ignoramuses. I was up on them. The last became the first.

"Stop acting so shocked. It's war, Bacon. There's two kinds of people, Pops always said: kings and pawns. Kings rule, pawns get used and kicked aside for the sake of the kingdom. I made myself a secret king and you another ignorant pawn." He bared his teeth, daring me to take offense.

"You knew Falcone would be back for revenge."

"Damn straight! After you went in the house, the boy and I started plotting. Having him on the inside was perfect. No love lost between him and the Carvers, you see that. We were a pair of ghosts. The Carvers on one side, Bat Falcone on the other and two little imps in the middle.

"The hard part was keepin' Lou in the dark. But she was still starin' into that light and couldn't see anything around it. So we played the next trick. The boy had nicked a gun from my father's whores and I already had mine. I sent Lou off on her errand. Then we hid in the fog until Falcone showed. Tiptoed up behind one on the outside! *Bang! Bang!* Tiptoed right out. The boy got one on the inside and there they went again. Idiots!

"By the time Lou got back, the shooting stopped. She had no idea." He had forgotten she was right there, as his eyes blazed with fiendish delight at his cunning. "Today Falcone came back and we watched. I knew he wouldn't let it go. Then the boy comes and says he's seen you again, this time working for Falcone, playing go-between, negotiating a cease-fire. That got me worried, a goddamn diplomat muddying the waters. Peace would only bring evil. How could I stop them from forging their new empire? I nearly gave up the whole scheme. But next we found you pacing around by the train stop. You looked so lost in the fog, in the middle of nothing. I could see you'd escaped and they were after you. You needed a ride.

"But I still didn't know what to do with you, until you told me the details of the meeting. And then Lou, my bright brilliant girl here, came up with her idea to join the gathering. It was a goofy idea, sure, but not how I saw it. Gasoline Creek was a fire waiting for a match. Meeting on the bridge would put 'em right in its path. All that singing and praying would distract them even more.

"But to keep them there until the fire came down, I had to get them blasting away again. I planned to get the two of you out there while I tiptoed in again. I was starting to hurt bad enough from this wound, so I'd have an excuse to hang back, then sneak in among 'em and—boom!" He waved the pistol in the air. "But then comes Chess Stetson to drag you off. Even so, the idea had its hooks in me."

I raised my hand. "Wait. It was supposed to be Stetson and me out on the bridge with Falcone. Stetson said he'd all but taken over the gang from Cobb and Molly and he was the new boss." I addressed the boy directly. "Then you came to the door saying it was all set, meaning that Cobb and Molly were out of the way. But you lied. You knew Stetson and Molly were fighting for the throne and that she still had it. You led us into that ambush before the bridge. Cobb Carver said as much."

"We were waiting to take him to the bridge when he came out Stetson's house," Tag said. "We almost didn't make it in time."

"My point is I wound up on the bridge with Molly."
I nodded at the boy, wanting an answer. "You tried to
fix it so she'd be the one who'd burn to death. Why?"

"My nephew's so clever." Tag laughed fondly. "Wish
you were my boy!"

"Your neph—what?" The world shuddered and
tipped.

"Take a good look. See anyone you know? That light
skin, his jawline, the shape of the ears. He's family.
He's a Carver."

True, I had seen something familiar about the boy's
face from the start, but I had been a little too busy
lately to pay closer attention.

"I was ten when he was born. Molly wouldn't tell
Pops and Mother who the father was, but after the
baby came, they copped to it fast. The handyman in
the cottage in the back— handsome Negro, always a
gent to me—even showed me how to use some of his
tools. My father, Danny and a couple of their bullies
paid him a visit the Saturday night after the baby was
born." He sighed. "I heard the poor man screaming.
Mother sat with me reading, trying to distract me, but
the screams were there behind the stories. I think they
took him to the rending plant. They gave the baby to
the whores to raise as their own and we all pretended.
The boy never knew about his father. Not until I told
him not long after Mother died. The day I left
Butchertown." He winked at the boy. "I came back and
we fixed it, didn't we?" The boy did not respond.

"You let me go out there alone," Lou croaked. "Did you want me to die, too?"

"It was your idea to start with, just like coming here. You wanted to go. You didn't say no. You wanted to atone, to get your lost child back, which'll never happen by the way, oh no. I didn't even have to try that hard. All I had to do was to whimper like a sick puppy. You lapped it right up."

"You were doing the Devil's work." Lou showed her teeth. "I came to bring life to this place, but you brought more death and misery!"

"I can still see you striding off into the fog, proud and sure, singing and swinging your torch. 'Glory, glory, hallelujah.' Then the boy and I got to work bringing the Hellfire. On a hot platter." He grinned with obscene pleasure. "Look at all this smoke and fire. Lord, how I do love it! Ain't it something? There's no saving Butchertown. This is a better fate. Hark! The cannons sound!"

Sure enough, another salvo, a dozen or so rounds, punched the air from close by. The dog leapt furiously against its chain.

"Hellzapoppin'! I am vengeance, Lord!"

Voices came circling around the house. Old Cobb Carver lumbered around the corner by the driveway, a big .45 in his right hand, his face dirty, false teeth missing, coatless, his knitted brown slacks ruined, his white shirt turned limp and gray, his piggy eyes more confused than ever.

Chess Stetson and Buckram, both singed and bullet grazed, strode in behind, standing with their boss against the common enemy, love him or not. Buckram looked like a torn-faced monster from a cave. Stetson was a savage fiend, jagged streaks of blood coursing down his sharp-boned, grizzled face.

None of them saw the four of us crouching there in the garden. Their attention was elsewhere, to our left. Stetson called out "Hey!"

Three men were hurrying across the yard as fast as they could, running from a nightmare. One of them was Bat Falcone.

Or what remained of him.

Chapter 24

Settling the Score

That Falcone was alive and standing after the fire on the bridge made for a grotesque miracle. He looked like a chicken cooked on one side only. The fire had seared him black and red on his left side; his hair had been burned off his large noble head, leaving raw, red scalp; his face was a mass of shriveled skin, his left eye melted shut. His fine pinstripe suit had crumbled to ash, his left hand a black claw. His right side remained intact, but only relatively. Gray ash had turned his suit the same color as the pinstripes. His remaining hair was ashen gray as well. His good eye glared as he raised a .38 revolver in his good hand.

Maurizio stood behind, lugging a BAR too big for him, braced next to a third gunman, armed with a pump-action shotgun. They had little left in them. But still they stood their ground, stood by their boss, Bat Falcone.

I yanked the gun out of Tag Carver's hand and threw myself on top of Lou. The shooting lasted seconds, felt like eternity. The air shimmered from the barrage. A bullet skated across my back; another exploded the concrete. Hot debris stung my face.

Then it stopped. My ears swollen and pinging, my hearing clogged, my nerves numb, I slowly got up, dust falling from me as I checked on Lou. "Has it stopped?" She lay uninjured, her face flat to the ground, staring across the plain of dirt, before placing her hand over her face, shuddering. "Has it stopped? Can we go now?"

Chess Stetson was standing over where Bat Falcone lay sprawled on his back. Maurizio was writhing on his side nearby, trying to sit up, both his shoulders shattered. His partner lay flat on his back, his body sinking like dough.

I joined Stetson, staring down at his former padrone.

Three bullets had stitched their way across Falcone's barrel chest. His remaining eye rolled about, looking for something to focus on. It finally found me. He mumbled in Italian. I knelt beside him to listen.

"Something about getting up to watch the sun rise," Stetson growled. "He liked to gather us all on the porch with him. Like we were all family."

Falcone grabbed my arm. "I want a priest! Yes! Bless me, Father! Forgive me, for I have sinned!"

He was convinced he would be soon off to Hell and I was the one who could save him. I struggled to recall the words I knew from listening to my father:

"O Almighty God, um with whom do live the spirits of just men made perfect . . . after they are delivered from their earthly persons; we humbly commend the soul—"

He shook his head, scowling. "No, no, Father, that is not right . . ."

"I don't speak Latin," I mumbled, remembering he was Catholic and I was not. But before I could tell him it would make no difference, Bat Falcone's eye dulled. A bubble of bloody saliva burst on his lips. His great chest went still.

I stood and turned to Stetson. His sleek, shiny suit was now burned and ripped all over. A bullet had scraped above his left eye, releasing another drying trickle of blood, which had coursed crookedly down into his mustache. Another had cut his left arm, turning the sleeve brown. He sported a most devilish grin.

"Last man I expected to see at the big showdown. Can't stay out of a fight, can ya, Bacon?" He gave me a hearty slap on the back. "I know how ya feel."

The remaining Carvers were still on their feet, victorious though badly shot up. Buckram had taken the worst of it, a direct hit high on his shoulder. His rifle slipped from his arms as the numbing shock wore off, his scar stretching across the whole left side of his face like melted rubber. He was smiling at me. Stetson set his Thompson down and rushed to him, his face softening, his voice as tender as the hand he placed on his pal's shoulder. "You all right?"

Meanwhile the mastiff had started barking again. The noise had reduced the poor beast to a cowering mass, but now that it was over, he was up and raging. His jaws snapped and drooled, fur bristled, whites showed around his eyes as he pulled at his chain. The chain hook yawed as the wood splintered.

His rage was directed at Cobb Carver, who stood near the garden wall, sagging like a tired troll, his pistol pointed down, his face uncomprehending. I doubt he had fired a shot.

"Hey! Pops!"

Tag Carver, the prodigal, stepped over the wall, limped towards his father.

"I'm home, Pops! Taggie-boo! Remember your youngest?" He waved a triumphant hand. "You know who did all this? I did! This is the Hell you deserve, murdering bastard!" His gestures were like his father's, though they looked so different from each other. Tag jabbed a bloody thumb at his chest. "I killed Danny! I smashed his face in! Me! I killed your golden boy!" He laughed. "I tricked you into destroying everything! I knew you were all stupid!"

But Cobb Carver seemed to hear neither his son nor the large dog that was barking at him. He was mumbling, his eyes fixed on me. Those bruises I gave him still hurt as fresh as the day I gave them. And he remembered.

"Piece-of-shit punk! I'm gonna finish you!" he said.

He raised the pistol, aimed it right at me. I raised mine.

But then the dog finally tore loose and took down Cobb Carver in one bound. His huge jaws closed around the old man's head, fangs biting through the skull, gnawing on his prey as though it were a bone. Cobb did not cry for long.

Meanwhile Tag staggered back and fell over the garden wall with a look of disappointment. Pops died not knowing his youngest son's great achievement.

Then another gun banged. Buckram, still on his feet, stiffened and sagged in Stetson's arms. Stetson called out his partner's name. For the last time Chess Stetson was caught flat-footed, this time fatally. As he started to lay his partner down, another shot hit him in the neck. Buckram slipped from his hands as he straightened up and took another one to the chest and a step back. Astonishment crossed his snaky countenance as he looked around for his killer. I looked too.

It was Molly Carver. She stood with her legs apart like an Old West shootist, aiming a small-caliber automatic in both hands at eye level, her teeth bared. I raised Tag's pistol, my hand shaking, aimed it straight at her, squeezed the trigger.

Click!

Tag's gun was empty. I glanced at the boy, but his hand was shaking. He could shoot anybody, but not the woman who was his mother. Meanwhile Molly had drawn her bead on me and before I could even duck—

Click!

I dropped my gun. Molly threw hers. It skipped painlessly off my shoulder. She took off down the driveway, alongside the house. I dashed after her. She went left, sprung up the side steps, flung open the kitchen door, vanished inside the house.

I caught up quick, I thought as I sprang up the steps. What I would do when I got my hands on her I had no idea, but it would hurt.

But once again I found myself staring into the little black eye of the Luger I had taken off the dead Chinese at the stockyard Friday night, clutched in Molly's shaking hands.

Molly prodded me out the door, down the steps. I raised my hands as she herded me across the driveway, the gun less than a yard from my face, her finger on the trigger. Maybe I can duck, my brain stupidly speculated. I shook all over, unable to even plead for mercy. My face muscles crimped and my eyelids fluttered. My stomach pushed up one way, my guts the other.

"Why didn't you leave like I told you?" Molly yelled. "Why did you stay? What are you doing here?"

The gun went off. The shot sounded flat and dull, with a metal twang undertone. A sharp puff of heat blew over my face, then nothing. There came shrieking, but not from me.

It came from Molly. I opened my eyes as she stumbled back, fell hard on the steps, her hands over her face. One hand was ripped open. A piece of metal poked out between her fingers from where blood spurted.

The Luger lay nearby, its barrel exploded and split. I never had the chance to clean it inside and out after picking it up at the bottom of that mud pile Saturday morning. Neither had Molly.

I stood in a stupor for a moment, not knowing what to do. I had only helped with the wounded long after the battle. Finally, I dashed into the house, into the kitchen, ran the hot water, found some towels and a pint of what I hoped was clean hooch. I stopped to pick up the phone, but the line was dead.

Then, as I put the phone down, I heard Molly screaming even louder. I dashed outside to find yet another horror.

It was the boy. He was standing over Molly, his face cold, his pistol in his hand, kicking her with his hobnailed boots, stomping on her ribs. I dropped everything and shoved him away.

"For chrissakes, cut it out! That's enough! For God's sake, what is it with this place? I don't understand any of you people!" He seemed not to hear me, staring down at his mother.

"Look, your friend Tag, he's hurt," I said. "Maybe you should go help him."

At last the boy showed feeling. He curled his mouth, tipping his head back in disdain, as though talking down to a fool.

"I don't give a shit about any of these people," he said in a burnt voice. "They can all die. Like they made my daddy die."

He turned, walked away, his step slow, gun loose in his hand, head down. He crossed the driveway, past the now-burning whorehouse, disappeared around the front corner of the old bungalow.

I did what I could for Molly, but she kept slapping my hands away as I tried to tend her wounds. Her fading beauty was beyond the help of makeup now, but even after all her cruel tricks I took no joy in her suffering. I made a pillow for her head out of the towels, set the pint next to her and left her in grubby delirium.

As I sloughed back down the driveway, I heard the familiar clacking and choking of an old car. I passed by the dead and wounded. Bat Falcone and his men lay where they had fallen. Maurizio was trying to sit up, crying and screaming, but unable to support himself on his arms.

Cobb Carver was missing. The mastiff had managed to drag old Cobb away to some private corner. I could hear other dogs yipping as they rushed to join him.

Finally—and this hurt to see in the most curious way—there was Chess Stetson sprawled facedown across Buckram as though to shield him, as I suspected he had time and again. Buckram's head was twisted back, his dead eyes fixed on me.

Lou Wheeler and Tag Carver were nowhere to be seen.

I reached the gateway to see the flivver miraculously clanking into the fog towards Oakland, with Lou behind the wheel. Tag was likely slumped in the front or folded in the back seat, his life draining away.

Let someone else catch him. Enough of running, of fighting, of killing. Enough of Butchertown. I sat on the low wall, buried my face in my hands and tried to empty my brain of the last—what—two, three, four days, a week? A month? A year? Butchertown felt like the only place I had ever known. The only place I would ever know, where time was torn into long bloody strips.

I tried remembering good places and good times I had known. The good things in life were there before and would be there after, I tried to tell myself. But I could not find them and doubted they ever existed. Those were dreams. This was a new permanent reality.

Soon, through humming darkness came distant sirens. Well, damn me a thousand times. Someone had taken interest at last. I would not have to clean up Butchertown all by myself.

As the sirens drew closer, my skin grew warm. I took my face out of my hands and saw the ground at my feet turning to gold. The light spread around and behind me, soft and silent. There lay my shadow, my right shoulder and the tousled top of my head. Then I looked up to see a blinding gold ball in a widening pitch of blue.

"Oh. It's you, you lazy bum. What kept you?"

When the first cops pulled up, they found a grown man sitting on a low brick wall among the dead and wounded, sobbing like a baby.

Epilogue:

Back Across the Bay

If you check the newspaper morgues for that 1922 August weekend, you will find only sidelong squibs and morgue items concerning my misbegotten weekend in Butchertown.

Sensational as those short two days and twelve hours were—and what newshound would turn his nose from such a scoop?—a big someone or someones somewhere ordered a thick rug thrown over the whole bloody mess, to be nailed and tacked down at all the corners and along the sides; tacked down so completely that it would be too much trouble to tear it up to get at that huge lump in the middle. It would be walked over repeatedly, until it was crushed down and remembered only as a bump on the road to progress.

I know because that rug was thrown over me.

The biggest news item was a column in the Oakland paper (and one in the two major San Francisco papers) covering the Gasoline Creek fire. That conflagration was impossible to miss, but "officials" rushed to brush it off as the work of youthful pranksters or the tobacco habits of careless foreign workers (who were always up to something nefarious). There was a paragraph about protests from East Bay Hill residents and "nature lovers." Others—those who were out of the path of the smoke—were said to have "enjoyed the late Fourth of July–type spectacle." "Officials continue to investigate" was the last I ever read about Gasoline Creek. All I know is that it was never allowed to catch fire again. Call it an improvement if you want, but I doubt the fish ever returned.

As for the war between the Carvers and Bat Falcone, it was mostly swallowed in the darkness around the fire. Both Danny and Cobb Carver received obituaries in the Oakland paper. Danny's murder became an accidental death in a street brawl that grew out of the Prohibition march on Friday, while Cobb was reported to have died of a broken heart the following Monday. His successor as mayor was someone I had never heard of. And there was nothing about Tag Carver or his poor sister Molly.

Bat Falcone received a tiny paragraph saying he died of a "self-inflicted gunshot" in a local hotel. The same story was repeated in the North Bay papers, adding that Falcone had been in poor health recently. His death received more coverage, or at least his funeral did. In his way he had been a big man in the North, where many seemed to mourn his passing without knowing the facts of it. Maybe they were content without them.

As for all the others who died, there remained only a silence deader than they were. Even Chess Stetson and Buckram, the two Great War heroes, were left unmentioned.

As for me, I was only permitted moments to enjoy the return of sunshine to the Bay Area before they caged me in a tiny cell. For four days I was drilled and grilled by city cops, county cops, state cops, all steaming in like dreadnoughts in brown and gray suits. They questioned me over and over down through my skin, into my bones, all in a closed, smoke-filled room, where I choked and coughed every time someone lit up. I turned down every cigarette they offered me. My lungs were so sore I had to plead with them to stop smoking just so I could talk. They found this amusing.

Even so, they could not shake me from my story, though they seem to mightily doubt it, especially my claim that I had killed no one except for that poor chump in the stockyard stairwell.

By the end of the third day, I noticed that the federal police had not shown their mugs. They almost certainly should have shown some interest in the bootlegging angle, but no one ever showed that badge or even mentioned them. They were being fenced out of this one.

It was while I mulling this over in my cell, scratching my six-day beard, that a lackey—someone I did not even know—from the San Francisco DA's office showed up to tell me that I had been fired, right from the cannon, and not to even bother showing my mug around the office. Photographs had been found. My conduct that weekend had brought public embarrassment to the DA's office. They had already sent my personal effects to my apartment.

The next morning, Friday, I was marched into a large smoke-filled conference room to face a group made up of my interrogators, joined by cops and other big shots from every city and town hugging the shores of the Bay.

The man at the head of the table, the state cop, the smallest but toughest of them, spoke first, waving a long cigar like a teacher's pointer. He hammered and stamped out his words like a factory machine rolling out simple parts made for running other machines.

"Bacon, what happened this last weekend didn't happen, see? It's been happening back east. In Chicago. New York, too. Blood running like a goddamn river over their boots, out the faucets. But it's never happened here in California, see? It's not happening now. And it's not going to happen, not anywhere in this state. Ever.

"With all the shit running back east, everyone's looking out here for something better: gold, sunshine, orange trees and more. And we—not just us—want to keep them looking, want to keep them coming just like you did. California could be a whole country by itself, but not if everybody looks and sees the same bloody shit they're standing in.

"So what happened last weekend? Shut up about it, got me? We got the papers quiet, but should some newshound come sniffing, you don't know. You didn't see, see? You weren't there. No matter what they say they know, they're wrong and you say it. You're as innocent as a baby lamb."

Then he looked around the table. "Boys?"

The boys all chimed in, the same song, variations on "Keep your big yammer shut." Threats pulsed to the surface here and there. The cop from Oakland pointed out I had been first on the scene at Danny Carver's murder, and given my relationship with his sister, "Maybe something happened between the two of you; maybe he didn't like you pawing his sister. You were pawing her, right? The pair of you were seen making big sparks on the Key train."

I could not say much of anything, mostly because every time I drew a breath I exploded in raucous coughing. Once I stammered out "Butchertown" but they cut me off.

"Evansville is a useful community in the Bay Area." The San Francisco chief's lips hardly moved beneath his pencil mustache. "Everyone here, the cities and

towns they represent, even San Francisco, count on
Evansville in small ways, big ways, all kinds of ways. A
lot of what we have gets made there. It's important in
ways maybe you can't see. After all, you only spent one
weekend there, a couple days, got me, pal? Maybe you
just wandered into the bad part of town; a young kid
like you, new to the area. It's like that flu. Who talks
about it, right?"

The state cop nodded curtly. The jail guard lifted me
to my feet and pushed me out the door. Some kind
stranger slipped twenty bucks and my watch into my
pocket, and from there I was out on the street, under a
blinding sun. Twenty bucks sounds like a pittance, but
I had lost almost everything, see? I walked the streets
of Oakland, a stranger in a secondhand ill-fitting
brown cotton suit, no collar for the shirt, no hat. I was
a no-name, down to my socks and underwear, which
didn't fit either. The shoes, their tops scuffed and torn,
had holes, were flat at the heels and a size too large.
My watch was the only thing left of the me that had
crossed the Bay only a week ago.

I walked to Broadway and stood on a corner, looking
to grab a street car or jitney to the ferry terminal,
squinting against the light, blind as a ground mole.

Choral singing came from somewhere nearby:
"Onward, Christian Soldiers." An uncomfortable
feeling swept over me. That song would always be a
sign of trouble to me.

Once I espied the group's location, standing brownly
across the street on the opposite train stop, I averted

my eyes so they would not get any ideas, as crusaders do when they make the eye-to-eye with outsiders. From among them there rose a voice that disturbed with its piercing familiarity.

Then the hymn ended. One of them started across the street straight for me. I made a hurried half turn towards the ferry dock. And just as I stepped off the curb—

"Paul! Paul, wait!"

Louise Wheeler trotted towards me, lifting her skirt. Her hair was back up in a bun, but she was no longer dressed like a starless mournful night, but in plain, dusty patched brown. She looked as reduced as I did, her face like chipped white china, her eyes standing out with hunger.

"What do you want?" I looked away, my shoulders up. "I've got a ferry to catch."

"To say I'm sorry. For abandoning you."

"Is that all you're sorry for?"

"And for hitting you."

She stopped a couple feet away, her eyes downcast.

"What happened to him?" I asked.

She shook her head. I wondered whether I should offer condolences.

"I'm not supposed to talk about it."

"Yeah, I received that lecture too."

She looked over her shoulder at the crowd on the opposite side. One of them, a dark-skinned young fellow in a newsboy cap and baggy gray suit, had stepped away and was waving at her. A Key train, destination Evansville, came rolling their way.

"You're not going back for more of that, are you?"

"They're all from there," she explained. "They live there and they're going home to try and rebuild. I owe them help after the mess I made."

"You didn't make all of it."

"I made enough," she said ruefully. "I have to consider what they need now. Not what I think they need. Another thing to atone for. My child's even further away from me now. God's path really is thorny."

Then she looked at me deeply, like she once did long ago. I took a step forward, but she held up her hand, took a step back.

"No, you don't have to come. I'm a do-gooder, Paul. That's who I am. I don't understand why the rest of the world isn't like me, but there it is. You're someone else. You did the best you could. We were both in the dark, but at least you knew it." Then she stepped forward again, this time close, putting her arms around me, pulling me close, holding me against her whole body, her face next to mine.

"May you always be kind to those God sends your way."

"And I hope you find your little boy," I said, but by then she had hurried away. Her train had arrived. Mine was on the way.

****

I stood on the aft deck of the ferry for a spell watching the East Bay hills recede. I had not seen nature's color in so long, the green vegetation seemed more miraculous than the sky and the sun. I felt homesick for the verdant mountains of my New York home.

The only flaw was the long brown smudge running along the shore, blanketed by a gassy red haze. Above the haze the factory smokestack, Butchertown's chief landmark, pointed defiantly at the sky, its fiery serpent tongue guiding the world in, a beacon for tomorrow.

I had my fill of that fast. Ahead waited clear blue sky over the hills and skyscrapers of San Francisco; the California I had come thousands of miles for.

The oceans winds were still up, though, and we were heading into heavy chop. The last thing I needed was my stomach rolling against the waves, and so I made for the boathouse.

The interior was empty at that time of day but for another group of black-clad Temperance people seated with their signs in a corner near the starboard bow, crouched like troops in the trenches, their faces grim.

I steered aft and recognized the ferry bartender from Friday night before he recognized me. Cannot say I blame him, what with my face a patch of purple lumps and two large bandages on my skull. I stared at him hard while his brain grinded away.

Finally, I said, "Friday night on the ferry coming over. You warned me, don't drink the booze in Butchertown. You were right." He burst out laughing, waving his hand as though pulling a card out of the air.

"You! Sure! Brother, you look like you rolled off the train from Pigtown." Then he frowned. "There's been rumble of some trouble last weekend."

"The poker game got kinda argumentive." I shrugged. "Lost my shirt and more." Lying no longer bothered me like it used to and it simplified matters, especially with strangers.

The bartender brought up a cardboard box and flipped it open: black stogies. The sight sent me into a raging coughing fit. As I stood gasping for breath, he asked if I was all right.

"I quit smoking." I brushed the box away with the back of my hand.

"Yeah," he said with a laugh. "You sound like you were suckin' smoke right outta that big smokestack." Then he teasingly wagged a finger. "Now don't tell me a few days in Butchertown turned you into one of them milk drinkers. Whooo-hee! I hate seein' a man go all snow pure."

I leaned over the bar, spoke in a phlegmy whisper. "Speakin' easy here, you wouldn't happen to have a little cough medicine available, would you now?"

"Hang there." He shot a glance at the Temperance crowd, then disappeared for a moment. He returned bearing two tall crystal glasses full of coffee-brown fizzy. He set one directly in front of me with fine mock dignity and held the other high.

"Your Coke, sir." He leaned forward and murmured out the side of his mouth, "Imported from Canada no less."

I laughed as we made a toast to bad behavior and the end of bad laws. The first swig turned my nerves to rose petals. The pain in my chest eased. I turned and looked out the forward window, sipped steadily, felt more like my old self with every passing minute.

As the city's gloomy canyons filled the window, I realized I had no idea what I was going back to, but it bothered me none. I would take any damn thing the world had to throw at me.

"C'mon," the barkeep whispered. "What really happened over there? Gimme the scoop."

"It was all stupid," I said. "Nothing but stupid."

THE END

Acknowledgments

As with all books, more than a few hands had a hand in this novel, guiding mine through the various drafts and rewrites. I would like to thank them all.

Chief among them stands David Corbett, a great writer and editor, who bravely served as developmental editor to help bring it home.

I also wish to thank John-Ivan ("He's Done It to Me Again!") Palmer; Don Herron; Tim Stookey (and the gang at Stookey's Club Moderne, San Francisco); Margaret Clark; St. Paul's Episcopal Church, Oakland (for a quiet sanctuary from the storm brewed by this gruesome novel); and Gray Brechin, whose book *Imperial San Francisco: Urban Power, Earthly Ruin* provided essential historical insight, thereby enriching the world of Butchertown.

Thanks also to Matt Chauvin's 20sjazz.com, Duke Ellington, Lee Van Cleef, and Ennio Morricone.

Acknowledgments

A very special thanks goes to Dave and Carla Ennis, owners, and Matthew Gordon, caretaker, of the unique property at 40th and Adeline in Emeryville. It was a good place to live and a fine location to reimagine as it might have been almost a century ago (and I apologize for any architectural changes I made).

I also wish to thank the Emeryville Historical Society, the Oakland Public Library History Room, the California Historical Society and, especially, the Berkeley Public Library.

In addition to Joel Friedman and the folks at Book Designer for the templates, I also wish to thank my excellent copyeditor, Marcus Trower, and my equally excellent proofreader Adam Rosen, both of whom found those last dropped words, loose buttons and stuck zippers. They, too, understood where this book was going and helped get it there.

And once again, Cathi Stevenson at Bookcover Express struck gold with her cover design.

Finally, I wish to thank most of all my darling wife, Elizabeth, whose faith and patience in me and my efforts, humble though they might be, both comforted and inspired, even when life in Butchertown had turned darkest. God bless and keep you, my darling!

About the Author

Thomas Burchfield was born in Peekskill, New York. His debut novel, the contemporary Dracula tale *Dragon's Ark*, won several awards in 2012. When not blogging on his "A Curious Man" webpage, he writes for such publications as *Bright Lights Film Journal*, *Filmfax* and *The Strand Magazine*. He lives in Northern California with his wife, Elizabeth.